"If I ever get involved with anyone again,"

Mariah told Miller, "it's going to be because I find someone I can't live without. I want to find the kind of passion that's overpowering...I want to lose control."

Overpowering passion.

The kind of passion that started wars and crumbled empires. The kind of passion that made it difficult for even a hardened expert like him to do his job. The kind of passion that made him want to break every rule and restriction he'd set for himself and pull this woman into his arms and cover her mouth with his own.

Dear Reader,

A new year has begun, and in its honor we bring you six new—and wonderful!—Intimate Moments novels. First up is *A Marriage-Minded Man?* Linda Turner returns to THE LONE STAR SOCIAL CLUB for this scintillating tale of a cop faced with a gorgeous witness who's offering him lots of evidence—about a crime that has yet to be committed! What's her game? Is she involved? Is she completely crazy? Or is she totally on the level—and also the perfect woman for him?

Then there's Beverly Barton's *Gabriel Hawk's Lady,* the newest of THE PROTECTORS. Rorie Dean needs help rescuing her young nephew from the jungles of San Miguel, and Gabriel is the only man with the know-how to help. But what neither of them has counted on is the attraction that simmers between them, making their already dangerous mission a threat on not just one level but two!

Welcome Suzanne Brockmann back with *Love with the Proper Stranger,* a steamy tale of deceptions, false identities and overwhelming passion. In *Ryan's Rescue,* Karen Leabo matches a socialite on the run with a reporter hot on the trail of a story that starts looking very much like a romance. *Wife on Demand* is an intensely emotional marriage-of-convenience story from the pen of Alexandra Sellers. And finally, welcome historical author Barbara Ankrum, who debuts in the line with *To Love a Cowboy.*

Enjoy them all, then come back next month for more excitement and passion—right here in Silhouette Intimate Moments.

Yours,

Leslie J. Wainger
Senior Editor and Editorial Coordinator

Please address questions and book requests to:
Silhouette Reader Service
U.S.: 3010 Walden Ave., P.O. Box 1325, Buffalo, NY 14269
Canadian: P.O. Box 609, Fort Erie, Ont. L2A 5X3

LOVE WITH THE PROPER STRANGER

SUZANNE BROCKMANN

Published by Silhouette Books

America's Publisher of Contemporary Romance

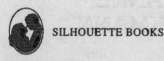

SILHOUETTE BOOKS

ISBN: 0-373-07831-5

LOVE WITH THE PROPER STRANGER

Books by Suzanne Brockmann

Silhouette Intimate Moments

Hero Under Cover #575
Not Without Risk #647
A Man To Die For #681
*Prince Joe #720
*Forever Blue #742
*Frisco's Kid #759
Love with the Proper Stranger #831

*Tall, Dark and Dangerous

SUZANNE BROCKMANN

wrote her first romance novel in 1992 and fell in love with the genre. She writes full-time, along with singing and arranging music for her professional a cappella singing group called Vocomotive, organizing a monthly benefit coffeehouse at her church and managing the acting careers of her two young children, Melanie and Jason. She and her family are living happily ever after in a small town outside of Boston.

For Mary Gray, Kirsten McDonough, Sylvia Micalone and all of the other wonderful Workcamp volunteers who have allowed me to help raise a hammer and build houses alongside them, even if only in spirit.

A Note from the Author

Shelter is one of the basic human needs. No one should be without it.

Each spring, thirty-five people from my community travel to the Appalachian Mountains as part of the "Cabell/Lincoln County Workcamp," to build and rebuild houses for people who are elderly, ill or underprivileged.

I became involved more than three years ago when I joined with a group of friends to start a monthly benefit coffeehouse to help raise money needed to pay for the trip south and for some of the building supplies.

I've yet to join the Workcampers on their weeklong "vacation" of hard work—my kids are still too young to participate and I can't take the time away from them. But I've seen in the eyes of my friends who *have* gone how empowering it is actually to take hammer in hand and make a visible difference in another person's life.

As they say at Workcamp, "Love works."

And it works both ways.

For more information, send an SASE to me at P.O. Box 5092, Wayland, MA 01778.

Suzanne Brockmann

Prologue

She laced his coffee with opium.

He wasn't supposed to drink coffee this late at night. The doctor had told him not to. But she knew how much it pleased him to cheat the doctor's rules just a little every now and then.

He smiled as she brought it to him, smiled again as he took a sip. He liked it sweet.

The opium wouldn't kill him. It was part of the ritual, part of the game. She'd given him enough to confuse him, enough to slow his wits, to keep him docile and in control as she prepared for her checkmate.

She kissed the top of his balding head and he smiled again, breathing a deep sigh of contentment—the king, relaxing after a hard day at the office, secure in his castle alongside his beautiful queen.

Tonight, this king would die.

Tony was breathing hard. John Miller could hear him clearly over the wire, his voice raspy and loud in the radio headset. Tony was breathing hard and Miller knew he was scared.

"Yeah, that's right. I'm FBI," Tony said, giving up his cover. Miller knew without a doubt that his partner and best friend was in serious, serious trouble. "And if you're as smart as your reputation says you are, Domino, then you'll order these goons to lay down their weapons and surrender to me."

Domino laughed. "I've got twenty men surrounding you, and you think I'm going to *surrender...?*"

"I've got more than twenty men on backup," Tony lied, as Miller keyed his radio.

"Where the *hell* is that backup?" Miller's usually unshakable control was nearing a breaking point. He'd been ordered to sit tight and wait here outside the warehouse until the choppers arrived in a show of force, but he couldn't wait any longer. He *wouldn't* wait.

"Jesus, John, didn't you get the word?" came Fred's scratchy voice over the radio. "The choppers have been rerouted—there's been an assassination attempt on the governor. It's code red, priority. You're on your own."

No choppers. No backup. Just Tony inside the warehouse, about to be executed by Alfonse Domino, and John Miller here, outside.

It was the one scenario Miller hadn't considered. It was the one scenario he wasn't ready for.

Miller grabbed the assault rifle from the floor of the van and ran toward the warehouse. He needed a miracle, but he didn't waste time praying. He knew full well that he—and Tony—didn't have a prayer.

"I quit."

The board of directors looked at her in stunned silence.

Marie Carver gazed back at the expressions of shock on the familiar faces and knew that those two little words she'd uttered had granted her freedom. It was that easy. That simple. She quit.

"I've made arrangements for my replacement," she told them, careful not to let her giddy laughter escape. She quit. Tomorrow she would *not* walk through the front doors and take the elevator up to her executive office on the penthouse floor. Tomorrow she would be in another place. Another city, another state. Maybe even another country. She passed around the hiring reports her secretary had typed up and bound neatly with cheery yellow covers. "I've done all the preliminary interviews and narrowed the candidates down to three—any one of which I myself would have utmost faith in as the new president of Carver Software."

All twelve members of the board starting talking at once.

Marie held up her hand. "Should you decide to hire an outside candidate," she said, "you would, of course, require my approval as the major stockholder of this company. But I think you'll be impressed with the choices I've given you here." She rapped the yellow-covered report with her knuckles. "I ask that you hold all of your questions until after you've read this. If any concerns remain unanswered, you can reach me at home until six o'clock this evening. After that, I'll remain in touch with my secretary, whom I've promoted to Executive Assistant." She smiled. "I appreciate your understanding, and will see you all at the next annual shareholders meeting."

She gathered up her briefcase and walked quickly out of the room.

* * *

The opium was working.

His pupils had retracted almost to a pinpoint and he was drooling slightly, blinking sleepily as he watched her dance.

This was the part she liked. This was where she showed him what he would never again have the chance to experience, to violate.

True, this one had been gentle. His soft, old hands had never struck her. He'd been careful not to hurt her. He'd given her expensive presents, fancy gifts. But the act itself would always be an act of violence, always despicable, always requiring punishment.

Capital punishment.

Her dress fell in a pool of silk at her feet, and she deftly stepped out of it. His eyes were glazed, but not enough to hide his hunger at the sight of her. He stretched one hand out toward her, but he didn't have the strength to reach her.

And still she danced, to the rhythm of the blood pounding through her veins, to the anticipation of the moment when he would gaze into her eyes and know without a doubt that he was a dead man.

Freedom.

It hit Marie like the coolness of the air that swept through the open door at the end of the hall. It felt fresh and clean, like that very spring breeze, bringing hope and life and renewal. Through that open door she could see her car, sitting out in the parking lot, ready for her escape.

"Mariah."

There was only one person on that board of directors who could slow her departure. Susan Kane. Aunt Susan. Marie turned, but kept moving, backward, down the hall.

Susan followed, her long, batik-patterned dress moving in the breeze, disapproval in her slate-blue eyes. "Mariah," she said again, calling Marie by her childhood nickname. "Obviously you've been planning this for some time."

Marie shook her head. "Only two weeks."

"I wish you had told me."

Marie stopped walking then, meeting the older woman's sternly unwavering gaze. "I couldn't," she said. "I didn't tell most of my own staff until this morning."

"Why?"

"The company doesn't need me anymore," Marie said. "It's been three years since the last layoffs. We've turned it around, Sue. Profits continue to rise—we're thriving. You know the numbers as well as I do."

"So take a vacation. Take a leave of absence. Sit back on your laurels and relax for a while."

Marie smiled ruefully. "That's part of my problem," she said. "I can't relax."

Susan's face softened, concern in her eyes. "Is your stomach still bothering you?"

"Among other things." Like, for instance, the fact that Marie was thirty-two years old and since her divorce four years ago, she had no life outside of the office. Like, the fact that she still worked long overtime hours to increase profits, to expand, to hire more people, even though the failing computer software company that her father's sudden fatal heart attack had thrust into her lap had long ago become a Fortune 500 business. Like, the fact that each morning she found herself walking into the new, fancy office building into which the company had recently moved, and she wondered what exactly was the point? What purpose did she serve by being here, by stressing herself out enough to develop stomach ulcers over the mundane, day-to-day operation of this business?

One day she was going to wake up, and she was going to be sixty years old and still walking into that building, still going home much too late to that sad excuse for a condo, still living out of boxes that she *still* hadn't managed to unpack.

And she'd look at her life, and all those meaningless, wasted years would stretch back into her meaningless, wasted past.

Because the truth was, even though she'd dutifully gotten her degree in business as her father had wanted, Marie had never wanted to run this company.

Shoot, it had taken years before she'd admitted that to herself. As far as knowing what she really wanted to do, Marie honestly didn't have a clue. But there was something that she did know.

She wanted to do more than keep a multimillion-dollar corporation up and running. She wanted to have a sense of real purpose. She wanted to be able to look back on her life and feel proud—feel as if she'd truly made a difference.

She was considering running for office. She was also thinking about joining the peace corps. She had found a list a mile long of volunteer organizations that desperately needed man power—everything from accountants for the Salvation Army to hands-on, hammer-wielding home builders for Foundations for Families.

But before she could do anything, she had to handle her stress.

Step one was cutting herself off from this company—breaking her addiction to this job and the company's addiction to her. She was going to do it cold turkey.

The company would survive. Marie knew they'd survive. Any one of her three job candidates would bring a freshness and vitality to the job that she'd lacked for nearly two years now. Whether or not Marie would survive was a different story...

"Where are you going?" Susan asked.

"I don't know," Marie admitted. "I'm just going to take my camera and go. I read in a book about stress reduction that I should take a few months and leave everything behind—including my name. This book recommended that I temporarily take on a new identity. Supposedly that'll help me distance myself from everything that's been causing my ulcers." She smiled. "I'm going to leave Marie Carver locked in my condo—along with all my doubts about my sanity and my worries that Carver Software will go into a nosedive the moment I leave town."

Susan pulled her in for a quick hug—an unusual display of affection. "The job will be yours again when you come back," the older woman whispered. "I'll make sure of that."

Marie pulled away, unable to answer. If she had her way, she'd never be back. If she had her way, Marie Carver and her damned ulcers would be gone forever.

She used the knife to cut off a lock of his hair.

He didn't have too much, just a light fringe of gray at the back of his head, but that didn't matter. It was the only thing of his that she would keep.

Besides the money.

He was handcuffed now. He'd let her do that willingly, thinking she was playing some new sex game, never suspecting he had only moments left to live.

But when she unsheathed the stiletto, there was a hint of consternation in his drug-glazed eyes.

"What are you doing?" he asked.

She shushed him with a kiss. He couldn't speak. He wasn't allowed to speak.

But he didn't know the rules. "Clarise?" he said, fear pushing past the opium, creeping into his voice, making it waver as she set the tip of the stiletto against his chest.

She felt a flash of regret.

Clarise. She liked that name a lot. It was a shame that she would only be Clarise for a few moments longer. She couldn't use that name again. And she wouldn't. She was too smart to make that mistake.

"This has gone far enough," he said, trying to hide his fear behind an air of authority. "Release me now, Clarise."

She smiled and leaned on the whisper-thin blade, sliding it deep into his heart, setting him forever free.

"Kill him."

Domino's order came before John Miller had reached the warehouse doors, and the gunshots—four of them in rapid sequence were amplified deafeningly through his headset.

Tony.

Tony was dead.

Miller knew it. He had no chance of saving his friend.

He had this tape, though, this tape of Domino giving the order to off a federal agent. He had enough evidence to put Domino on death row. Blasting his way through that warehouse door at twenty to one odds would only get himself killed, too.

He knew that as well as he knew his own heartbeat.

But the heart that was pounding in his chest wasn't

beating with a recognizable rhythm. And the red cloud of rage that covered his eyes didn't obscure his vision, but rather made it sharper, clearer.

Tony was dead, and the son of a bitch who ordered it done was *not* going to make his escape in a powerboat, losing himself in South America, outside of the FBI's jurisdiction. No, Alfonse Domino was going to burn in hell.

Miller hit the warehouse door at full run, bringing his gun up and into position at his hip, shouting in rage at the sight of Tony's crumpled body lying on the cold, blood-soaked concrete, shooting the surprise off the faces of Alfonse Domino and his men.

She had her airline ticket all ready, under an assumed name, of course. A temporary name.

Jane Riley. Plain Jane. Plane Jane. The thought amused her and she smiled. But only briefly. She knew she had a noticeable smile, and right now she had no desire to be noticed.

Her hair was under a kerchief for the occasion, and she wore a dowdy camel-colored jacket she'd picked up at a secondhand store downtown.

She took nothing of Clarise's with her. Nothing but the money and her collection. Nine locks of hair.

She traveled light, boarding the plane to Atlanta with only a tote bag that held several novels she'd picked up at the airport shop and two hundred thousand dollars in cash. The rest of the money was already in her Swiss bank account.

In Atlanta, she'd catch a train to who knows where. Maybe New York. Maybe Philadelphia.

She'd catch a show or two, take her time deciding

exactly who she wanted to be. Then she'd get her hair cut and colored, shop for a new wardrobe to match her new personality, pick a new town in a new state, and start the game all over again.

And then she'd have ten locks of hair.

Chapter 1

John Miller's heart was pounding and his mouth was dry as he awoke with a start. He stood up fast, trying hard to get his bearings, reaching automatically for his gun.

"John, are you all right?"

Christ, he was in his office. He'd fallen asleep with his head on his desk, and now he was standing in his office, with his side arm drawn and his hands shaking.

And Daniel Tonaka was standing in the doorway watching him. Daniel was expressionless, as he often was. But he was gazing rather pointedly at Miller's weapon.

Miller reholstered his gun, then ran both hands across his face. "Yeah," he said. "Yeah, I'm fine. I just fell asleep—or something—for a second."

"Maybe you should go home and go to bed."

Bed. Yeah, right. Maybe in some other lifetime.

"You look like hell, man," Daniel continued.

Miller *felt* like hell. He needed a case to work on. As

long as he was working, the dreams weren't so bad. It was this damned in-between time that was unbearable. "I just need some more coffee."

Daniel didn't say anything. He just looked at Miller. He was relatively new to the bureau—just a kid. He was hardly twenty-five years old, with a young handsome face, high cheekbones and deep brown, exotically shaped eyes that announced his part-Asian parentage. Those eyes held a wisdom that extended far beyond his tender years. And true to the wisdom in his eyes, the kid always knew when to hold his tongue.

Daniel Tonaka could say more with his silence and maybe a lift of one of his dark eyebrows than twenty other men could say if they talked all day.

Miller had had half a dozen new partners since Tony, but Daniel was the only one who had lasted for any length of time. Next week it would be, what? Seven months? The kid deserved some kind of award.

Miller knew quite well the reputation he had in the bureau. He was "The Robot." He was a machine, an automaton, letting nothing and no one get in the way of his investigation. He was capable of putting everyone around him into a deep freeze with a single laser-sharp look. Even before Tony had died, Miller had kept his emotions to himself, and he had to admit he'd played his cards even closer to his vest over the past few years.

He was aware of the speculation about his lack of close friends within the bureau, the whispered conversations that concluded he was incapable of emotion, devoid of compassion and humanity. After all, a man who so obviously didn't possess a heart and soul couldn't possibly feel.

Some of the younger agents would go well out of their way to avoid him. Hell, some of the *older* agents did the same. He was respected. With his record of arrests and successful investigations, he'd have to be. But he wasn't well liked.

Not that a robot would give a damn about that.

Daniel stepped farther into Miller's office. ''Working on the Black Widow case?''

Miller nodded, gazing down at the open file on his desk. He'd been studying the photos and information from the latest in a string of connected murders before he'd fallen asleep.

And dreamed about Tony again.

He sat back down in his chair, grimacing at his stiff muscles. Christ, everything ached. Every part of him was sore. He desperately needed sleep, but the thought of going home to his apartment and sinking into his bed and closing his eyes was unbearable. The moment he closed his eyes, he'd be back outside that warehouse. He'd dream about the night that Tony died, and he'd watch it happen all over again. And for the four thousandth time, the choppers would never come. For the four thousandth time, Miller would arrive too late. For the four thousandth time, blowing Domino's ass straight to hell *still* wouldn't make up for the fact that Tony's brains were smeared across the concrete.

God, the stab of guilt and loss he felt was still so sharp, so piercing. Miller tried to push it away, to bury it deep inside, someplace from which it would never escape. He tried to put more distance between himself and this pain, these emotions. He could do it. He *would* do it. He was, after all, the robot.

Miller took a swig from a mug of now-cold coffee, trying to ignore the fact that his hand was still shaking. ''The killer did her last victim about three months ago.'' The coffee tasted like something from a stable floor, but at least it moistened his mouth. "Which means she's probably preparing to make another go of it. She's out there somewhere, hunting down husband number eight. At least we think it's number eight. Maybe there've been more we just don't know about."

"What if she's decided she's rich enough?"

"She doesn't kill for the money." Miller picked up the picture of Randolph Powers, knife blade protruding from his chest as he gazed sightlessly from his seat at the dinner table. "She kills because she likes to." And she was getting ready to do it again. He knew it.

"I haven't had time to look at this file," Daniel admitted, sitting down on the other side of the desk, pulling the report toward him. "Are we sure this is the same woman?"

"Exact M.O. The victim was found in the dining room, cuffed to the chair, with the remains of dinner on the table." Miller ran his fingers through his hair. God, he had a headache. "Opium was found in his system in the autopsy. The entire house was wiped clean of fingerprints. The only photo was a wedding portrait—and the bride's veil was over her face. It's her."

Daniel skimmed the report. "According to this, Powers married a woman named Clarise Harris two and a half weeks prior to his death." He glanced up at Miller. "The honeymoon was barely over. Didn't she usually wait two or three months?"

Miller nodded, rummaging through his desk drawers for his bottle of aspirin. "She's getting impatient." Jackpot. Miller twisted off the aspirin bottle's cap—empty. "Damn. Tonaka, do you have any aspirin in your desk?"

"You don't need aspirin, man. You need sleep. Go home and go to bed."

"If I wanted free advice, I would've asked for it. I think what I asked for was aspirin."

The deadly look Miller gave Daniel was designed to freeze a man in his tracks.

But Daniel just smiled as he stood up. "You know, I really hope we're partners for a good long time, John, because I cannot for the life of me imitate that look. I've tried. I practice every night in my bathroom mirror, but..." He shook his head. "I just can't do it. You have a real God-given talent there. See you later."

Daniel closed the door on the way out and Miller just sat, staring after him, wishing...for what?

If the kid had been Tony, Miller might have told him about the nightmares, about the fact that he was too damn scared even to try to sleep. If the kid had been Tony, Miller might have told him that this morning when he'd gotten on the bathroom scale, he'd found he'd lost twenty pounds. Twenty pounds, just like that.

But Daniel Tonaka *wasn't* Tony.

Tony was gone. He'd been dead and gone for years. Years.

Miller reached for the phone. "Yeah, John Miller. Put me through to Captain Blake."

It was time to get down to real work on this Black Widow case. Maybe then he could get some damned sleep.

Garden Isle, Georgia, was the best kept secret among the jet set. The beaches were covered with soft white sand. The sky was blue and the ocean, although murky with mineral deposits, was clean. The town itself was quaint, with cobblestone streets and charming brick houses and window boxes that overflowed with brightly colored flowers. Most of the shops were exclusive, the restaurants trendy and four-star and outrageously expensive—except if you knew where to go.

And after two months on Garden Isle, Mariah Robinson knew exactly where to go to avoid the crowds. She loaded her camera and her beach bag into the front basket of her bike and headed toward the beach.

Not toward the quiet, windswept beach that was only several yards from her rental house, but rather toward the usually crowded, always happening beach next to the five-star resort.

Most of the time, she embraced the solitude, often reveling in the noise-dampening sound of the surf and the raucous calls of the seabirds. But today she felt social. Today, she *wanted* the crowds. Today, just on a whim, she wanted to use her camera to take photographs of people.

Today she was meeting her friend, Serena, for lunch at one of those very same four-star restaurants.

But she was more than an hour early, and she took her bike with her onto the sand. She set it gently on its side and spread her beach blanket alongside it. There was a reggae band playing in the tent next to the resort bar even this early in the morning, and the music floated out across the beach.

She sat in the sun, just watching the dynamics of the people around her.

Some sunbathers lay in chaise lounges, their noses buried in books. Others socialized, talking and flirting in large and small groups. Men and women in athletic gear ran up and down the miles of flat, hard sand at the edge of the water. Others walked or strolled. Still others paraded—clearly advertising their trim, tanned bodies, scantily clad in designer bathing suits.

Mariah took out her camera, focusing on a golden retriever running next to a muscular man in neon green running shorts. She loved dogs. In fact, now that she wasn't shut up in an office each day from dawn till dusk, she was thinking about getting one and—

"Fancy meeting you here this early."

Mariah looked up but the glare from the bright sun threw the face of the woman standing next to her into shadows. It didn't matter. The crisp English-accented voice was unmistakable.

"Hey," Mariah said, smiling as Serena sat down next to her on her blanket.

"I thought you'd sworn off the resort beach," Serena continued, looking at Mariah over the tops of her expensive sunglasses.

Serena Westford was older than Mariah had originally thought when they'd first met a few weeks ago—she was closer to forty than thirty, anyway. Her smile was young though. It was mercurial and charming, displaying perfect white teeth. Her hair was blond with wisps escaping from underneath the big straw hat she always wore, and her trim body was that of a twenty-four-year-old.

She was as cool and confident as she was beautiful. She was everything Mariah wished she could be. Everything Marie Carver wished she could be, Mariah corrected herself. But Marie Carver had purposely been left behind in Phoenix, Arizona. Mariah Robinson was here in Georgia, and Mariah was happy with her life. She went with the flow, calm and relaxed. No worries. No problems. No stress. No jealousy.

Serena was wearing a black thong bathing suit, covered only by a diaphanous short wrap that fluttered about her buttocks and thighs in the ocean breeze, leaving only slightly more than nothing to the imagination. Despite the fact that Serena Westford was no longer a schoolgirl, she was one of the minuscule percentage of the population who actually looked *good* in a thong bikini.

Mariah let herself hate her friend—but only for a fraction of a second. So what if Mariah was destined never to wear a similarly styled bathing suit? So what if Mariah was the exact physical opposite of petite, slender, golden Serena? So what if Mariah was just over six feet tall, broad shouldered, large breasted and athletically built? So what if her hair was an unremarkable shade of brown curls, always messy and impossible to control? So what if her eyes were brown? Light brown, not that dark-as-midnight intriguing shade of brown, or cat green like Serena's.

Mariah was willing to bet that behind Serena Westford's cool, confident facade, there lurked a woman with a thousand screaming anxieties. She probably worked out two hours each day to maintain her youthful figure. She probably spent an equal amount of time on her hair and makeup. She was probably consumed with worries and stress, poor thing.

"I just came down here to violate the photographic rights of these unsuspecting beachgoers," Mariah told her friend, unable to hide a smile.

The two women had first met when Mariah took Serena's picture here on the resort beach. Serena had been less than happy about that and had demanded Mariah hand over the undeveloped film then and there. What could have been an antagonistic and adversarial relationship quickly changed to one of mutual respect as Serena explained that while in the peace corps, she'd spent a great deal of time with certain tribes in Africa who believed that being photographed was tantamount to having one's soul kidnapped.

Mariah had surrendered the film, and spent an entire

afternoon listening to Serena's fascinating stories of her travels around the world as a volunteer humanitarian.

They'd talked about Mariah's work for Foundations for Families, too. Serena had mentioned she'd seen Mariah getting dropped off by the Triple F van in the evenings. And they'd talked about the grassroots organization that used volunteers to help build affordable homes for hardworking, low-income families. Mariah spent three or four days each week with a hammer in her hand, and she loved both the work and the sense of purpose it gave her.

"Hey, I got a package notice from the post office," Mariah told her friend. "I think it's my darkroom supplies. Any chance I can talk you into picking it up for me?"

"If you had a car, you could pick it up yourself."

"If I had a car, I would use it once a month, when a heavy package needed to be picked up at the post office."

"If you had a car, you wouldn't have to wait for that awful van to take you over to the mainland four times a week," Serena pointed out.

Mariah smiled. "I like taking the van."

Serena looked at her closely. "The driver *is* a real hunk."

"The driver is happily married to one of the Triple F site supervisors."

"Too bad."

Serena's sigh of regret was so heartfelt, Mariah had to laugh. "You know, Serena, not everyone in the world is husband hunting. I'm actually very happy all by myself."

Serena smiled. "Husband hunting," she repeated. "The biggest of the big game." She laughed. "I like that image. I wonder what gauge bullet I'd need to bring one down..."

Mariah gathered up her things. "Let's go have lunch."

* * *

She would know him when she saw him, but she simply hadn't seen him yet. He would have money. Lots of money. Enough so that when she asked for the funds for the down payment on a house, he wouldn't hesitate to give it directly to her. Enough so that he would open a checking account in her name—an account she would immediately start draining. She would transfer the money to dummy accounts out of state.

She had the system set up so that anyone following the paper trail would be stopped cold, left high and dry.

She'd sit on the cash for a week or two, then make the deposits into her Swiss bank accounts.

Three million dollars. She had three million dollars American already in her Swiss accounts.

Three million dollars, and nine locks of hair.

Yes, she'd know him when she saw him.

"Garden Isle, Georgia," the agent named Taylor said as he looked around the table from Daniel Tonaka to Pat Blake, the head of the FBI unit, and finally to John Miller. "It's her. The Black Widow killer. It's got to be."

He slid several enlarged black-and-white photos across the conference table, one toward Blake and the other toward Miller and Daniel. Miller sat forward slightly in his chair, picking it up and angling it away from the reflections of the overhead lights. He couldn't seem to hold it steady—his hands were shaking—and he quickly put it down on the table.

"She's going by the name Serena Westford," the young agent was saying. "She came out of nowhere. Her story is that she spent the past seven years in Europe—in Paris—but no one seems to know her over there. If she *was* living there, she wasn't paying taxes, that's for sure.''

The photograph showed a woman moving rapidly, purposefully across a parking lot. She was wearing a hat and sunglasses, and her face was blurred.

Miller looked up. "What's your name again?"

The young man held his gaze only briefly. "Taylor. Steven Taylor."

"Couldn't you get a better picture than this, Taylor?"

"No, sir," he said. "We're lucky we even got this one. It was taken with a telephoto lens from the window of the resort. It's the best of about twenty that I managed to get at that time. Any other time I tried to take her picture, she somehow seemed to know there was a camera around and she covered herself almost completely. I have about five hundred perfect pictures where her face is nearly entirely obscured by enormous sunglasses or her hat. I have five hundred other perfect shots of the back of her head."

"Yet you're certain this woman is our Black Widow." Miller didn't hide his skepticism.

Daniel shifted in his seat. "I believe it's her, John. Hear him out."

Miller was usually unerringly accurate when it came to reading people. He knew for a fact that Patrick Blake disliked him despite his record of arrests. And he knew quite clearly that Steven Taylor was afraid of him. Oh, he was polite and respectful, but something about his stance told Miller clear as day that Taylor was going to request a transfer off this case now that he knew Miller was aboard.

Daniel Tonaka, on the other hand, had never been easy to read. He was unflappable, with a quirky sense of humor that surfaced at the most unexpected moments. As far as Miller could tell, Daniel treated every person with whom he came into contact with the same amount of courtesy and kindness. He treated everyone from a bag lady to the governor's wife with respect, always giving them his full attention.

Daniel had spoken up to say he had a hunch or a feeling about a suspect or a case only a handful of times, and all of those times he'd been right on target. But this time he'd used even stronger language. He *believed* Serena Westford was the Black Widow.

Miller looked expectantly at Steven Taylor, waiting for him to continue.

Taylor cleared his throat. "I, um, used the computer to search out the most likely locations the Widow would choose for her next target," the young man told him. "She prefers small towns with only one or two resorts nearby. I programmed the computer to ignore everything within two hundred miles of the places she either met or lived with her previous victims, and narrowed the list down to a hundred and twenty-three possibilities. From there, I accessed resort records and used a phone investigation to query the resort staff, searching for female guests under five feet two inches, traveling alone, staying for extended lengths of time.

"Frankly, there was a great deal of luck involved in finding Serena Westford. She'd arrived at the Garden Isle resort only two days prior to our call. When it became clear she was traveling under an alias, I went to Georgia myself to try to further identify the suspect." He shook his head ruefully. "But as you can see, in all of the pictures we have of the Black Widow, her face is covered."

"But her legs aren't," Daniel pointed out. "Steve got plenty of pictures of Serena Westford's legs."

"Her legs are visible in some of the other photos we

found in the victims' houses," Taylor said. "We have no pictures of the Black Widow's face, but we have plenty of photos of her legs." He looked at Daniel and grinned. "Tonaka had the idea to take those pictures and *these* pictures and run a computer comparison. According to the computer, there's a ninety-eight percent chance that the Black Widow's legs and Serena Westford's legs are one and the same."

Miller glanced at Daniel. Damn, the kid was good at finding creative alternatives. "A computer match of legs won't hold up in a court of law as proof of identity," he commented.

"No kidding," Taylor said, quickly adding, "Sir. But it's enough to convince *me* that there should be a further investigation."

Miller passed the photograph to Captain Blake, and again his hands shook. The older man glanced at him, eyebrows slightly raised.

Miller turned back to Taylor. "Tell me more," he commanded.

"When Serena first arrived, she had traces of bruising beneath her eyes," Taylor continued. "I'd dare to speculate that that was from recent plastic surgery—probably a nose job to alter her appearance."

"We've been talking about the possibility of flying husband number seven's former housekeeper to Garden Isle," Pat Blake interrupted, "but if the Widow *has* had extensive plastic surgery, there's no way she could make a one hundred percent positive ID. I want no room for reasonable doubt. This one isn't going to walk away."

Miller nodded. What they needed was to catch the killer in the act.

"She's recently rented a beach house on Garden Isle," Taylor continued. "That's a clear indication that she's intending to stay, although at this point, I don't believe she's targeted her next victim. I've compiled a list of all of the people—both men and women—whom our suspect has had contact with over the past several weeks. Out of forty-seven people, twenty-eight have since left the island. They were there only on vacation, and they've gone home. Out of the other nineteen, one in particular stands out.''

Taylor took a series of photos from his file, spreading them out on the table.

''Her name is Mariah Robinson,'' he said. ''Or so she says. According to our files, no such person exists. We've identified her as Marie Carver, former CEO of Carver Software out of Phoenix, Arizona.''

Miller leaned forward to look at the photographs. One was of a tall young woman with shoulder-length dark hair, wearing a bathing-suit top and shorts, seated on a beach blanket. Another bikini-clad woman was sitting next to her, her face obscured by a huge straw hat.

The woman in the hat had to be Serena Westford. Her barely there bikini was designed to make blood pressures rise, yet it was the woman sitting next to her that drew Miller's eyes.

''Marie Carver—or Mariah Robinson as she calls herself—lives alone in a rented house on the island,'' Taylor continued. ''She spends most of her time on a private beach taking nature photographs. She has a darkroom in her cottage. Every few days, she goes off island—I don't know where. I haven't had the opportunity yet to follow her. She and Serena seem pretty tight.''

Mariah Robinson was more than tall, Miller realized. She was an Amazon—a goddess. She had to be only an inch or two shorter than his own six feet two inches. She was as tall as a man, but built entirely like a woman. Her breasts were full and generously proportioned to the rest of her body. Her hips were appropriately wide—enough so that she was probably self-conscious, hence the shorts. Her legs were impossibly long and well muscled.

Another picture caught her riding an ancient bicycle. She was going up a slight hill and standing above the seat, muscles straining in her legs, breasts tight against the cotton of her T-shirt.

Christ, what a body. There was so damned much of her.

Serena Westford was their Black Widow suspect. She had allegedly lured seven men to their deaths with her searing sexuality. She was a femme fatale in the most literal sense.

Yet it was this other woman, Mariah Robinson, who made Miller stand at attention. Of course, he'd always been a breast-and-leg man. And from what he could see from these pictures, she had more than enough of both. Enough for a man to sink into and lose himself in for a solid year or two.

God, what was wrong with him? He didn't usually have this kind of reaction to the female suspects in a case. Apparently, it had been too long since his last sexual encounter. Way too long. Back even before Daniel came on as his partner. Miller couldn't even remember when it was, or even whom he'd been with.

Maybe that was why he wasn't sleeping. Maybe he *would* finally be able to sleep if a woman was in bed with him. Maybe all he needed was a little sexual relief.

Except the reason he *hadn't* had sex since forever was because none of the women he'd met during that time had managed to turn him on.

Yet here he was, having a definite physical reaction from surveillance photos of a murderess's best friend, who also happened to be living under an alias. What the hell was wrong with him?

And wasn't it just his luck that it wasn't going to be the goddess, but the murderess who was probably going to end up in his bed? And *that* sure as hell wasn't going to make him sleep any better.

Miller picked up the fifth photo. It was a close-up of Mariah Robinson's face.

She was pretty in a sweet, girl-next-door kind of way. Her face was heart shaped, with broad cheekbones and a strong, almost pointed chin. Her mouth was generous and wide. Her smile revealed straight white teeth and made dimples appear in her cheeks. Her eyes were light colored—Miller couldn't tell from the black-and-white photo if they were blue or light brown. But they sparkled with some secret amusement, as if she were laughing at him.

Miller felt a swirl of anticipation deep in his gut. It was sexual energy combined with something else, something deeper and far more complicated. Something that made his pulse quicken. Something he couldn't identify.

Captain Blake smoothed one hand along the top of his nearly bald head as he shuffled through his copy of the file. "How long do you think it'll take till we can get a cover in place for an agent to portray potential husband material?" he asked.

"A week," Taylor answered. "Two at the most. In order to match the profiles of the previous victims, we'd need to find an agent who could pose either as a much older man or a man in poor health. We'd need to provide fictional background, complete with financial records and heavily padded bank accounts. You can bet Serena will run a credit check on anyone she's considering targeting.

We'll need to prep the agent, set up protection and a surveillance team—"

Miller sat forward. "I could be ready to go down to Garden Isle tomorrow."

Taylor stared at him, unable to hide his expression of surprise. "*You?* You're not old enough."

"Husband number three was only twenty-nine years old," Daniel pointed out mildly. "And husband six was in his mid-thirties."

"Both were in extremely poor health, one in a wheelchair."

Miller took two copies of his file from his briefcase, handed one to Blake and tossed the other onto the table in front of Steven Taylor. "Meet Jonathan Mills," he said. "I'm thirty-nine years old. Recently in remission after a long struggle with Hodgkin's disease—that's a kind of cancer of the lymph system."

Taylor opened the file and quickly skimmed Miller's investigation summary. His eyes widened. "You actually intend to *marry* this woman...?"

"If I don't, she won't try to kill me."

"You're going to *be* her husband," Taylor said. "You're actually planning to *sleep* with her...?"

Even Daniel had a hint of curiosity in his dark brown eyes as he waited for Miller's answer.

Pat Blake shook his head. "Should I not be hearing this?"

"Don't worry, Captain, the marriage will be legal. She'll be my wife," Miller said. "And I'll make a point to practice safe sex." He smiled. "Of course, in *her* case, that means no knives in bed." He stood up, scooping the photos and files off the table, and looked at Blake. "Am I good to go?"

The older man nodded. "Let's do it."

Daniel and Steven Taylor got to their feet, and Miller turned to leave the room.

"One moment, if you don't mind, John," Blake said. He waited until the younger agents had left his office, then stood up and closed the door behind them. "You look like crap."

Miller knew Blake hadn't missed the fact that his hands were shaking. "Too much coffee," he said. "I'm fine, but thanks for your concern."

Blake nodded, clearly not buying it for one second. "I know we haven't exactly been friends down through the years, John. I've always just figured I'll stay out of your way, let you do what you do best, and you'll continue to give me the highest success record in the Bureau. But if you've got some kind of problem, maybe there's something I can do to help."

Miller met his superior's eyes steadily. "I just want to get to work."

"Do you have anyone at all you can talk to, Miller?"

"Will that be all, sir?"

Blake sighed. "I'm not supposed to give you a warning, but after this one's over, I'm bringing you in for a full psychological evaluation. So go on, get out of here. And try to spend a least *some* of your time on that resort island with your eyes closed and your head on a pillow."

Miller *had* to protest. "Over the past eighteen months my efficiency has *increased*—"

"Yeah, because you work twenty-two hours each day." Blake sighed again. "Go to Georgia, John. Catch this killer. Get the job done and make the world safe again for rich, dirty old men. But be ready to be stuck under a shrink's microscope when you get back."

Blake turned toward his desk, and Miller knew the conversation was over. He let himself out, aware that his pulse was racing, the sound of blood rushing through his veins roaring in his ears. Psych evaluation. Christ, he didn't stand a chance. Somehow, over the next few weeks, he was going to have to teach himself to sleep again—or face the new nightmare of a psychological evaluation.

God, he needed another cup of coffee.

He was halfway down the hall that led to the lounge when he heard voices coming from one of the tiny windowless cubicles assigned to the less experienced agents. He heard what's-his-name's voice. Taylor. Steven Taylor's voice.

"He's a time bomb, about to explode. You know that as well as I do. You wouldn't *believe* the rumors that are circulating about John Miller. Talk is that he's on the verge of some kind of breakdown."

"Do you always listen to rumors?" It was Daniel, and there was a hint of amusement in his voice.

"Not usually, no. But the man looks *terrible*—"

Daniel's voice was gentle now. "He's a living legend, Steve. He's the best there is. He looks terrible because he's got insomnia. It gets worse when he's between investigations. But believe me, he'll be fine. Don't request a transfer—you'll be able to learn a lot from this guy. Trust me on this one."

"Humph." Taylor didn't sound convinced. "Did you see the way his hands shook? No way do I want to be under the command of some flaky insomniac James Bond has-been who's on the edge. No, I'm outta here. Haven't you heard that his partners have a way of dying on him?"

Miller stepped into the room. "If you've got a problem with me, Taylor," he said coldly, "come and tell me to my face."

A flush of embarrassment darkened Taylor's cheeks as

he gazed at him in surprise. His eyes lost their focus for a second or two, and Miller knew that he was replaying his words in his mind, recalling all the harsh things he'd said that Miller had no doubt overheard.

Time bomb. Flaky insomniac. James Bond has-been.

"Excuse me, sir," Taylor said, making a quick exit out of the room.

That was one agent *he* was never going to see again. Miller turned to Daniel Tonaka. "Mind stepping into my office with me?"

Daniel didn't look perturbed, but then again, Daniel never did.

Miller went out into the corridor, leading the way back to his office. He went inside, then turned and waited for Daniel to join him.

"What's up?" Daniel asked evenly.

Miller closed the door and immediately lit into him. "If I hear you discussing my personal life with another agent ever again, you will be transferred off my team so fast, you won't know what hit you."

He'd truly caught Daniel off guard, and a myriad of emotions flashed across the young man's face. But he quickly recovered. "I was unaware that you believed your inability to sleep was a secret around here."

"I know damn well that it's no secret," Miller said coolly. "But it's not your business to discuss."

Daniel nodded and even managed to smile. "Okay. I can respect that, John. And I apologize for offending you."

Miller opened his office door. "Just be ready to leave first thing in the morning."

"I will." Daniel paused and smiled again before he went out the door. "I'm glad we had this little time to talk and straighten things out."

Miller didn't let himself smile until he'd closed his office door behind Daniel. *I'm glad we had this little time to talk...* Hell, other men would've wet themselves. *Taylor* sure as hell would've—it was just as well he wasn't going to be hanging around, getting in the way.

Miller tossed his briefcase onto a chair and the photos Taylor had taken onto his desk. The blurred picture of Serena Westford had been on top, but it slid off the pile, and Mariah Robinson's laughing eyes peeked out at him.

Tomorrow he was going to be in Garden Isle, Georgia, and he was "accidentally" going to bump into Mariah Robinson. For the first time in weeks, he felt wide-awake with the buzz of anticipation.

Chapter 2

There was a dog on the beach, frolicking in the surf in the predawn light.

There was a dog—and a man.

It wasn't such a rare occurrence for a dog and its master to be on the beach outside of Mariah's cottage. The stretch of sand was nearly seven miles long, starting down by the resort, and ending at the lighthouse on the northernmost tip of the island. Ambitious runners and power walkers often provided a steady stream of traffic going in both directions.

No, finding a dog and a man on the beach wasn't odd at all, except for the fact that it wasn't yet even five o'clock in the morning.

Mariah had risen early, hoping to get some photos of the deserted beach at sunrise.

There was still time—she could ask them to move away, off farther down the beach. But the man was sitting in the sand, his back slumped in a posture of exhaustion, his head in his hands. And the dog was having one hell of a good time.

Mariah moved closer. The wind was coming in off the water, and neither dog nor man was aware of her presence. She settled herself on her stomach in the sand and propped her camera up on her elbows as she focused her lens on the dog.

It was a mutt and probably female. Mariah could see traces of collie in the animal, along with maybe a little spaniel and something odd—maybe dachshund. Her coat was long and shaggy—and right now almost entirely soaked. She had short legs and a barrel-shaped body, a long, pointed nose and two ears that flapped ungracefully around her head. She may not have been eligible to win any beauty contests, but Mariah found herself smiling at her expression of delight as she bounded in and out of the waves. She could swear the dog was full-out grinning.

Her master, on the other hand, was not.

He stood up slowly, painfully, as if every movement hurt. He moved as if he were a hundred years old, but he wasn't an old man. His crew-cut hair was dark without even a trace of gray, and the lines from the glimpse she saw of his face seemed more from pain than age.

As he straightened to his full height, Mariah saw that he was tall—taller even than she was by at least a few inches. He wore sweatpants and a windbreaker that seemed to fit him loosely, as if he'd recently lost weight or been ill.

Together, man and dog made a great picture, and Mariah snapped shot after shot.

The dog bounded happily up to the man.

"Hey, Princess. Hey, girl." His voice was carried on the wind directly to Mariah. "Time to go back."

His voice was low and resonant, rich and full.

Dog and master were silhouetted against the red-orange sky, making a striking picture. Mariah moved her camera up to snap another photo, and the dog turned toward her, ears up and alert. She launched herself in Mariah's direction, and the man turned, too.

"Stop," he commanded. He spoke softly, just one single word, but the dog pulled up. She backed off slightly, her entire backside wagging as she grinned at Mariah.

Mariah looked from the dog to the man.

The man was far better-looking—or at least he would be if he smiled.

His hair was dark and severely cut close to his scalp, almost as if it was growing in after he'd shaved his head. Despite the austerity of his crew cut, he was a strikingly handsome man. His features looked almost chiseled, the bone structure of his face more elegant than rugged. His eyebrows were thick and dark, and right now forming a rather intimidating scowl over eyes that she guessed were brown. His chin quite possibly was perfect, his lips generously full, but his nose was large and slightly crooked.

On closer scrutiny, Mariah realized that it was possible some people might not have found this man worthy of a second glance. Actually, he wasn't conventionally handsome—he'd certainly never grace the cover of a men's fashion magazine. But there was something about his looks that she found incredibly appealing.

Or maybe it wasn't his looks at all, Mariah thought with a smile, remembering how the young woman in the natural food store on the mainland had spoken of cosmic reverberations and auras. Maybe as far as auras went, his was a solid ten.

As he stepped closer, she saw in the pale morning light that his face was lined with weariness and gray with fatigue. Still, despite that and his too-short hair, she found him to be remarkably attractive.

"Hi," Mariah said, sitting up and brushing the sand off the front of her T-shirt. His eyes followed the movement of her hand, and she became self-consciously aware of the fact that she'd only thrown a pair of shorts on underneath the T-shirt she'd worn to bed. She wasn't wearing a bra and she didn't have the body type that allowed for such wardrobe omissions. The only times she didn't bother to put on a bra were mornings like this, when she was certain she would be alone.

But she'd been wrong. Right now, she most definitely was not alone.

"I'm sorry," she said, trying to fold her arms across her chest in a casual manner. "I didn't mean to intrude."

Dear God, would you listen to her? She was *apologizing* for being on her own stretch of beach.

She didn't have to apologize for that. And she certainly shouldn't bother to apologize for her missing bra. Despite the man's earlier scowl, it was clear from the way that his gaze kept straying in the direction of her breasts that he, for one, was not in the least put out by her lack of underwear.

He pulled his gaze away from her long enough to glance up at the cottage. "Is this your place?"

Mariah nodded. "Yeah," she said. "I'm renting it for the season."

"Nice," he said, but his eyes were back on her, sweeping along the lengths of her bare legs, skimming again across her body and face. "I hope we didn't disturb you. The dog can get loud—she's still young."

"No, I woke up to catch the sunrise on film."

He glanced up at the sky. The sun was already above

the horizon and climbing fast. "I'm sorry," he said. "We were in your way."

"It's all right."

He held out one hand, offering to help her up.

Taking his hand meant she'd have to unfold her arms. But there was no way she'd be able to get to her feet with her arms folded anyway.

What the heck, Mariah thought, reaching up to clasp his hand. With a face like his, this man had no doubt seen a vast array of female bodies, and probably wearing far less than a worn-out T-shirt. She was nothing new, no big deal.

He, on the other hand, was a very, *very* big deal. He pulled her up from the sand, and she found herself standing much too close to him. But when she moved to back away, he steadied her with his other hand, his fingers warm against her elbow.

He was tall, with shoulders that went on forever and a broad chest that tapered down to a narrow waist and slim hips and... Embarrassed, Mariah quickly brought her eyes back to his face.

His eyes were blue. They were electric, brilliant, neon blue. And they sparked with the heat of attraction. Dear God, he found *her* attractive, too.

"Is it just you?" the man asked, and Mariah gazed up at him stupidly, wondering *what* he was talking about.

"Renting the house," he added, and she understood.

"Yes," she said, gently pulling free and putting some distance between them. "I'm here by myself."

He nodded. God, whoever he was, he was *so* serious. She'd yet to see him smile.

"How about you?" she asked. "Are you vacationing with your family?"

He shook his head. "No, I'm here alone, too." He

motioned vaguely down the beach. "I'm staying at the resort, at least temporarily. I was thinking about renting one of the houses up on this part of the beach. I'm getting tired of room service—I'd like to have my own kitchen."

"It's a trade-off," Mariah told him. "Renting a house is more private, but you lose the benefits of having a hotel maid. And if you're not careful about cleaning up after yourself in the kitchen... Well, the variety of insect life you can attract is immense. You can't leave *anything* out. Not even a plate with crumbs on it. You have to keep all the food in the refrigerator—or in plastic containers. But as long as you don't mind doing that, it's great."

He nodded. "Maybe I'll stick with room service for a while longer."

Princess the dog inched forward and pressed her cold nose against the back of Mariah's knee. "Yikes!" Mariah exclaimed.

"Princess, back," the man said sharply.

"She was just playing," Mariah protested as the dog immediately obeyed. "It's okay—she just startled me. I don't mind. She's...an unusual mix."

There was a glint of amusement in his eyes. "You're unusually tactful. But it's okay. She's not a mix of anything. She's a pure mutt, and she knows it. There's no ego involved—for either one of us."

"She does what you say," Mariah said. Princess gazed up at her, tongue lolling from her mouth, eyes sharp, ears alert, tail thumping slightly even though she was sitting down. She seemed to understand every word of the conversation. "That's worth more than a pedigree."

"She was well trained," he told her. "I...inherited her from a friend a few years ago."

He glanced out over the ocean as if trying to hide the sudden sadness in his eyes. Or maybe she only imagined she saw such an emotion there—when he looked back at her, it was gone.

He held out his hand. "I'm Jonathan Mills."

His fingers were warm and large and made her own hand seem slender and practically petite. "I'm..." She hesitated for a moment, uncertain of which name to give him. "...Mariah Robinson," she decided. It wasn't as if she were telling a lie. It had become true. Over the past two months, she'd acted less and less like Marie Carver and more and more like Mariah Robinson. At least more like the Mariah Robinson she'd heard about from her grandmother. The Mariah her own childhood nickname had come from.

He was still holding her hand, but his gaze had dropped to her breasts again.

"Are you here for the week?" she asked.

He looked up, and for half a second, Mariah thought she saw a flash of embarrassment in his eyes—embarrassment that he'd been caught staring. But it, too, was quickly gone. This man was a master at hiding his feelings.

"I'm here until my hair grows back in," he told her.

Mariah gently pulled her fingers free from his grip. "Well, that's one way to handle a bad hair day."

Jonathan Mills almost smiled. Almost, but not quite. He ran one hand across his short hair. "Actually, today's a rather good hair day, if you want to know the truth."

God, had she insulted him? "I'm sorry, I didn't mean that your hair looks bad...or anything..." Her voice trailed off.

He finally smiled. "It's okay. I know exactly what it looks like, and it looks much better than it did a few days ago."

He had a nice smile. It was only a small smile, barely

playing about the corners of his elegantly shaped lips, but it was very nice just the same.

He looked down at the camera she was holding, its strap still encircling her arm. "Are you a professional photographer?" he asked.

Mariah shook her head. "No, no, I'm... Not." God, what was her problem? It had been two decades since she was a seventh grader, so why was she suddenly acting like one? "It's a hobby."

Was it her imagination, or had Jonathan Mills just gone another shade paler?

"I've got a camera, too," he said, "though I've got to confess I'm not sure I can get it to work. I bought it a few years ago and don't use it much. Would you mind if I brought it over some time? Maybe you could show me how it works."

Would she mind? "Of course not."

He looked down the beach in the direction of the resort. "I think I better go," he said.

He *was* more pale. And perspiration was beading on his upper lip. He wiped it away with the back of his hand. The morning sun was hot, but it wasn't *that* hot.

"Are you all right?" she asked.

He pressed his temples with both hands. "I'm not sure. I'm feeling a little...faint."

He was a stranger. Mariah knew she shouldn't invite him into her house. But it couldn't hurt to bring him up so he could sit for a minute in the shade on her deck, could it?

"Why don't you come up to the house and sit in the shade?" she suggested. "I've got some iced tea in the fridge."

Jonathan nodded. "Thanks."

His entire face was slick with sweat as he followed Mariah up toward the cottage.

Even Princess was subdued, trailing after them quietly.

Mariah walked backward, watching him worriedly. "You're not, like, having a heart attack on me, are you?"

Whatever was happening, he was hurting. His lips twisted in a smilelike grimace. "My heart's fine."

Mariah could see that it took him some effort to speak, so she didn't ask any other questions. He staggered slightly, and she quickly moved to help him, unthinkingly supporting him by putting her arm around his back and his arm across her shoulders.

He was warm and he was solid and he was pressed against her side from her underarm all the way to her thighs. She may have reached for him unthinkingly, but now that she was in this rather intimate position, she could do nothing *but* think.

When was the last time she'd walked arm in arm with a man like this?

Never.

The thought flashed crazily through her mind as she misinterpreted her own silent question. She'd walked arm in arm with plenty of men—although not recently—but she'd never walked arm in arm with a man like this.

Jonathan Mills was different from all of the men she'd ever known. Including Trevor. Maybe especially Trevor.

"I'm really sorry about this," he murmured as they reached the stairs that led to her deck.

"Can you make it up here?" Mariah asked.

But he'd already started to lower himself down so that he was sitting on the third step. He shook his head. "Can you do me a favor?"

"I can try."

"Call my assistant at the resort. His name's Daniel

Tonaka. Room 756. Will you ask him to come and please pick me up?''

"Of course."

Mariah took the steps up two at a time, leaving Princess sitting and worriedly watching her master.

It didn't take long to make the phone call. She woke Daniel Tonaka up, but he snapped instantly awake. She gave him directions, and he told her he was on his way. Mariah had to wonder. Did this happen often?

She poured a plastic tumbler of iced tea as she spoke on the phone, then carried it back to the deck. "It shouldn't take him much more than ten minutes to get over here from the resort...."

Jonathan Mills was no longer sitting on the stairs. He wasn't on the deck, and she would have seen him if he'd come into the house...

Down in the sandy yard, Princess barked sharply. Mariah went halfway down the stairs and then she saw Jonathan.

He was crumpled in the sand, out cold.

At first she thought he was dead, he was lying there so completely motionless. She set the glass of iced tea down on the stairs but knocked it over in her haste to get down to him as quickly as possible.

She found the pulse in his neck beating slowly and steadily and she breathed a sigh of relief. His skin was warm and the stubble from his chin felt rough against her fingers. When was the last time she'd touched a man's face? Surely not an entire five years, back before Trevor finally left? Still, she honestly couldn't remember.

"John," she said softly, trying to rouse him but not wanting to shout in his ear.

He groaned and stirred, but didn't open his eyes.

Mariah could feel the early morning sun already beating down on her head and her back. "John," she said again, louder this time, touching his shoulder. "Come on, wake up. We've got to get you out of the sun."

He was a large man, but Mariah was no lightweight herself, and she was able to hoist him up by taking hold under both arms. As she dragged him toward the shade, he roused slightly, trying to help her. He opened his eyes, but quickly shut them, wincing against the brightness of the sun.

"God, what happened?"

"I think you fainted," she told him.

There was a bit of shade at the side of the house, and he sank to the ground.

"Can you sit up?" she asked.

He shook his head. "Still dizzy."

He lay on his back, right there on the sandy ground. His eyes were closed, and he had one arm thrown across them as if for added protection from the brightness. There were bits of gravel and sand stuck to the side of his face, and Mariah gently brushed them off.

"John, I'm going to go get some cold towels," she told him. "Don't try to stand up, all right?"

"Yeah," he managed to say.

Mariah dashed back up the stairs and into the house. She grabbed two hand towels from the linen closet, stopping only to dampen one with cool water in the kitchen sink.

Jonathan hadn't moved when she reached him, but he did open his eyes again at the sound of her footsteps. "I'm really sorry about this," he said. His eyes were so blue.

Mariah sat down next to him, lifting him slightly so that his head was off the hardness of the ground and resting instead in her lap. She pressed the cool towel against his forehead and he closed his eyes. "I really hope whatever this is, it's not contagious."

Another flash of blue as he looked up at her. "It's not. I'm...not contagious, I promise. I haven't been sleeping that well and... I'm really sorry about this," he said again.

Someday their children would marvel at the story of the way they'd met....

Where had *that* thought come from? It had simply popped into Mariah's mind. Their *children?* What was *that* about? Still, she had to admit, this made one heck of a good story. They meet on the beach, and he turns green and passes out. It certainly was different, at any rate.

"I don't know what happened," he admitted. "I was sitting on the steps, and I was positive I was going to get sick to my stomach, so I stood up and..." He laughed, but it was painful-sounding, embarrassed. "I don't think I've ever fainted before."

He seemed to want to sit up, so Mariah helped him. She could tell with just one touch that he was a mass of tension, a giant bundle of stress. She could feel it in his body, in his shoulders and neck, even see it in the tightened muscles in his face. Gently, she massaged his shoulders and back, wishing she had the power to teach this man in one minute all that she'd learned in the past two months, all the relaxation techniques and stress reduction exercises that had helped her.

"God, that feels good," he breathed.

"There's a licensed masseur at the resort," Mariah told him. "You should definitely schedule some time with him. You're *really* tense."

He was starting to relax, the tightness in his shoulders melting down to a more tolerable level. He sighed and she saw that his eyes were closed as he sat slumped forward, forehead resting in his hands.

"Don't fall asleep yet," Mariah leaned closer to whisper. "I think your friend just pulled up in front of the house."

Her lips were millimeters away from the softness of his ear, and on a whim, she closed the final gap, brushing her lips gently against him in the softest of kisses.

His eyes opened again, and he turned to stare at her, as if she'd taken a bite out of him instead.

Mariah felt her cheeks heat with a blush. Obviously, she'd finally lost her mind. It was the only explanation she could come up with, the only reason she had for kissing this stranger who'd fainted in her yard.

But his eyes seemed to soften as he saw her blush, and with that softness came an almost haunting vulnerability.

That vulnerability was something she instinctively knew that he usually kept hidden. He kept a lot hidden, she knew that, too. There was quite a bit about this man that she recognized, that seemed familiar.

"Wow, John, are you okay?"

Daniel Tonaka was a man of slightly shorter than average height. But he was stronger than his lean build suggested. He leaned over and easily helped Jonathan to his feet.

Daniel looked at Mariah. "What happened?"

"I don't know." She shook her head, gracefully rising and helping Daniel support John as they headed toward his car. "He walked out here from the resort, along the beach. We were talking, and then suddenly, wham-o. He started to sweat and then he passed out."

"I just need some breakfast," John insisted as they helped him into the passenger seat. "I'm all right."

"Yeah, man, you look about as all right as roadkill."

Mariah reclined the seat slightly, then leaned across John to fasten his seat belt. Her breasts brushed his chest, and when she glanced down at him, his eyes were open again, and he was looking directly at her.

"Thank you," he said, giving her one of his almost smiles.

Mariah's mouth was dry as she backed out of the car and closed the door.

"Come on, Princess," Daniel said.

The dog jumped into the car, taking a surefooted stance on the back seat.

"Thank you very much, Miss...?" Daniel called to her. "I'm sorry, I've forgotten your name."

"Robinson," she told him. "Mariah Robinson."

Jonathan Mills lifted a hand in a weak wave as the car pulled away.

Mariah looked at her watch. It wasn't even 6:00 a.m. The day had barely just begun.

She saw them through the window of the resort health club.

She worked out for several hours early each morning—earlier than most other people used the resort facility. She was here only to tone and strengthen her body. She wasn't here to flash her spandex-clad reflection in the mirrors on the wall, to catch the attention of some healthy, weight-lifting, muscle-bound man.

No, the man she was looking for wasn't going to be found pumping iron.

A car pulled into the parking lot alongside the building—the only thing moving in the early-morning stillness. As she worked her triceps, she watched a young Asian man help another man out of that car and toward the wing that held the more expensive rooms. A dog trotted obediently behind them.

The older man was bent over, his shoulders stooped as if from fatigue or pain. His skin had a grayish cast. Yet there was still something about him that caught her eye.

She set down her weights and moved closer to the window, watching until they moved out of sight.

Mariah Robinson belonged to him.

The game had begun early this morning, and already he'd gotten much further than he'd hoped.

John Miller pulled to a stop in Mariah's driveway. He took a deep breath, both amused and disgusted by the sensation of anticipation that was flowing through him.

This woman was his way to get closer to a suspected killer. No more, no less.

He tried to tell himself that the anticipation he was feeling was from being under cover, from closing in on the Black Widow. And those flowers he had on the car seat next to him were all part of his plan to make friends with a woman who was close to his suspect.

Miller had ordered a dozen roses yesterday—a thank-you gift for helping him—before he'd even met Mariah Robinson, as she was currently calling herself. But as he'd gone into the florist's to pick them up this afternoon, he'd spotted a display of bright yellow flowers—great big, round flowers that brought huge, colorful splashes of brilliance into the room.

He'd known instantly that Mariah would prefer wild-looking flowers like that over hothouse roses. On a whim, he'd canceled the roses and bought a huge bouquet of the yellow flowers instead, mixed together with a bunch of daisies and something delicate and white called baby's breath.

He should've stomped down his impulse and bought the damned roses. The roses were part of his plan. The roses said an impersonal thanks. But the yellow flowers echoed the memory of Mariah's gentle hands touching his face, her strong, slender fingers massaging his shoulders, her lips brushing lightly against his ear.

And that was trouble.

The yellow flowers had nothing to do with catching Serena Westford and everything to do with the unmistakable heat of desire that had flooded him as he'd gazed into Mariah's soft brown eyes.

She was everything her picture had shown and more.

And now he was going to walk into her house with these stupid flowers and lie to her about who he was and why he was here. But the biggest lie of all would be in denying the attraction that had flared between them. Jonathan Mills was only to become Mariah's friend. It was John Miller who wanted to take this woman as his lover and lose himself in her quiet serenity for the entire rest of the year.

It was John Miller who'd found himself unable to tear his eyes away from the soft cotton of Mariah's T-shirt as it clung revealingly to her body out on the beach that morning. He'd caught himself staring more than once, and he could only hope that she hadn't noticed.

But he knew damn well that she had. He'd seen the slight pink of her blush on her cheeks.

Miller got out of the car and, carrying the flowers with him, went to Mariah's front door and rang the bell.

There was no answer.

He knew she was home—Daniel had been out on surveillance all day and had just called saying that Mariah was back home after an afternoon of running errands in town. Sure enough, her bike was leaning against the side of the house.

Miller went around toward the back, toward the beach, and nearly ran smack into Mariah.

She'd come directly from the ocean. Her hair was wet, her dark curls like a cap against her head. Her skin glistened from the water, and her tank-style bathing suit was plastered to her incredible body. The sun sparkled on a bead of water caught in her eyelashes as her eyes widened in surprise.

"John! Hi! What are *you* doing here?"

God, she was gorgeous. Every last inch of her was fantastic. But she wrapped her towel around her waist as if self-conscious of the way she looked in a bathing suit.

He held out the yellow flowers. "I wanted to thank you for helping me this morning."

She took the flowers, but barely looked at them. Her attention was fully on him, her gaze searching his face. "Are you all right? You didn't walk all the way out here, did you?"

"No, I drove."

"By yourself?" She looked over his shoulder at the car, parked in her drive.

"I'm feeling much better," he said. "It was just...I don't know, low blood sugar, I guess. I didn't have much dinner last night, and I didn't have anything to eat before I left the resort this morning. But I had some breakfast and even managed to catch a few hours of sleep after Daniel gave me a ride back to my room."

"Low blood sugar," she repeated her gaze never leaving his face.

She clearly didn't believe him. It was the perfect opening for him to begin to tell her Jonathan Mills's cover story. But the words—the lies—stuck in his throat, and for the first time in his life, he almost couldn't do it.

What was wrong with him? This was the part of being under cover that he always enjoyed—getting close to the major players in the game. He'd never thought of his cover story as lies before. It was, instead, the new truth. His cover became his new reality. He *was* Jonathan Mills.

But as he looked into Mariah's eyes, he couldn't push John Miller away. No doubt the fatigue and the stress of the past few years were taking their toll.

"Actually," he said, clearing his throat, "it was probably a combination of low blood sugar—and the fact that I've just finished a course of chemotherapy." He ran his fingers through his barely there hair as he watched realization and horror dawn in Mariah's eyes. He should have felt a burst of satisfaction, but all he felt was this damned twinge of guilt. He hardened himself. He was the robot, after all.

"Oh," she said.

"Cancer," he told her. "Hodgkin's. The doctors caught it early. I'm...I'm lucky, you know?"

She was looking down at the flowers now, but her gaze was unfocused. When she glanced back up at him, he could see that she had tears in her eyes. Tears of compassion, of sympathy. He knew he'd moved another step closer to his goal, but robot or not, he felt like a bastard.

"Would you be interested in that glass of iced tea I offered you this morning?" she asked, blinking back the tears and forcing a friendly smile.

Miller nodded. "Thanks."

Mariah led the way up the stairs to her deck, her hips swaying beneath her beach towel. Miller let himself look. Looking was all he was going to be able to do, God help him.

"These flowers are beautiful. I've never seen anything like them before." She gestured toward a round, umbrella shaded table, surrounded by cushioned chairs. "Why don't you sit down?"

"Thanks."

Mariah carried the flowers into the kitchen and set them down on the counter. Cancer. Jonathan Mills had cancer. He'd just finished a course of *chemotherapy*.

She gripped the edge of the counter, trying hard to keep her balance.

Talk about stress. Talk about pain. Talk about problems. Her own petty problems were laughable compared to having an illness that, left unchecked, was sure to kill him. And even with the treatment, there was still a pretty big chance that he wouldn't survive.

Cancer. God. And *he* was the one bringing *her* flowers.

Mariah took a moment to put them in water, gathering the strength she needed to go back out onto the deck and make small talk with a man who was probably going to die.

Taking a deep breath, she took two glasses from the cabinets and filled them with ice, then poured the tea. *Cancer.*

Somehow, she was able to smile by the time she carried the glasses back out to the deck.

But he wasn't fooled. "I freaked you out, didn't I?" John asked as she set the glass down in front of him. "I'm sorry."

Mariah sat down across from him, arranging her towel so that it covered most of her legs, grateful that he wasn't going to ignore the fact that he'd just told her he was so desperately ill. "Are you able to talk about it?" she asked.

He took a sip of his iced tea. "Sometimes it seems as if it's all I've talked about for the past year."

"If you don't want to, it's—"

"No, that's all right. I guess I...wanted you to know. I haven't always made a habit of doing nosedives into the sand at the drop of a hat." He took a deep breath and forced a smile. "So. I'll give you the *Reader's Digest* version. I was diagnosed with Hodgkin's disease, which is a form of cancer of the lymph nodes. Like I said, my doctors caught it early—I was stage one, which means the cancer hasn't metastasized. It hasn't spread. The survival rate is higher for patients with stage one Hodgkin's. So I took the treatments, did the chemo—which made me far sicker than the Hodgkin's ever did—and here I am, waiting for my hair to grow back in." He paused. "And to find out if I'm finally out of danger."

Mariah remembered the tension she'd felt in his shoulders. Was it any wonder this man was a walking bundle of nerves? He was waiting to find out if he was going to live or die. He looked exhausted, sitting there across from her, the lines in his face pronounced.

"No wonder you're not eating well. You're probably not sleeping very well, either," she said. "Are you?"

Something shifted in his eyes, and he looked out at the ocean, shimmering at the edge of the sand. He didn't answer right away, but she just waited, and he finally turned back to her. "No," he said. "I'm not."

"Is it that you can't fall asleep?" she asked. "Or after you fall asleep, do you wake up a few hours later and just lie there, thinking about everything, worrying...?"

"Both," he admitted.

"I used to do that," she told him. "Two hours after I fell asleep, I'd be wide-awake, lying in bed, suffocating underneath all these screaming anxieties...." She shook her head. "That's not a fun way to live."

"I have nightmares." Miller heard the words leave his mouth, and it was too late to bite them back. Jonathan Mills didn't have nightmares. The nightmares were John Miller's albatross. They belonged to Miller alone. He drank the last of his iced tea and stood up. "I really didn't mean to stay long. I know you probably have things to do. I just wanted to thank you for...everything."

Mariah stood up, too. "You know, I have a book on stress reduction techniques that I could lend you, if you want."

A book. She could lend him. How perfect was that? He could drop by to return it some afternoon—while Serena Westford just happened to be visiting. What a coincidence. Serena meet Jonathan Mills. John, this is Serena...

"Thanks," Miller said. "I'd like that."

With the swish of her towel against her legs, she disappeared into the darkness of the house. The book must've been right in the living room because she came out almost immediately.

He took it from her, glancing quickly at the cover, which read *101 Innovative Ways to Relieve Stress.* "Thanks," he said again. "I'll bring it back in a few days."

"Why don't you keep it," she said. "I've gotten pretty good at most of the exercises in there. Besides, I can always pick up another copy."

Miller had to laugh as his perfect plan crumbled. "Don't you get it? I *want* to return it. It gives me an excuse to come back out here."

Mariah's soft brown eyes got even softer, and John was reminded of the way she'd looked at him this morning after she'd gently kissed his ear. "You don't need an excuse to come over," she told him quietly. "You're welcome here. Any time."

Miller tried to force a smile as he thanked her. What was wrong with him? he wondered again as he walked around to his car. He should be feeling triumphant. She liked him—that couldn't have been more obvious. This was working out perfectly.

Feeling like an absolute bastard, he put the car in gear and drove away.

Chapter 3

Mariah was on the roof when she saw Serena's sports car pull up in front of the Foundations for Families building site.

"Hel-lo!" Her friend's bright English accent carried clearly up to her.

Mariah used the back of her hand to wipe the perspiration from her forehead. Tomorrow she was going to have to remember to bring a sweatband—the weather forecast had predicted more of this relentless heat. She was dirty and hot, with stinging salt and sunblock dripping into her eyes, and her back was starting to ache.

But she was surrounded by people who laughed and sang as they worked. Today she was driving nails alongside Thomas and Renee, the man and woman who would own this house, watching the pride they took in being able to help build the home that would shelter them and their two daughters—Jane Ann and Emma.

Foundations for Families started each day with a minute of silent meditation, of joining hands and closing their eyes, just taking a moment to touch base with the powers that be—God, or Mother Nature, or even Luke Skywalker's Force—it didn't matter which. Meals were something out of an old-fashioned barn raising with sandwiches and lemonade provided by volunteers. And each day, Thomas and Renee would call to Mariah and thank her by name—sometimes even enveloping her in an embrace as she left to go home.

Mariah couldn't remember ever being happier.

Down on the ground, Serena shaded her eyes to gaze up at her. "What time are you done here?"

Mariah rested her hammer against her work boot and unfastened her water bottle from her belt. She took a long swig before answering. "My shift ends at six," she said.

"Good. Then you can meet me at seven, at the resort," Serena decided. "We can eat at the grill out by the pool, then prowl the bars, husband hunting as you so aptly put it."

The resort. Where Jonathan Mills was staying. Except Mariah was almost certain he wasn't the type to hang out in a bar. Still, she was almost tempted to go over there. Almost.

She hooked her water bottle back onto her belt and hefted her hammer. "Sorry. Can't," she told her friend, glad she had an excuse. She wasn't the type to hang out in bars, either. They were noisy, crowded and filled with smoke and desperation. "I'm coming back out here tomorrow. I've got to be up early in the morning. Laronda scheduled a building blitz. We're gonna get this sucker watertight by sundown."

Serena looked at the rough plywood that framed the modestly sized house and skeptically lifted an elegant eyebrow. "You're kidding."

"Nope," Mariah said cheerfully. "Of course, we could always use more volunteers. I don't suppose you're interested…?"

"Not on your life." Serena snorted. "I did my share—in Africa fifteen years ago, with the peace corps."

The peace corps. Funny. Mariah knew Serena had spent nearly eighteen months with the peace corps— building roads and houses, working in a part of Africa where electricity hadn't found its way to this very day. They'd talked about it quite a bit, but Mariah *still* couldn't picture the elegant blonde actually getting her hands dirty digging latrines. Serena? No, she just couldn't imagine it. Still, why would the woman lie? And she spoke of her time in the corps with such authority.

"Sure I can't talk you into having some fun tonight?" Serena asked.

Mariah shook her head. "I'm having fun right now," she told her friend.

"You," Serena said, "are one seriously twisted woman." She called back over her shoulder as she headed toward her car, "Don't forget about my party Friday night."

"You know, Serena, I'm not really the party type…"

But Serena had already climbed behind the wheel, starting her car with a roar.

Mariah didn't want to go to any party. She'd been to several of Serena's affairs before and stood uncomfortably while Serena's chic resort friends talked about nothing of any substance. The weather. The stock market. The best place to rent jet skis.

Last time, she'd left early and vowed to make up an excuse if Serena ever invited her again. She'd have to think up something convincing…

But she wasn't going to think about it right now. She had a house to build. No worries. No problems.

Mariah got back to work.

Miller was running on empty.

He'd awakened before dawn, after only a few hours of rest, jarred out of sleep by an ominous dream. It wasn't his usual nightmare, but it was a dream filled with shadows and darkness, and he knew if he fell back to sleep, he'd soon find himself outside that damned warehouse.

So he'd made himself a cup of coffee, roused Princess and headed down the beach, toward Mariah's cottage.

The first glimmer of daybreak had been lighting the sky when he'd reached the part of the strand where he'd met Mariah two mornings ago. And as he'd watched, the light in her beach house went off, and she came outside, shouldering a backpack.

She climbed on her bicycle and rode away, down the road toward town, before he was even close enough to call out to her.

He stayed for a while, hoping she would return, but she hadn't. Later, he'd found her bike, locked to a rack by the public library.

Having to wait for her to come back was frustrating, but Miller had been on stakeouts that had literally lasted for months, and he knew how to curb his impatience. He'd set up camp under the shade of a brightly colored beach umbrella, lathered himself with sunblock and waited.

He'd spent the first part of the morning reading that book Mariah had lent him. It was one of those touchy-feely books that urged the reader to become one with his or her emotions, and to vent—to talk or cry. Emotional release was necessary—according to the author, a Dr.

Gerrard Hollis from California, of course—before the anxiety causing stress could be relieved.

Miller flipped through the chapters on breathing exercises and self-hypnosis techniques, focusing instead on the section about reducing stress through sex. There was nothing like regularly scheduled orgasmic release—according to the esteemed Dr. Hollis, whoever the hell he was—to counter the bad effects of stress on the human nervous system.

Each of the exercises outlined in the book—and this section went on for an entire detailed chapter—were designed to be both physically and emotionally relaxing. They were also designed to be done either by a couple, or by an individual. Women could make use of certain "assistive" devices if they so desired, Dr. Hollis pointed out.

Miller had gotten a hell of a lot of mileage out of thinking about Mariah performing those exercises, with or without assistive devices.

But she still hadn't returned by lunchtime, and Miller had gone back to the resort. He'd spent the afternoon helping Daniel fine-tune the surveillance equipment the younger man had planted in Serena Westford's rented house. Yesterday, around noon, their suspect had gone off island. Instead of following her, assuming that if she was going over the causeway to the mainland she was planning to stay for a while, Daniel had used the opportunity to hide miniature microphones in key spots in Serena's home.

Their surveillance system was up and running.

And now Miller was back outside Mariah's house, watching the sun set, wondering where she had gone, feeling slightly sick to his stomach from fatigue.

He heard the squeak of her bicycle before he saw her.

As he watched, she turned up her driveway, getting off her bike and pushing it the last few feet up the hill. She put down the kickstand, but the sandy ground was too soft to hold it up, and she leaned it against the side of the house instead.

She slipped her arms out of her backpack and tossed it down near the foot of the stairs leading up to her deck. And then, kicking her feet free from a pair of almost ridiculously clunky work boots, she pulled her T-shirt over her head and headed directly toward the ocean.

As Miller watched, she dropped her shirt on the sand and crash-dived into the water. She didn't notice him until she was on her way back out. And then she saw Princess first.

Mariah's running shorts clung to her thighs, their waistband sagging down across her smooth stomach, the pull of the water turning them into hip huggers. The effect was incredibly sexy, but she quickly hiked her shorts up, pulling at the thin fabric in an attempt to keep it from sticking to her legs.

"John," she said, smiling at him. "Hi."

She was wearing some kind of athletic bra-type thing, the word "Champion," emblazoned across her full breasts. There was nothing she could do to keep *that* wet fabric from clinging, but she seemed more concerned with keeping her belly button properly concealed.

And Miller couldn't think of anything besides the exercise that Dr. Hollis called "Releasing Control." And the one the good doctor called "Pressure Cooker Release." And something particularly intriguing that was cutely labeled "Seabirds in Flight." It was a damned good thing *his* shorts weren't wet and clinging to *his* body.

"Hey." Somehow he managed to make his voice

sound friendly—and as if he *wasn't* thinking about how incredible it would be to reenact that famous beach scene in *From Here to Eternity* with this woman right here and now. "Where've you been all day?"

"Were you looking for me?" She couldn't hide the pleasure in her voice or the spark of attraction in her eyes.

Miller felt that same twinge of something disquieting and he forced it away. So she liked him. Big deal. "I came by this morning," he told her.

The waves tugged again at her shorts, and she came all the way out of the water to stand self-consciously, dripping on the sand. She had no towel to cover herself this time, and she was obviously uncomfortable about that. But she leaned over to greet Princess, enthusiastically rubbing the dog's ears.

"I went over to the mainland," she told Miller, rinsing her hands in the ocean. "I volunteer for Foundations for Families, and I was working at a building site. We got the vinyl siding up today."

"Foundations for Families?"

She nodded, squeezing the water out of her ponytail with one hand. "It's an organization that builds quality homes for people with low incomes. The houses are affordable because of the low-interest mortgages Triple F arranges, and because volunteers actually build the houses alongside the future home owners."

Miller had heard of the group. "I thought you had to be a carpenter or an electrician or a professional roofer to volunteer."

She narrowed her eyes at him. "And how do you know I'm not one?"

Miller covered his sudden flare of alarm with a laugh. She wasn't challenging him or questioning him. She hadn't suddenly realized he knew all about her background through his FBI files. She was teasing. So he teased her back. "Obviously because I'm a sexist bastard who archaically thinks that only men can be carpenters or electricians or roofers. I apologize, *Miz* Robinson. I stand guilty as charged."

Mariah smiled. "Well, now that you've confessed, I can tell you that I'm *not* a carpenter. Although I *am* well on my way to being a professional roofer. I've helped do ten roofs since I got here a couple of months ago. I'm not afraid of heights, so I somehow always end up working there."

"How many days a week do you do this?"

"Three or four," she told him. "Sometimes more if there's a building blitz scheduled."

"A building *blitz?*"

"That's when we push really hard to get one phase of the project finished. Today we blitzed the siding. We've had weeklong blitzes when we start and finish an entire house inside and out." She glanced at him. "If you're interested, you could come along with me next time I go. I've got tomorrow off, but I'm working again the day after that."

"I'd like that," he said quietly. The uneasiness was back—this time not because he was deceiving her, but because his words rang with too much truth. He *would* like it. A lot.

Means to an end, he reminded himself. Mariah Robinson was merely the means to meeting—and catching—Serena Westford.

But Mariah smiled almost shyly into his eyes and he found himself comparing them to whiskey—smoky and light brown and intoxicatingly warming.

"Well, good. I leave early in the morning—the van picks me up at six. You could either meet me here or downtown in front of the library." She looked away from him and glanced up at the sky. The high, dappled clouds were streaked with the pink of the setting sun. "Look at how pretty that is," she breathed.

She was mostly turned away from him, and he was struck by the soft curve of her cheek. Her skin would feel so smooth beneath his fingers, beneath his lips. Her own lips were slightly parted as she gazed raptly out at the water, at the red-orange fingers of clouds extending nearly to the horizon, lit by the sun setting to the west, to their backs.

And then Miller followed her gaze and looked at the sky. The clouds were colored in every hue of pink and orange imaginable. It *was* beautiful. When was the last time he'd stopped to look at a sunset?

"My mother loved sunsets," he said, before he even realized he was speaking. God, what was he telling her? About his *mother...?*

But she'd turned to look at him, her eyes still so warm. "Past tense," she said. "Is she...?"

"She died when I was a kid," he told her, pretending that he had only said that because he was looking for that flare of compassion he knew was going to appear in her eyes. Serena Westford, he reminded himself. Mariah was a means to an end.

Jackpot. Her eyes softened as he knew they would. She was an easy target. He was used to manipulating hardened, suspicious criminals. Compared to them, Mariah Robinson was laughably easy to control. One mention of his poor dead mother—never mind that it was true—and her eyes damn near became filled with tears.

"I'm so sorry," she murmured. She actually reached for his hand and gently squeezed his fingers before she let him go.

"She always wanted to go to Key West," Miller said, watching her eyes. "She thought it was really great that the people on Key West celebrate every single sunset— that they stop and watch and just sit quietly for a few minutes every evening. God, I haven't thought about that in years."

Mariah gave him another gentle smile, and he knew he was lying to himself. He was doing it again. This was *his* background, *his* history, not Jonathan Mills's cover story. He was telling her about his mother because he wanted to tell her. He'd known Tony for nearly two decades, and the topic had never come up in their conversations. Not even once. He knew this girl, what? Two days? And he was telling her about his mother's craziest dream.

They'd planned to rent a car and drive all the way from New Haven down to Key West. But then she'd gone and died.

Mariah was silent, just watching the sky as the last of the light slipped away. Who was controlling whom? Miller had to wonder.

"Do you have plans for this evening?" he asked.

She turned to scoop her T-shirt up off the sand. "A friend wanted me to go barhopping, but I turned her down. That's not exactly my idea of fun. Besides, I'm beat. I'm going to have a shower, a quick dinner, and then sit down with a good book with my feet up."

"I should go," Miller murmured. He definitely had to go. Serena Westford was probably that friend, and if she was out, she probably wasn't going to be dropping by tonight. He'd come back in the morning when the sun was up, when the soft dusk of early evening wasn't throwing seductive shadows across everything.

"Oh, I almost forgot," Mariah said. "I picked something up for you on the mainland this morning."

She hurried back up the beach toward the backpack she'd left at the bottom of the stairs. Miller followed more slowly. She'd picked something up for him?

"Wait a sec," she said, bounding up the stairs, carrying the heavy-looking backpack effortlessly. "I want to turn on the deck light."

Princess followed her up the stairs.

"Hey, what are you doing?" he heard Mariah say to Princess. "You can't go in there. My rental agreement distinctly says no dogs or cats. And I hate to break it to you, babe, but you're definitely a dog. I know you don't believe me...."

The light came on as Miller started up the stairs. It was one of those yellow bug lights, easy on the eyes. It cast a golden, almost fairy-tale-like glow on the deck.

Mariah had her backpack on the table as she unzipped one of the compartments. He stopped halfway up the stairs, afraid to get too close, fighting the pull that drew him toward her. Means to an end, he reminded himself.

"There's a Native American craft shop on the mainland," she told him as she drew a heavy tool belt out and set it on the table. "I love going in there—they've got some really beautiful jewelry and some fabulous artwork. But when I went past this morning, I was thinking about you and I went in and bought you *this*." She pulled a bag out of her pack and something out of that bag.

It was round and crisscrossed with a delicate string of some kind, intricately woven as if it were a web. A feather was in the center, held in place by the string, and several other longer feathers hung down from the bottom of the circle.

Miller didn't know what the hell it was, but whatever

t was, Mariah had bought it for *him*. She'd actually
bought him a *gift*.

"Wow," he said. "Thanks."

She grinned at him. "You don't have a clue what this
is, do you?"

"It's, um, something to hang on the wall?"

"It's something to hang on the wall by your bed," she
told him. "It's a dream catcher. Certain Southwestern
Native American tribes believed having one near while
you slept would keep you from having nightmares." She
held it out to him. "Who knows? Maybe they're right.
Maybe if you hang it up, you'll be able to sleep."

Miller had to climb the last few steps to take the dream
catcher from her hands. He wasn't sure what to say. He
couldn't remember the last time anyone had bought him
anything. "Thank you," he managed. She had been
thinking about him today. They'd only met twice, and
she had been thinking about him....

That was good for the case, he tried to tell himself, but
he knew the real truth. It had nothing to do with Serena
Westford and everything to do with this sudden ache of
desire he couldn't seem to ignore.

For the briefest, wildest moment, he actually considered following through on his urges to make his relationship with Mariah a sexual one. But even he couldn't do
that. Even he wasn't enough of a son of a bitch to use
her that way.

Still, when Miller opened his mouth to take his leave,
he found himself saying something else entirely. "I
haven't had dinner yet. Can I talk you into joining me?
There's a fish place right down the road...?"

"I'm really not up to going out," Mariah told him.
"But I've got a swordfish steak in the fridge that I was
going to throw on the grill. I'd love it if you'd join me."

She didn't give him time to respond. "I've *got* to take a shower," she said, pushing open the sliding door that led from the deck into the house. "I'll be quick—help yourself to a beer or a soda from the kitchen."

She was inside the house before he could come up with a good reason why he *shouldn't* stay for dinner. But there were plenty of reasons. Because eating here, in the seclusion of her cottage, was too intimate. Because he wasn't sure he'd be able to maintain this pretense of wanting to be only friends. Because the thought of her in the shower while he was out here waiting was far too provocative. Because he didn't trust himself to keep his distance.

But Miller didn't say anything.

Because, despite the fact he knew he was playing with fire, he wanted to stay here with Mariah Robinson more than he'd wanted anything in years.

"Car alarms," John said as he helped Mariah carry the last of the dishes back into the kitchen. "The company makes car alarms, and in the late eighties the business boomed. I took over as CEO when my father retired. I've been gone too long—I need to get back to work in a month or two."

Mariah leaned back against the sink. "How have the sales figures been since you've left?"

He shrugged. "Holding steady."

"Then you don't *need* to do anything," she told him. "Particularly not throw yourself back into the rat race before you're physically ready. Give yourself a break."

He smiled very slightly. "I still look pretty awful, huh?"

"Actually, you look much better." Over the past few days, his hair had grown in quite a bit more. Mariah figured he must be one of those men who needed a cut every two weeks or so because his hair grew so quickly. It was dark and thick and he now looked as if he'd intentionally gotten a crew cut rather than as if he'd been attacked by a mad barber with an electric razor.

His skin looked a whole lot less gray, too. He actually had some color, as if he'd been out in the sun for part of the day.

His eyes were a different story. Slightly bloodshot and bleary, he still looked as if he hadn't slept in weeks.

"Did you get a chance to look at that book I gave you?" she added.

"Yeah." He couldn't hide his smile. "It was... educational. Particularly the chapter about stress reduction through sex."

Mariah felt her cheeks heat with a blush. "Oh, God," she said. "I forgot all about that chapter. He *does* go into some detail, doesn't he? I hope you didn't think I was—"

"I didn't think anything," he interrupted her. "It's all right. I was just teasing."

She laughed giddily. "And I was just going to ask you into the living room to try out one of my favorite stress relieving exercises, but now I'm not sure how you'll take that invitation."

"It wouldn't happen to be the exercise called "Pressure Cooker Release," by any chance?" he asked.

She knew exactly which one he was talking about, and she snorted, feeling her face turn an even brighter shade of red. "Not a chance." But maybe after she got to know him quite a bit better...

He smiled as if he was following the direction of her thoughts. Jonathan Mills had the *nicest* smile. He didn't use it very often, but when he did, it softened the harsh lines of his face and warmed the electric blue of his eyes.

She found herself smiling back at him almost foolishly.

He broke their gaze, glancing away from her as if he were afraid the heat that was building in both of their eyes had the potential to burn the house down.

Pressure cooker release indeed.

Mariah waited for a moment, but he didn't look back at her. Instead, he poured himself another mug of decaf, adding just a touch of sugar, no milk.

The conversation had been heading in a dangerously flirtatious and sexually charged direction. John had started it, but then he'd just as definitely ended it. He'd stopped them cold instead of continuing on into an area peppered with lingering looks and hot sparks that could jolt to life a powerful lightning bolt between them.

Mariah didn't know whether to feel disappointed or relieved.

Jonathan Mills had proven himself to be the perfect dinner guest. He'd started the gas grill while she was in the shower and had even put together a salad from the fresh vegetables she'd had in the refrigerator.

He was clearly good at fending for himself in a kitchen. He had to be—he'd told her over dinner that he'd never been married. He'd told her quite a bit more about the successful business he'd inherited.

What she couldn't figure out was why no woman had managed yet to get her hooks into such an attractive and well-to-do man.

Not that Mariah was looking to get involved on any kind of permanent basis. She wasn't like Serena, eyeing every man who came her way for eligibility and holding a checklist of whatever characteristics she required in a husband. Money, Mariah thought. Serena wouldn't want a man if he didn't have plenty of money. John had that, but he also had cancer. Serena probably wouldn't be very interested in acquiring a man who was fighting a potentially terminal illness.

Nobody would.

Who would want to risk becoming involved with a man who had Death, complete with black robe and sickle, hovering over him?

Mariah cleared her throat. "Well," she said, "if you're interested in giving it a try, the relaxation exercise I'm thinking about is one I found extremely effective and…"

He looked a little embarrassed. "I don't know. I've never been very good at that kind of thing. I mean, it's never worked for me in the past and—"

"What can it hurt to try?"

John met her eyes then. He laughed halfheartedly, sheepishly. "I really don't have much patience for doing things like lying on your back and closing your eyes and having someone tell you to imagine you're in some special place with a waterfall trickling and birds singing. I've never been to a place like that and I can't relate at all and—"

Mariah held out her hand. "Just try it."

He looked from her face to her hand and back, but didn't move. "I should just go."

She stepped closer and took his hand. "I promise it won't hurt," she said as she led him into the living room.

Miller knew he shouldn't be doing this. This kind of touchy-feely stuff could lead to actual touching and feeling. And as much as he wanted that, it wasn't on his agenda.

He was here to catch a killer, he reminded himself. Mariah was going to provide his introduction to that killer. Her role was to be that of a mutual friend. A *friend*, not a lover. A means to an end.

As Mariah passed a halogen lamp, she turned the

switch, fading the light to an almost nonexistent glow. It was a typical rental beach house living room. Sturdy furniture with stain-resistant slipcovers. Low-pile, wall-to-wall carpeting. Generic pictures of lighthouses and seabirds on the walls. A rental TV and VCR all but chained to the floor. White walls and plain, easy-to-clean curtains.

But Mariah had been here for two months, and she'd added touches of her own personality to the room.

A wind chime near the sliding glass doors, moving slightly in the evening breeze. Books stacked on an end table—everything from romances to military nonfiction. A boom box and a pile of CDs on another end table. A crystal bird on a string in front of a window, sparkling even in the dim light. A batik-print throw across the couch. The bouquet of bright yellow flowers he'd brought her just a few mornings ago.

She released his hand. "Lie down."

"On the floor?" God, he hated this already. But he did it, lying on his back. "And close my eyes, right?"

"Mmm-hmm."

As he closed his eyes, he heard her sit on the couch, heard her sandals drop to the floor as she pulled her long legs up underneath her.

"Okay, are your eyes closed?"

Miller sighed. "Yeah."

"Okay, now I want you to picture yourself lying in a special place. In a field with flowers growing and birds flying all around and a waterfall in the distance..."

Miller opened his eyes. She was laughing at him.

"You should see the look on your face."

He sat up, rubbing his neck and shoulders with one hand. "I'm glad I entertained you. Of course, now my stress levels are so high I may never recover."

Mariah laughed. It was a husky, musical sound that warmed him.

"Lie down here on the couch," she said, moving out of his way and patting the cushions. "On your stomach this time. I'll rub your back while we do this, get those stress levels back down to a more normal level—which for you is probably off the scale, right?" She stopped, suddenly uncertain. "What I meant to say was, I'll rub your back if you *want*..."

Miller hesitated. Did he want...? God, yes. A back rub. Mariah's fingers on his neck and shoulders... He moved up onto the couch. Surely he was strong enough to keep it from going any further.

"Thanks," he said, resting his head on top of his folded arms.

"It'll be easier if you take your shirt off," she told him, "but you don't have to if you don't want to," she added quickly.

Miller turned to look up at her. "This is just a back rub, right?"

She nodded.

"You're doing me a favor. Why wouldn't I want to make it easier for you?"

Mariah was blunt. "Because people sometimes misinterpret removing clothes as a sign that something of a sexual nature is going to follow."

He had to smile. "Yeah, well, that's mostly true, isn't it?"

She sat down next to him, on the very edge of the couch. "If I was going to come on to you, I would be honest about it. I would tell you, 'Hey. John, I'm going to come on to you now, okay?' But that's not what I'm doing here. Really. We just met. And if *that* weren't enough, you have issues. *I* have issues."

"You have issues?" he asked. Did they have something to do with the reason why she'd traveled more than halfway across the country to live under an assumed name?

"Not like yours. But yeah. I do. Doesn't everyone?"

"I guess."

She was remarkably pretty, sitting there above him like that, her clean, shiny hair falling in curls and waves down to her shoulders.

She'd put on a pair of cutoff jeans and a tank top when she came out of the shower. She smelled like after-sun lotion, sweet and fresh.

Miller pulled his T-shirt over his head, rolling it into a ball and using it, along with his arms, as a pillow. As he shifted into position, he could feel Mariah's leg pressed against him. It felt much too good, but she didn't move away, and he was penned in by the back of the couch. He had nowhere to go.

But then she touched him, her fingers cool against the back of his neck, and he forgot about trying to move away from her. All he wanted was to move closer. He closed his eyes, gritting his teeth against the sweet sensation.

"This is supposed to make you relax, not tighten up," Mariah murmured.

"Sorry."

"Make a fist," she told him.

Miller opened his eyes, lifting his head to look back at her. "What?"

She gently pushed his head back down. "Are you right- or left-handed?"

"Right-handed."

"Make a fist with your right hand," she said. "Hold it tightly—don't let go."

"Am I allowed to ask why?"

"Yeah. Sure."

"Why?"

"Because I'm telling you to. You agreed to do this exercise, and it won't work unless you make a fist. So do it."

"I never agreed to do anything," he protested.

"You gave your unspoken consent when you lay down on this couch. Make a fist, Mills." She paused. "Or I'll stop rubbing your back."

Miller quickly made a fist. "Now what?"

"Now relax every other muscle in your body—but keep that fist tight. Start with your toes, then your feet. You've surely done that exercise where you relax every muscle, first in your legs and then your arms and then all the way up to your neck?"

"Yeah, but it doesn't work," he said flatly.

"Yes, it does. I'll talk you through it. Start with your feet. Flex them, flex your toes, then relax them. Do it a couple of times."

She ran her fingers through his hair, massaging the back of his head and even his temples. Christ, it felt heavenly.

"Okay, now do the same thing with your calves," she told him. "Tighten, then relax. You know, this is actually an exercise from a Lamaze childbirthing class. The mothers-to-be learn to keep the rest of their bodies relaxed while one muscle is tensed and working hard. Of course they can't practice with the actual muscle that's going to be contracting, so they contract something else, like a fist." Her voice was soft and as soothing as her hands. Despite himself, he felt his tension draining away. He actually felt himself start to relax. "Okay, tighten and relax the rest of your legs. Are you doing it? Are you loose?''

He felt her reach down with one hand and touch his legs, shaking them slightly.

''That's pretty good, John. You're doing great. Relax your hips and stomach…and your rear end. And don't forget to breathe—slow it down, take your time. But keep that fist tight.''

Miller felt as if he were floating.

''Okay, now relax your shoulders and your arms. Relax your left hand—everything but that right fist. Keep holding that.''

He could feel her touching him, her hands light against his back, caressing his shoulders and arms.

''Relax the muscles in your face,'' she told him softly. Her husky, musical voice seemed to come from a great distance. ''Loosen your jaw. Let it drop open.

''Okay, now relax your right hand. Open it up as if you're setting everything free—all of your tension and stress. Just let it go.''

Let it go.

Let it go.

Miller did as she commanded, and before he could stop himself, he sank into a deep, complete, dreamless sleep.

Chapter 4

Mariah woke up, heart pounding, sure she'd been dreaming.

But then she heard it again. A strangled, anguished cry from the living room. She nearly knocked over the lamp on her bedside table as she lunged for it, using both hands to flip the switch.

Four fifty-eight. It was 4:58 in the morning.

And that was Jonathan Mills making those noises out in her living room.

He'd fallen asleep on her couch. He'd lain there motionless, as thoroughly out cold as if he'd been hit over the head with a sledgehammer. Mariah had stayed up reading for as long as she could, but had finally given in to her own fatigue. She hadn't had the heart to wake him and send him home.

She'd put an old blanket under the patio table for Princess to curl up on and covered John with a light sheet before she went to bed herself.

He cried out again, and she went out into the hall, turning on the light.

He was still asleep, still on the couch. He'd thrown off the sheet, shifting onto his back. Perspiration shone on his face and chest as he moved restlessly.

He was having a nightmare.

"John." Mariah knelt next to him. "John, wake up."

She touched him gently on the shoulder, but he didn't seem to feel her. His eyes opened, but he didn't even seem to see her. What he *did* see, she couldn't imagine—the look of sheer horror on his face was awful. And then he cried out, a not quite human sounding "No!" that ripped from his throat. And then the horror turned to rage. "No!" he shouted again. *"No!"*

He grabbed her by the upper arms, and Mariah felt a flash of real fear as his fingers bit harshly into her. For one terrifying moment, she was sure he was going to fling her across the room. Whoever it was he saw here in her place, he was intending to hurt and hurt badly. She tried to pull away, but he only tightened his grip, making her squeal with pain.

"Ow! John! God! Wake up! It's me, Mariah! Don't—"

Recognition flared in his eyes. "Oh, *God!*"

He released her, and she fell back on the rug on her rear end and elbows. She pushed herself away from him, scooting back until she bumped into an easy chair.

She was breathing hard, and he was, too, as he sat, almost doubled over on the couch.

The shock in his eyes was unmistakable. "Mariah, I'm sorry," he rasped. "What the hell happened? I was... God, I was dreaming about—" He cut himself off abruptly. "Did I hurt you? God, I didn't mean to hurt you...."

Mariah rubbed her arms. Already she could see faint bruises where his fingers had pressed too hard in the soft underside of her upper arms. "You scared me," she admitted. "You were so *angry* and—"

"I'm sorry," he said again. "Oh, God." He stood up. "I better go. I'm so sorry...."

As Mariah watched, he turned to search for his T-shirt. He couldn't find it and he had to sit down on the couch again for a moment because he was shaking. He was actually physically shaking.

"You don't ever let yourself get good and angry," Mariah realized suddenly. "Do you?"

"Do you have a shirt I can borrow? Mine's gone."

"You don't, do you?" she persisted.

He could barely meet her eyes. "No. Getting angry doesn't solve anything."

"Yeah, but sometimes it makes you *feel* better." She crawled back toward him. "John, when was the last time you let yourself cry?"

He shook his head. "Mariah—"

"You don't cry, either, do you?" she said, sitting next to him on the couch. "You just live with all of your fear and anger and grief all bottled up inside. No wonder you have nightmares!"

Miller turned away from her, desperate to find his shirt, desperate to be out of there, away from the fear he'd seen in her eyes. God, he could have hurt her so badly.

But then she touched him. His hand, his shoulder, her fingers soft against the side of his face, and he realized there was no fear in her eyes anymore. There was only sweet concern.

Her face was clean of any makeup and her hair was mussed from sleep. She was wearing an oversize T-shirt that barely covered the tops of her thighs, exposing the full length of her statuesque legs. Her smooth, soft skin seemed to radiate heat.

He reached for her almost blindly, wanting only... what? Miller didn't know what he wanted. All he knew was that she was there, offering comfort that he couldn't keep himself from taking.

She seemed to melt into his arms, her face lifted toward his, and then he was kissing her.

Her lips were warm and soft and so incredibly sweet. He kissed her harder, drinking of her thirstily, unable to get enough.

Her body was so soft, her breasts brushing against his chest, and he pulled her closer. She fit against him so perfectly, the room seemed to spin around him. He wanted to touch her everywhere. He wanted to pull off her shirt and feel her smooth skin against his.

He pulled her back with him onto the couch and their legs intertwined. Not for the first time that night, Miller wished he'd worn shorts instead of jeans.

He shifted his weight and nestled between the softness of her thighs, nearly delirious with need as he kissed her harder, deeper.

This was one hell of a bad mistake.

She pushed herself tightly against him, and he pushed the thought away, refusing to think at all, losing himself in her kisses, in the softness of her breast cupped in his hand.

She was opening herself to him, so generously giving him everything he asked for, and more.

And he was going to use her to satisfy his sexual desires, then walk away from her without looking back the moment she introduced him to Serena Westford—her friend, his chief suspect.

He couldn't do this. How could he do this and look

himself in the eye in the mirror while he shaved each morning?

But look where he was. Poised on the edge of total ecstasy. Inches away from paradise.

He pulled back, and she smiled up at him, hooking her legs around him, her hands slipping down to his buttocks and pressing him securely against her.

"John, don't stop," she whispered. "In case you haven't noticed, I *am* coming on to you now."

"I don't have any protection," he lied.

"I do," she told him. "In my bedroom." She reached between them, her fingers unfastening the top button of his jeans. "I can get it...."

Miller felt himself weaken. She wanted him. She couldn't be any more obvious about it.

He let her pull his head down toward hers for another kiss, let her stroke the solid length of his arousal through the denim of his jeans, all the while cursing his inability to keep this from going too far.

He was a lowlife. He was a snake. And after all was said and done, she would hate him forever.

Somehow, Miller found the strength to pull back from her, out of her arms, outside the reach of her hands. "I can't do this," he said, nearly choking on the words. He sat on the edge of the couch, turned away from her, running his shaking hands through his hair. "Mariah, I can't take advantage of you this way."

She touched his back gently, lightly. "You're not taking advantage of me," she said quietly. "I promise."

He turned to look at her. Big mistake. She looked incredible with her T-shirt pushed up and twisted around her waist. She was wearing high-cut white cotton panties that were far sexier than any satin or lace he'd ever seen. She wanted to make love to him. He could reach for her and have that T-shirt and those panties off of her in less than a second. He could be inside of her in the time it took to go into her bedroom and find her supply of condoms.

He had to look away before he could speak.

"It's not that I don't want to, because I do," he told her. "It's just..."

Miller could feel her moving, straightening her T-shirt, sitting up on the other end of the couch. "It's all right. You don't have to explain."

"I don't want to rush things," he said, wishing he could tell her the truth. But what *was* the truth? That he couldn't make love to her because he was intending to woo and marry a woman she considered one of her closest friends?

He had to stop thinking like John Miller and start thinking like Jonathan Mills. He had to *become* Jonathan Mills, and his reality—and the truth—would change, too. But he'd never had so much trouble taking on a different persona before.

"I'm not ready to do more than just be friends with you, Mariah. I just got out of the hospital, my latest test results aren't even in and..." He broke off, staring out the window at the dawn breaking on the horizon, Jonathan Mills all but forgotten. "It's morning."

As Mariah watched, John stood up, transfixed by the smear of color in the eastern sky.

"I slept until morning," he said, turning to look at her. He smiled—a slight lifting of one side of his mouth, but a smile just the same. "Whoa. How'd *that* happen?"

She smiled back at him. "I guess you're going to have to admit that my silly relaxation exercise worked."

He shook his head in wonder, just gazing at her. She

could still see heat in his eyes and she knew he could see the same in hers.

He looked impossibly good with his shirt off and the top button of his jeans still unfastened. He was maybe just a little bit too skinny, but it was clear that before his illness he'd been in exceptionally good shape.

She could guess why he didn't want to become involved with her. He was just out of the hospital, he'd said. He didn't even know if he was going to live or die. And if he thought he was going to die…

Another man might have more of a live-for-today attitude. But John refused to take advantage of her. He was trying to keep her from being hurt, to keep her from becoming too involved in what could quite possibly be a dead-end relationship in a very literal sense.

But it was too late. She already was involved.

It was crazy—she should be pushing to keep her distance, not wanting to get closer to him. She didn't need to fall for some guy who was going to go and die. She should find his shirt for him, and help him out the door.

But he found his shirt on his own, on the floor next to the couch. He slipped it on. "I better go."

He didn't want to leave. She could see it in his eyes. And when he leaned over to kiss her goodbye—not just once, but twice, then three times, each kiss longer than the last—she thought he just might change his mind.

But he didn't. He finally pulled away, backing toward the door.

"I'd love it if you came over for dinner again tonight," she told him, knowing that she was risking everything—*every*thing—with her invitation.

Something shifted in his eyes. "I'm not sure I can."

Mariah was picking up all kinds of mixed signals from him. First those lingering goodbye kisses, and now this evasiveness. It didn't make sense. Or maybe it made perfect sense. Mariah wasn't sure which—she'd never been this intimate with someone dealing with a catastrophic illness before.

"Call me," Mariah told him, adding softly, "if you want."

He looked back at her one more time before going out the door. "I want. I'm just not sure I should."

Serena went through the sliding glass doors, past the dining table and directly into the kitchen, raising her voice so that Mariah could hear from her vantage point on the deck. "Thank God you're home. I'm so thirsty, I was sure I was going to die if I had to wait until I got all the way to my place."

"Your place is not *that* much farther up the road." Mariah glanced up from the piles of black-and-white photographs she was sorting as Serena sat down across from her at the table on the deck, a tall glass of iced tea in hand.

"Three miles," Serena told her after taking a long sip. "I couldn't have made it even one-*tenth* of a mile. Bless you for keeping this in the icebox, already chilled. I was parched." She leaned forward to pull one of the pictures out from the others, pointing with one long, perfectly manicured fingernail. "Is that me?"

Mariah looked closely. Ever since her initial meeting with Serena, she had tried to be careful not to offend her friend by taking her picture. Or rather, she had tried not to offend Serena by letting her *know* her picture was being taken. Mariah had actually managed to get several excellent photographs of the beautiful Englishwoman— taken, no less, with one of those cheap little disposable cameras. Serena was incredibly photogenic, and in color, even on inexpensive film, her inner vibrance was emphasized. Mariah was careful to keep those pictures hidden.

But yes, that was definitely Serena, caught in motion at the edge of a particularly nice shot of the resort beach, moments before a storm struck. "You must've walked into the shot," Mariah said.

Serena picked it up, looking at it more closely. "I'm a big blur—except for my face." She lifted her gaze to Mariah. "Do you have any copies of this?"

Mariah sifted through the pile that photo had been in. "No, I don't think so."

"How about the negative? You still have that, right?"

Mariah sighed. "I don't know. It might be down in the darkroom, but it might've been in the batch I just brought over to B&W Photo Lab for safekeeping."

"Safekeeping?" Serena's voice rose an octave in disbelief. "Forgive me for being insensitive, but, Mariah sweetheart, no one's going to want to steal your negatives. You know I love you madly, dearest, but it's not as if you're Ansel Adams."

Mariah laughed. "I bring them to B&W for storage. I don't have air-conditioning here, and the humidity and salt air are hell on film."

Serena slipped the photo in question into her purse. "You realize, of course, that I'm going to have to kill you now for stealing my soul," she said with a smile.

"Hey, you were the one who stuck your soul into my shot," Mariah protested. "Besides, I'll get the negative next time I'm over at B&W. You can have it, and your soul will be as good as new."

"Do you promise?"

"I promise. Although it occurs to me that you might want to get yourself a more American approach to having your picture taken. You're not living in Africa anymore."

"Thank God." Serena took another sip of her drink. "So. How are you?"

"Fine." Mariah glanced suspiciously at the other woman. "Why?"

"Just wondering."

"Don't I look fine?"

Serena rested her chin in the palm of her hand, studying Mariah with great scrutiny. "Actually, you don't look half as fine as I would have thought."

Mariah just waited.

"You're not going to tell me a thing, are you?" Serena asked. "You're going to make me ask, aren't you? You're going to make me pull every little last juicy detail out of you."

Mariah went back to work. "I don't know what you're talking about."

"I'm talking about the man."

"What man?"

"The one I saw leaving your house at five-thirty this morning. Tall, dark and probably handsome—although I'm not certain. I was too far away to see details."

Mariah was floored. "What on earth were *you* doing up at five-thirty in the morning?"

"I get up that early every morning and go over to use the resort health club," Serena told her.

"You're kidding. Five-thirty? *Every* morning?"

"Just about. This morning the tide was low, so I rode my bike along the beach. And as I went past your place, I distinctly saw a man emerging from your deck door. I'm assuming he wasn't the refrigerator repairman."

"No, he wasn't." Mariah didn't look up from her photos.

"Well...?"

"Well what?"

"This is the place in the conversation where you tell me who he is, where you met him, and any other fascinating facts such as whether he was any good in bed, and so on and so forth?"

Mariah felt herself blush. "Serena, we're just friends."

"A friend who happens to stay until dawn? How modern of you, Mariah."

"He came over for dinner and fell asleep on my couch. He's been ill recently." Mariah hesitated, wanting to tell Serena about Jonathan Mills, but not wanting to tell too much. "His name is John, and he's very nice. He's staying over at the resort."

"So he's rich," Serena surmised. "Medium rich or filthy rich?"

"I don't know—who cares?"

"*I* care. Take a guess."

Mariah sighed in exasperation. "Filthy rich, I think. He inherited a company that makes car alarms."

"You said he's been ill? Nothing serious, I hope."

Mariah sighed again. "Actually, it *is* serious. He's got cancer. He's just had a round of chemotherapy. I think the prognosis is good, but there's never any guarantees with something like this."

"What did you say his name was?"

"Jonathan Mills."

"It's probably smart to keep your distance. If you're not careful, you could end up a widow. Of course, in his case, that means you'd inherit his car alarm fortune, so it *could* be worse—"

"*Serena!*" Mariah stared at her friend. "Don't even *think* that. He's *not* going to die."

The blonde was unperturbed. "You just told me that he might." She stood up. "Look, I've got to run. Thanks for the tea. See you later tonight."

Mariah frowned. "Later...tonight?"

"My party. You've forgotten, haven't you? Lord, Mariah, you're hopeless without your date book."

"No, I'm *relaxed* without my date book. Oh, that reminds me—can I borrow your car this afternoon? Just for an hour?"

Serena looked at her watch. "I'm getting my hair done at half past two. If you want to drive me to the salon, you can use the car for about an hour then."

"Perfect. Except I'm not sure I can make it to the party—I'm tentatively scheduled to have dinner again with John." Except she wasn't. Not really. She'd asked, but he'd run away.

"Bring him. Call him, invite him to my party, and bring him along with you. I want to meet this *friend* of yours. No excuses," Serena said sternly as she disappeared down the deck steps.

Mariah gazed after her. Call him. Invite him to the party. Who knows? Maybe he'd actually agree to go.

He was the one. The gray-faced man from the resort. She'd recognized him right away.

The fact that he'd spent the night with that silly cow only served to make him even more perfect.

Tonight she would begin to cast her spell.

Tonight she would allow herself to start thinking about the dinner she would serve him.

Oh, it was still weeks away—maybe even months. But it was coming. She could taste it.

And tomorrow morning, she would go shopping for the perfect knife.

The message light on his telephone was blinking when Miller returned to his suite of rooms after lunch.

Daniel had the portable surveillance equipment set up in the living room. The system was up and running when Miller came in. Daniel was wearing headphones, listening intently, using his laptop computer to control the volume of the different microphones they'd distributed throughout Serena Westford's house. The DAT recorder was running—making a permanent record of every word spoken in the huge beach house.

"Lots of activity," Daniel reported, his eyes never leaving his computer screen. "Some kind of party is happening over at the spider's web tonight."

"I know." Miller picked up the phone and dialed the resort desk. "Jonathan Mills," he said. "Any messages?"

"A Mariah Robinson asked to leave voice mail. Shall I connect you to that now, sir?" the desk clerk asked.

"Yes. Please."

There was a whirr and a click, and then Mariah's voice came on the line.

"John. Hi. It's me, Mariah. Robinson. From, um, last night? God, I sound totally lame. Of course you know who I am. I just...I wanted to invite you to a party that a friend is having tonight—"

"Jackpot," Miller said.

Daniel glanced in his direction. "Party invitation?"

Miller nodded, holding up his hand. Mariah's message wasn't over yet.

"...going to start at around nine," her voice said, "and I was thinking that maybe we could have dinner together first—if you're free. If you want to." He heard her draw in a deep breath. "I'd really like to see you again. I guess that's kind of obvious, considering everything that happened this morning." She hesitated. "So, call me, all right?'' She left her phone number, then the message ended.

Miller really wanted to see her again, too. *Really* wanted to see her again.

Daniel glanced at him one more time, and Miller realized he was standing there, staring at nothing, listening to nothing. He quickly hung up the phone.

"Everything all right?" Daniel asked.

"Yeah." He was well aware that Daniel had said not one word about the fact that Miller hadn't come back to the hotel last night until after dawn. The kid hadn't even lifted an eyebrow.

But now Daniel cleared his throat. "John, I don't mean to pry, but—"

"Then don't," Miller said shortly. "Not that it's any of your business, but nothing happened last night." But even as he said the words, Miller knew they were a lie. Something *had* happened last night. Mariah Robinson had touched him, and for nearly eight hours, his demons had been kept at bay.

Something very big had happened last night.

For the first time since forever, John Miller had slept.

Mariah was dressing up.

She couldn't remember the last time she'd worn anything besides shorts and a T-shirt or a bathing suit. She'd gone to Serena's other parties in casual clothes. But tonight, she'd pulled her full collection of dresses—all four of 'em—out of the back of her closet. Three of them were pretty standard Sunday-best, goin'-to-meeting-type affairs, with tiny, demure flowers and conservative necklines.

The fourth was black. It was a short-sleeved sheath cut fashionably above the knee, with a sweetheart neckline that would draw one's eyes—preferably Jonathan Mills's eyes—to her plentiful assets. Her full breasts were, depending on her mood, one of her best features or one of her worst. Tonight, she was going to think positively. Tonight they were an asset.

She briefly considered sheer black stockings, but rejected them in place of bare legs and a healthy coating of Cutter's—in consideration of the sultry evening heat.

Usually when she went out with a man, she wore flats, but Jonathan Mills was tall enough for her to wear heels. They might make her stand nose to nose with him, but she *wouldn't* tower over him.

Since the moment he'd called to tell her that he wasn't available for dinner but he'd love to go to the party with her, Mariah had been walking on air. She was ridiculously excited about seeing him again—she'd thought about almost nothing else all afternoon.

She couldn't remember the last time she'd felt this way. Even in college, when she was first dating Trevor, she hadn't felt this giddy.

Even the dark cloud of anxiety cast by John's potentially terminal illness didn't faze her tonight. They'd caught the cancer early, he'd told her. The survival rate for this type of cancer was high. He was going to live. Positive thinking.

Mariah felt another surge of anticipation as she slipped into her shoes and stepped back to look at herself in the mirror.

She looked...sexy. She looked...well proportioned. It was true that those proportions were extra large, but they had to be to fit her height. And in this case, she was using her body to her advantage. In this dress, with this neckline, she had cleavage with a capital *C*. All that without a WonderBra in sight.

The doorbell rang, and she smoothed the dress over her hips one last time, leaning closer to check her lipstick.

Ready or not, her date had come.

Praying that she wasn't coming on too strong, what with the attack of the monster cleavage and all, Mariah opened her front door.

"Hi," she said breathlessly.

John's eyes skimmed down her once, then twice, then more slowly, before coming back to rest on her face as he smiled. "Wow. You look...incredible."

She stepped back and opened the door wider to let him in.

"Incredibly tall," he added as he noted the heels that put them eye to eye.

Was that a compliment? Mariah took it as one. "Thank you," she said, leading the way into the kitchen. "I'm ready to go, but I wanted to show you something first."

He was dressed a whole lot more casually than she, in a faded pair of jeans, time-softened leather boat shoes and a sport jacket over a plain T-shirt.

"I think I might be underdressed," he said.

"Don't worry about it. Knowing Serena's friends, there'll be an equal mix of sequined gowns and tank tops over swimsuits." Mariah opened the door to the basement.

"Serena?" he asked.

"Westford," she told him, turning on the switch that lit the stairs going down. "She lives a little more than three miles north, just up the road."

"Is she one of the Boston Westfords? Funny, maybe I know one of her brothers."

Mariah shook her head, poised at the top of the stairs. "She hasn't talked about Boston. Or any brothers. When we met, she *did* give me a business card with a Hartford hotel, but I think that was only a temporary address. I think she lived in Paris for a few years." She started down, careful of the rough wooden steps in her heels. "Aren't you coming?"

"Into the basement? Is your darkroom down there?"

"My darkroom's down here," Mariah told him, "but that's not what I want to show you."

She turned on another light.

The ceiling was low, and both she and John had to duck to avoid pipes and beams. But it was a nice basement, as far as basements went. The concrete floor had been painted a light shade of gray and it had been carefully swept. Boxes were neatly stacked on utility shelves that lined most of the walls.

A washer and dryer stood in one corner, along with a table for folding laundry. Another corner had been walled off to make the darkroom.

But she led him to the open area of the basement, where an entire concrete-block wall and the floor beneath it had been cleared. Only one box sat nearby, in the middle of the room on top of a broken chair.

Mariah reached inside and pulled out one of the plates she'd bought dirt cheap at a tag sale that afternoon, when she's borrowed Serena's car. It was undeniably one of the ugliest china patterns she'd ever seen in her life. She handed it to John.

He stared at it, perplexed.

"It occurred to me this morning that you probably never give yourself the opportunity to really vent," she explained.

"Vent."

"Yes." She took another plate from the box. "Like this." As hard as she could, she hurled the china plate against the wall. It smashed into a thousand pieces with a resounding and quite satisfying crash.

John laughed, but then stopped. "You're kidding, right?"

"No." She gestured to the plate in his hands. "Try it."

He hesitated. "Don't these belong to someone?"

"No. Look at it, John. Have you ever eaten off something that unappetizing? It's begging for you to break it and put it out of its misery."

He hefted it in his hand.

"Just do it. It feels...liberating." Mariah took another plate from the box and sent it smashing into the wall. "Oh, *yeah!*"

John turned suddenly and, throwing the plate like a Frisbee, shattered it against the wall.

Mariah handed him another one. "Good, huh?"

"Yeah."

She took another herself. "This one's for my father, who didn't even *ask* if I wanted to spend nearly seven years of my life working eighty hour weeks, who didn't even *try* to quit smoking or lose weight after his doctor told him he was a walking heart attack waiting to happen, and who died before I could tell him that I loved him, the bastard." The plate exploded as it hit the wall.

John threw his, too, and reached into the box for another before she could hand him one.

"This one's the head of the bank officer who wouldn't approve the Johnsons' loan for a Foundations for Families house even when the deacons of their church offered to co-sign it, all on account of the fact that she's a recovering alcoholic and he's an ex-con, even though they both have good, steady jobs now, and they both volunteer all the time as sponsors for AA."

The two plates hit the wall almost simultaneously.

"We only have time for one more," Mariah said, breathing hard as she prepared to throw her last plate of the evening. "Who's this one for, John? You call it."

He shook his head. "I can't."

"Sure you can. It's easy."

"No." He glanced at the plate he was holding loosely in his hands. "It gets too complicated."

"Are you kidding? It simplifies things. You break a plate instead of someone's face."

"It's not always that easy." He gazed searchingly into her eyes as if trying to find the words to explain. But he gave up, shaking his head. Then he swore suddenly, sharply. "This one's for me." He threw the plate against the wall so hard that shards of ceramic shot back at them. He moved quickly, shielding her.

"Whoa!" Mariah said. She wasn't entirely sure what he meant by that, but he was catching on.

"I'm sorry. *God*—"

"No, that was *good*," she said. "That was *very* good."

He had a tiny piece of broken plate in his hair, and she stepped toward him to pull it free.

He smelled delicious, like faintly exotic cologne and coffee.

"We should get going," he murmured, but he didn't step back, and she didn't, either, even after the ceramic shard was gone.

As Mariah watched, his gaze flickered to her mouth and then back to her eyes. He shook his head very slightly. "I shouldn't kiss you."

"Why not?" He'd shaved, probably right before he'd come to pick her up, and his cheeks looked smooth and soft. Mariah couldn't resist touching his face, and when she did, he closed his eyes.

"Because I won't want to stop," he whispered.

She leaned forward and brushed his lips with hers. With her heels on, she didn't even need to stand on her toes. She kissed him again, as softly and gently as before, and he groaned, pulling her into his arms and covering her mouth with his.

Mariah closed her eyes as he kissed her hungrily, his tongue possessively claiming her mouth, his hands claiming her body with the same proprietary familiarity.

But just as suddenly as he'd given in to his need to kiss her, he pulled himself away, holding her at arm's length. "You're dangerous," he gasped, half laughing, half groaning. "What am I going to do with you?"

Mariah smiled.

"No," John said, backing even farther away. "Don't answer that."

"I didn't say anything," she protested.

"You didn't have to. That wicked smile said more than enough."

Mariah started back up the stairs. "What wicked smile? That was just a regular smile."

When she reached the top of the stairs, she realized he wasn't behind her.

"John?" she called.

From the basement, she heard the sound of a shattering plate.

"Did that help?" she asked with a smile, as he came up the stairs.

He shook his head. "No." His expression was so somber, his eyes so bleak, all laughter gone from his face. "Mariah, I'm...I'm really sorry."

"Why, because you want to take some time before becoming involved? Because you're trying to deal with a life-threatening illness? Because it's so damn unfair and you're mad as hell? Don't be sorry about that.'' She gazed at him. "We don't have to go to this party. We can stay here and break some more plates." She paused. "Or we could talk."

He tried to smile, but it didn't quite cancel out the sadness in his eyes. "No, let's do it," he said. "I'm ready to go." He took a deep breath. "As ready as I'll ever be."

Chapter 5

Serena Westford. She was small and blond and green-eyed with a waist Miller could probably span with his hands. Her fingernails were perfectly manicured, her hair arranged in a youthful style. She was trim and lithe, dressed in a tight black dress that hugged her slender curves and showed off her flat stomach and taut derriere to their best advantage. She had sinewy muscles in her arms and legs that, along with that perfect body, told of countless hours on the Nautilus machine and the StairMaster.

She was beautiful, with a body that most men would die for.

But Miller knew more than most men.

And even if she wasn't his only suspect in a string of grisly murders, he *still* wouldn't have wanted to give her more than a cursory glance.

But she *was* his suspect, and even though he didn't want to look at anyone but Mariah, he smiled into Serena's cat green eyes. He'd come into this game intending to do more than smile at this woman. He was intending to marry her. Until death—or attempted murder—do us part.

Of course, his plan depended quite a bit on Serena's cooperation. And it was entirely possible that she wouldn't hone in on what Mariah was clearly marking as her territory with a hand nestled into the crook of his elbow. Serena was probably a killer, but Miller's experience had taught him that even killers had their codes. She may not hesitate to jam a stiletto into a lover's heart, but hitting on a girlfriend's man might not be acceptable behavior.

And that would leave Miller out in the cold, forced to bring in another agent to do what? To play the part of his even more terminally ill friend? A buddy he'd met in the oncology unit of the hospital?

God, if Serena wouldn't take his bait, the entire case could well be lost. Still, he found himself hoping...

But Serena smiled back at him and held his hand just a little too long as Mariah introduced them, and Miller knew that he was looking into the eyes of a woman who had no kind of code at all. If she was interested, and he thought that she was, she would do what she wanted, Mariah be damned.

"Look at us," the blond woman said, turning back to Mariah. "We're wearing almost exactly the same thing tonight. We're twins." She flashed a glance directly into Miller's eyes, just so that he knew she was well aware of the physical differences between the two women.

Miller forced himself to smile conspiratorially back at Serena, knowing that Mariah was going to see the exchange, knowing that she was going to interpret it as friendliness. At first.

Later, when she'd had time to think about it, Mariah would realize that he'd been flirting with her friend right from the start.

"You wouldn't happen to be from the Boston area, would you?" he asked Serena. "I know a Harcourt West-ford from my Harvard days—his family came from...I think it might've been Belmont."

"No, as a matter of fact, I've never even been to Boston."

She was lying. She'd met, married and murdered victim number six in Hyannisport, out on Cape Cod. The victim's sister had told investigating officers that her brother and his new wife—she was using Alana as an alias back then—frequently went into Boston to attend performances of the BSO.

"Help yourself to something from the bar," Serena directed them. "And the caterer made the *best* crab puffs tonight—be sure you sample them."

As Serena moved off to greet other arriving guests, she glanced back at Miller and blew him a kiss that Mariah couldn't see.

"Are you okay?" Mariah's fingers gently squeezed his upper arm. "You look a little pale."

He met her eyes and forced a smile. "I'm fine."

"Why don't you sit down and I'll get us something to drink?"

"You don't have to do that." He didn't want her to go. He didn't want to have to use the opportunity to watch Serena, to smile at her when he caught her eye.

"I don't mind," Mariah told him. "What can I get you?"

"Just a soda."

"Be right back."

Miller couldn't stop himself from watching her walk

away, knowing that by the time she came back, he'd be well on his way toward destroying the easy familiarity between them.

There were chairs along the edge of the deck, but he didn't sit down. If he sat down there, he wouldn't be able to see Serena Westford where she was standing on the other end of the wide deck, at the top of the stairs that led down to the beach.

He made his way to one of the more comfortable looking lounge chairs instead. He'd have a clear view of Serena from there.

Serena was watching him. He could feel her glancing in his direction as he gingerly lowered himself into one of the chairs. From the corner of his eye, he saw her lean closer to the man she was talking to. The man turned to look over at the bar and nodded. As he walked away, Miller sensed more than saw Serena heading in his direction.

His cover flashed through his mind like words scrolling down a computer screen. He was Jonathan Mills. Harvard University, class of '80. M.B.A. from NYU in 1985. Car alarms. Hodgkin's. Chemotherapy. Never married. Facing his own mortality and the end of his family line.

Forget about Mariah. God knows she'd be better off without a man like him in the long run. He was "The Robot," for God's sake. What would a woman who was so incredibly warm and alive want with a man rumored to have no soul?

"Are you feeling all right?" Serena's cool English voice broke into his thoughts. He glanced over to find her settling onto the chair next to his. "Mariah was telling me how you've recently been ill."

There was an unmistakable glint of interest in her eyes.

Miller nodded. "Yeah. I have been." Across the deck

he could see Mariah, a glass of something tall and cool in each hand, held in conversation by the same man who'd been talking to Serena earlier. She glanced at him, but he looked away before she could meet his eyes.

"How awful," Serena murmured.

"Mariah didn't tell me anything at all about *you*," Miller countered, knowing that everything she was about to tell him about herself would be a lie.

In the past, this game of pretend had had the power to excite him, to invigorate him. She would lie to him, and he would lie to her, and the game would go on and on and on until one of them slipped up.

It wouldn't be him. It never was him.

But tonight he didn't want to play. He wanted to turn back the clock and spend the next one hundred years of his life reliving this morning's dawn, with Mariah in his arms, the taste of her kisses on his lips.

"I think our Mariah has something of a crush on you," Serena told him. "I don't think she was eager for you to meet me."

Meaning that it was an indisputable fact that the moment Miller met Serena, he would turn away from Mariah, and—in Serena's opinion—rightly so.

This woman's self-confidence and ego were both the size of the Taj Mahal.

Miller leaned closer to Serena, feeling like Peter in the Garden of Gethsemane. "I don't really know her—not very well. We just met a few days ago, and... I know we're here together tonight, but we're really just friends. She seems very nice, though."

Meaning, he hadn't made up his mind about anything.

"Tell me," Miller said, "what's a woman like you doing on Garden Isle all by yourself?"

Meaning Serena was definitely interesting and attractive to him with her petite, aerobicized body and her gleaming blond hair and killer smile.

Serena smiled.

The game had moved into the next round.

Mariah felt like a giantess. Standing next to Serena, she felt like a towering football linebacker despite the dress and heels. Maybe *because* of the dress and heels. She felt as if she'd dressed up like this in an attempt to fool everyone into thinking she was delicate and feminine, but had failed.

Miserably.

John and Serena were deep in a conversation about Acapulco. Mariah had never been to Acapulco. When had she had the time? Up until just a few months ago, she hadn't gone anywhere besides the office and to the occasional business meeting up in Lake Havasu City or Flagstaff.

Feeling dreadfully left out, but trying hard not to let it show, Mariah shifted her weight from one Amazon-sized leg to another and took a sip of her wine, wishing the alcohol would make her feel better, but knowing that drinking too much would only give her a headache in the morning.

This evening was *so* not what she'd hoped. Silly her. She'd never even considered the fact that Jonathan Mills would take one look at Serena and be smitten. But he was obviously infatuated with Mariah's friend. He'd watched the blond woman constantly, all evening long. The few times Mariah had been alone with him, he'd talked only about Serena. He'd asked Mariah questions about her. He'd commented on her hair, her house, her party, her shoes.

Her *tiny* shoes. Oh, he didn't say anything about size,

but Serena's feet were small and feminine. Mariah hadn't worn shoes that size since third grade.

All those signals she'd thought she'd picked up from him were wrong. Those kisses. Had he kissed her first, or had she kissed him? She couldn't remember. It was entirely possible that she had made the first move this morning on the couch. She *knew* she'd made the first move down in the basement.

And each time she'd kissed him, he'd told her in plain English that he thought they should just be friends.

But did she listen? Nope, not her. But she was listening now. It was all that she could do—she had nothing worth adding to the conversation. Acapulco. Skiing in Aspen. John and Serena had so much in common. So much to talk about. Art museums they'd both been to in New York...

Serena seemed just as taken with John as he was with her. In spite of the fact that she herself had warned Mariah about becoming involved with a man who could very well die, Serena looked for all the world as if she was getting ready to reel John in.

Some friend.

Of course, Mariah had told Serena that she and John were just that—friends. Still, Mariah had the sense that even if she'd told her friend that she was already well on her way to falling in love with this man, Serena wouldn't have given a damn.

Neither John nor Serena looked up as Mariah excused herself quietly and went back to the bar.

The hard, cold fact was that Mariah didn't stand a chance with John if Serena decided that she wanted him for her own. And it sure seemed as if she wanted him.

Disgusted with all of them—herself included—Mariah set her empty glass down on the bar, shaking her head when the bartender asked if she wanted a refill. No, it was time to accept defeat and beat a retreat.

The bartender had a pen but no paper, so Mariah quickly wrote a note on a napkin. "I'm partied out, and I've got to be up early in the morning. I've gone ahead home—didn't want you to feel obligated to drive me. Enjoy the rest of party. Mariah."

She folded the napkin in half and asked the bartender to bring it to John in a minute or two.

Chin up, she silently commanded herself as she took off her shoes and went barefoot down the stairs that led to the beach. Jonathan Mills wasn't the man she'd thought he was anyway. He was just another member of the jet set, able to talk for hours at a time about nothing of any importance whatsoever. Frankly, she'd expected more of him. More depth. More soul. She'd thought she'd seen more when she'd looked into his eyes.

She'd thought she'd seen a lover, but she'd only seen the most casual of acquaintances.

She headed down the beach, toward home, determined not to look back.

"John." There was the briefest flare of surprise in Daniel Tonaka's eyes as he opened the door to his hotel room and saw Miller standing on the other side. "Is there a problem?"

Miller shook his head. What the hell was he doing here? "No. I..." He ran his hand through his too short hair. "I saw that your light was still on and..." And what? "I couldn't sleep," he admitted, then shrugged. "What else is new?"

What was new was his admitting it.

Daniel didn't comment, though. He just nodded, opening the door wider. "Come in."

The hotel suite was smaller than Miller's room, but

decorated with the same style furniture, the same patterned curtains, the same color rug. Still, it seemed like another planet entirely, strange and alien. Miller stood awkwardly, uncertain whether to sit or stand or beat a quick exit before it was too late.

He remembered the way he used to go into Tony's room without even knocking, the way he'd simply help himself to a beer from Tony's refrigerator. He remembered the way they'd pick apart every word spoken in the course of the night's investigation, hashing it out, searching for the hidden meanings and subtle clues, trying to figure out from what had—or hadn't—been said, if their cover had been blown.

They'd done the same thing in high school, except back then the conversation had been about girls, about basketball, about the seemingly huge but in retrospect quite petty troubles they'd had with the two rival gangs that ruled the streets of their worn-out little town. They'd often been threatened and ordered to choose sides, but Tony had followed Miller's lead and remained neutral. They were Switzerland, for no one and against no one.

Switzerland. God, Miller hadn't thought about *that* in ages.

"Can I get you something to drink?" Daniel asked politely. "A beer?"

"Are you having one?"

Daniel shook his head. "I don't drink." He paused. "I thought you knew that."

Miller gazed at him. "I knew that when you were around me, you chose not to drink. I didn't want to assume that held for all the times you *weren't* with me."

"I don't drink," Daniel said again.

"I shouldn't have bothered you. It's late—"

"Be careful about coming on too strong with the suspect," Daniel warned him.

Miller blinked. "Excuse me?"

The kid's lips curved slightly in amusement. "I figured that's why you came over here, right? To ask my opinion about where you stand with Serena Westford?"

Miller didn't know why the hell he was here. He turned toward the door. "I'll let you get back to whatever you were doing."

"John," Daniel said, "sit down. Have a soda." He unlocked the little self-service refrigerator and crouched down to look inside. "How about something without any caffeine?"

Miller found himself sitting down on the edge of the flower-patterned couch as Daniel set a pair of lemon-lime sodas on the coffee table.

Daniel sat across from him and opened one of the cans of soda. "I listened in on most of your conversations," he said. "I think it went well—Serena kept talking about you even after you left. She was asking people if they knew you. She's definitely interested. But she kept referring to you as Mariah's friend, John, and it was more than just a way to identify you. I got the feeling that she's getting off on the idea of stealing you away from her friend."

Miller gazed at his partner. He'd never heard Daniel talk quite so much—and certainly not unless his opinion had been specifically solicited. "Yeah, I got that feeling, too," he finally said.

"What are you going to do about it?" Daniel asked.

"What do *you* think I should do?"

It was clear that Daniel had already given this a great deal of thought. "The obvious solution is for you to see the friend again. Play Serena's game. Hook her interest even further by making it seem as if you're not going to be an easy catch." The kid gazed down at the soda can in his hands as if seeing the bright-colored label for the first time. "But that doesn't take into consideration other things."

Other things. "Such as?"

Daniel looked up, squarely meeting Miller's gaze. "Such as the fact that you really like this other lady. Mariah. Marie. Whatever she wants to call herself."

Miller couldn't deny it. But he could steer the conversation in a slightly different direction. "Mariah invited me to go out to the Triple F building site tomorrow morning." Of course, that had been *before* he'd ignored her so completely at Serena's party.

Daniel nodded. "What are you going to do?"

"I don't know."

Miller had never hesitated over making this kind of a decision before. If he had a choice to do something that would further him in his case, by God, he'd do it. No questions, no doubt. But here he was wavering for fear of hurting someone's feelings.

It was absurd.

And yet when he closed his eyes, he could still see Mariah, hurt enough to leave the party without him, but kind enough to write a note telling him she was leaving. He could see her, head held high as she went down the stairs to the beach.

He'd left the party soon after and followed her to make sure she'd arrived home safely. He'd sat in his car on the street with his lights off and watched her move about her house through the slats in her blinds. He watched her disappear down the hall to her bedroom, unzipping the back of that incredible dress as she went.

She'd returned only a moment later, dressed in the same kind of oversize T-shirt that she'd worn to bed the night before. When she'd curled up on the couch with a book he'd driven away—afraid if he stayed much longer he'd act on the urge to get out of the car, knock on her door and apologize until she let him in.

And once she let him in, he knew damn well he'd end up in her bed. He'd apologize and she'd eventually accept. He'd touch her, and it wouldn't be long until they kissed. And once he kissed her, there'd be no turning back. The attraction between them was too hot, too volatile.

And then she would *really* be hurt—after he slept with her, then married her best friend.

So he'd make damn sure that he wouldn't sleep with her.

He'd show up in front of the library tomorrow at 6:00 a.m. He'd see her again—God, he wanted to see her again—but in public, where there'd be no danger of intimacies getting out of hand. Somehow he'd make her understand that their relationship was to be nothing more than a friendship, all the while making Serena believe otherwise. Then Serena could "steal" him from Mariah without Mariah getting hurt.

Miller stood up. "I'm going to do it. Figure I'll be out of the picture all day tomorrow."

Daniel rose to his feet, too. "I'll stay near Serena." Miller turned to leave, but Daniel's quiet voice stopped him. "You know, John, we could do this another way."

His cover was all set up. He was here, he was in place. And all of his reasons for not going ahead would be purely personal. He'd never pulled out of a case for personal reasons before and he sure as hell wasn't about to start now.

"I haven't come up with a better way—or a quicker way—to catch this killer," he flatly told his partner. "Let's do this right and lock her up before she hurts anyone else."

Chapter 6

Mariah saw him as soon as she rounded the corner.

Jonathan Mills was sitting on the steps to the library, shoulders hunched over, nursing a cup of coffee.

He couldn't have been waiting for her—not after last night. Not after he'd been visibly dazzled by Serena.

And yet she knew there was no one else he could have been waiting for. She was the only one on all of Garden Isle who regularly volunteered for Foundations for Families. Occasionally there would be a group of college students on vacation, but the Triple F van would pick them up over by the campground.

Mariah briefly considered just riding past. Not stopping. Flagging the van down near the drugstore or the post office. Leaving her bike...where? This bike rack in front of the library was the only one in town.

Maybe if she ignored him, he'd go away.

But Mariah knew that that, too, wasn't any kind of

solution, so she nodded to him briefly as she braked to a stop.

He stood up as if every bone in his body ached, as if he, too, hadn't had an awful lot of sleep last night.

"I realized as I was getting ready to meet you here that I don't have a tool belt," he told her.

Her own belt was in her backpack, weighing it down, and she slid it off her shoulders and onto the sidewalk as she positioned her bike in the rack. She didn't know what to say. Was he actually serious? Did he really intend to spend the day with her?

Her cheeks still flushed with embarrassment when she thought about last night. And the night before. She'd actually thought he was as attracted to her as she was to him. She'd gone and thrown herself at him and...

She could think of nothing worse than spending the entire day with this man, yet she couldn't simply tell him to go home. She couldn't bring herself to do it. Yes, she'd resolved last night that she'd have nothing more to do with him. Yes, she'd come to the conclusion that he was far more shallow and self-absorbed than she'd previously thought. Still, she couldn't tell him to go away.

"I couldn't sleep again last night," he told her, "and I was lying there in bed, listening to the radio. I had it tuned in to that college station on the mainland, and they were playing this song—these two women singing with guitars, it was really nice. But it was the words that got to me. There I was, listening to the lyrics of this song, something about getting out of bed and getting a hammer and a nail or something like that, and I couldn't stop thinking about you. It was as if they wrote this song about you."

Mariah turned and really looked at him for the first time. He was dressed in jeans, sneakers and a T-shirt. He looked as if he'd climbed out of bed without a shower or a shave. His chin was rough with his morning beard, and he wore a baseball cap on his head, covering his hair. It was silly, actually. His hair was still too short to be rumpled from sleep.

But she knew the song he was talking about. It was a wonderful song, a thoughtful song, a not-at-all shallow song. "That was the Indigo Girls," she said.

"Was that who they were? It was good. I liked them. I never used to listen to music…you know, *before.*"

Before he'd been diagnosed with cancer. Cancer—the reason she couldn't just tell him to go away. He could very well be living the last of his days right now. Who was she to tell him he couldn't spend his time doing exactly as he pleased?

"Mariah, I'm really sorry about last night. I didn't realize I was neglecting you, and then you were gone and—"

"I think my expectations were too high," she admitted. "You had no way of knowing."

"I really want to be your friend," he said quietly.

Mariah turned and looked at him. He'd told her point-blank that he wanted to be her friend before, too. Was it his fault that she hadn't listened? Was it his fault that her feelings already were much stronger than mere friendship?

"Please let me come with you today," he added.

Mariah could see the Triple F van approaching, and she shouldered her backpack.

"All right," she said, knowing that she was a sucker. *He* wanted to be friends. So she'd spend the day with him because *he* wanted to be friends, never mind the fact that every moment she was with him made her like him even more. Want him even more. As more than just a friend.

The really stupid thing was that she would have turned another man down. But for Jonathan Mills, with his sad smile, his startlingly heaven blue eyes and his catastrophic illness, she was ready to cut a great deal of slack.

Even though she knew damn well she was going to live to regret it.

Miller was getting into the rhythm. Take a nail, tap it gently, then drive it in.

He'd never really had much of an opportunity to work with a hammer before. It fitted well in his hand, though. Almost as well as his gun did.

Mariah glanced over at him, wiping ineffectively at a river of sweat that streamed down her face despite the sweatband she wore. "Tired yet?"

"I'm fine."

When they'd first arrived, she'd set him up in a lawn chair in the shade, like some kind of invalid. Like the invalid he was *supposed* to be.

But he'd been unable to sit and watch. Even though it jeopardized his cover as a weak and ailing man, it hadn't been long before he'd begged an extra hammer and was working alongside Mariah.

They were inside the little house, putting plasterboard up, turning the framed-off and already electrically wired areas into real rooms. They'd completed the living room, with several more experienced members of the volunteer building crew cutting out the holes for the electrical outlets and the light switches. They'd worked their way down the hall and into the larger of two bedrooms. The place was starting to look like a home. Sure, the seams had to be taped, and the tape and the nail heads covered with spackle, then sanded before the rooms could be painted, but all of its promise gleamed through.

The owners of the house, a tall black man named Thomas and a slender, proud-looking woman named Renee, kept wandering through every time they took a break, holding hands like a pair of wide-eyed schoolchildren, going from room to room.

"Glory be," Thomas kept saying, tears in his eyes. He'd never owned his own home before, never thought he'd be able, he kept saying. He'd even stopped at one point to pull Miller into his arms, giving him a heartfelt hug of thanks.

Miller knew why Mariah liked this work. He'd caught her with a tear or two in her own eyes more than once. And when everyone on the work crew wasn't busy fighting back tears of joy, they were singing. They sang anything and everything from current pop tunes to spirituals as the radio's dial got moved back and forth, depending on who was in control at the moment. Miller even found himself joining in once or twice when the Beatles came on. He remembered the Beatles from when he was very young. To his surprise, he still knew almost all of the words to their songs.

But as the sun was rising in the sky, the little house was starting to heat up. Miller had long since pulled his shirt off. He wished to hell he'd worn shorts instead of these jeans. It had to be near ninety—and the mercury was climbing.

Mariah set down her hammer and took off her T-shirt. She was wearing another athletic bra—a sweatshirt-colored gray one this time. She used her shirt to mop her face and then hung it over her tool belt.

Miller tried not to watch her, but it was damned hard.

He drove another nail into the wall, narrowly missing hitting his thumb.

In the other bedroom, someone turned the radio to a classical station.

"Mozart," Miller said, barely aware he'd spoken aloud. He looked up to find Mariah watching him. "His clarinet concerto," he continued, giving her a half smile. "My mother loved this piece. She swore that listening to Mozart would make you smarter."

"I've heard that, too," Mariah said. "The theory being that the complexity of the music somehow expands your ability to reason."

"Lemonade break," Renee said cheerfully, carrying two tall glasses into the room.

Mariah put down her hammer and took one of the plastic glasses as John took the other. He nodded his thanks to Renee, then sat down next to Mariah on the dusty plywood floor.

Mariah drained half her glass in one long drink. "God," she gasped, catching her breath, "what I *really* need is a hosing down. Can it get any hotter?"

"Yes."

Mariah laughed. "That was *not* the correct answer." She leaned her head back against the newly erected plasterboard and pressed the cool plastic against her neck as she closed her eyes.

Miller let himself stare. As long as her eyes were closed, he could take the opportunity to drink her in. Her eyelashes were about a mile long. They rested, thick and dark, against her sun-kissed cheeks. She had a sprinkling of freckles on her nose. Freckles on her shoulders and across her chest, too.

He looked up to find her eyes had opened. She'd caught him doing all but drooling. Perfect.

But she didn't move away. She didn't reprimand him.

"Thomas and Renee can't wait to move in."

It took him a moment to realize what she was talking about.

"This is a really nice little house," Mariah continued. "It's a popular one—I've helped build at least seven just like it."

Miller nodded. "I lived in a house with a layout almost exactly like this when I was a kid."

Mariah pulled her knees up to her chest, her eyes sparking with interest. "Really?"

"Yeah, it's almost weird walking through here." He pointed down the hall. "That was my bedroom, next to the bathroom. This one was my mother's."

Mariah was watching him, waiting for him to tell her more. He knew that once again he'd already said too much, but her eyes were so warm. He didn't want her to stop looking at him that way.

Besides, he'd figured out a way to make it work—this odd blending of his background and the Jonathan Mills cover story. As Mills, he would have the same background as Miller, except when he was eleven, when his mother died, he hadn't gone into foster care. He— Mills—had gone to live with his fictional estranged father, the king of the car alarms. It would work.

"I can still remember how the kitchen smelled," he told Mariah. "Ginger and cinnamon. My mother loved to bake." He glanced up at the white plasterboard they'd just used to cover the wall opposite the closet, gesturing toward it. "She also loved books. That whole wall was covered with bookshelves and *filled* with books. Everything and anything—if it was any good, she read it." He smiled at Mariah. "She was kind of like you."

As he said the words, he realized how accurate they

were. Physically, Mariah looked nothing like his mother. His mother had been average height and willow thin. But their smiles had the same welcoming glow, the same unconditional acceptance. When he was with Mariah, he felt accepted without question. It was something he hadn't felt in years.

"She worked as a secretary," he told Mariah. "Although she swore she was four times smarter than her boss. I remember, even though it was expensive, we kept the house heated well past seventy degrees all winter long. She would get so cold. I used to walk around in T-shirts and shorts, and she'd be wearing a sweater and scarf." He smiled, remembering. "And then there was the year she let me pick the color we were going to paint the living room. I must've been six, and I picked yellow. Bright yellow. She didn't try to talk me out of it. People's eyes would pop out of their heads when they came into the house."

"When did she die?" Mariah asked softly.

"A few days before I turned eleven."

"I'm sorry."

"Yeah, I was, too."

"You talk about your mother, but you've never said anything about your father," she said quietly.

Miller's real father had died in Vietnam. He was a medic who'd been killed evacuating a bombed Marine barracks, two weeks away from the end of his tour of duty.

He shrugged. "There's not much to say. He and my mother were divorced," he lied. "I went to live with him after she died." He shifted his weight, changing the subject. "We always talk about me. You've never really told me about yourself."

"My life has been remarkably dull."

"You mentioned your father dying of a heart attack," he pointed out. "And at dinner the other night, you told me you'd once been married, but you didn't go into any detail."

"His name was Trevor," she told him. "We were married right out of college. We parted due to irreconcilable differences in our work schedules, if you can believe *that*. He wanted kids and I couldn't schedule them in until late 1999. So he left."

Miller was quiet, just waiting for her to say more.

"He married again about six months after we split," she said. "I ran into him downtown about a year ago. He had two little kids with him. His new wife was in the hospital, having just delivered number three."

She was silent for a moment.

"I looked at Trevor and those kids and I tried to feel really bad—you know, that could have been my life. Those could have been my cute little kids. Trevor still could've been my husband...."

"But..." he prompted.

"But all I could feel was *relieved*. And I realized that I had married Trevor because I couldn't really think of a good reason *not* to marry him. I loved him, but I'm not sure I was ever really *in* love with him. I never felt as if I'd die if he didn't kiss me...."

She trailed off, and Miller found himself staring at her, memorizing her face as she in turn stared down at the empty glass in her hands.

"If I ever get involved with anyone again, it's going to be because I find someone I can't live without. I want to find the kind of passion that's overpowering," she told him. "I want to lose control."

Lose control. Overpowering passion.

The kind of passion that started wars and crumbled

empires. The kind of passion that made it difficult even for a hardened expert like Miller to do his job. The kind of passion that made him want to break every rule and restriction he'd set for himself and pull this woman into his arms and cover her mouth with his own.

She was talking about the kind of passion that flared to life between them even when they did no more than sit and quietly talk. It was a one-of-a-kind thing, and Miller hated the fact that he couldn't take it further— push it to see where it would lead.

Mariah was quiet, lost in her own thoughts.

Miller tried not to watch her. Tried, and failed.

"Mariah!" One of the little girls—one of Thomas and Renee's young daughters—came skidding into the room. "Jane Ann climbed way, *way* up into the big ol' tree in the backyard and now she can't get down!" the girl wailed. "Papa says he's too big—the branches up that high won't hold him. And Mama's got no head for heights. And Janey's crying cause she can't hold on much longer!"

Mariah scrambled to her feet and ran.

Miller was right behind her.

A crowd had gathered beneath the shade of the monstrously large tree that dominated the quarter acre plot. It was a perfect climbing tree, with broad, thick branches growing well within even a child's reach of the ground. But the branches became narrower as they went up the trunk. And up where Janey was sitting and howling like a police siren, way up near the top of the tree, the branches were positively delicate-looking.

Mariah moved quickly, navigating her way up through the branches effortlessly and efficiently. But she was no lightweight herself. Despite the fact that she'd told him she was good with heights, good at climbing, this was going to be tricky.

"Mariah!" Miller called. "We can call the fire department for help."

She only glanced down at him very briefly. "I think Jane Ann wants to come down right now, John," she told him. "I don't think she wants to wait for the fire truck to arrive."

He didn't know what to do—whether to climb up after her, or wait there on the ground, hoping that if she or the child slipped, he could somehow cushion their fall. He turned to the girl's father.

"Thomas, didn't I see some kind of tarp out front? Thick plastic—it was blue, I think—the kind of thing you'd use to cover a roof that's not quite watertight, in the event of rain?"

Thomas didn't understand.

"If we stretched it tight, it could break the girl's fall," he explained. "We could try to catch her if she slips."

Thomas gave a curt order and two teenaged boys ran quickly to get the tarp.

Miller looked up into the tree. Mariah was moving more slowly now, more carefully. He could hear the soothing rise and fall of her voice as she spoke to the little girl, but he couldn't make out the words. But the girl was finally quiet, so whatever Mariah was saying was working to calm her.

The boys came back with the tarp, and everyone but Miller took an end, pulling it taut, ready for disaster. Miller, instead, started up into the tree.

Mariah had climbed as far as she dared and she held out one hand to the little girl. Her other arm was securely wrapped around the rough trunk of the tree. Miller knew she was willing the child to move closer, just a little bit closer, so that she could grab hold of her.

Slowly, inch by inch, Jane Ann began to move.

There was an audible sigh of relief from the ground as Mariah pulled the child close to her and the girl locked her arms around Mariah's neck.

But the worst was not yet over. Mariah still had to get back down—this time with the added weight of an eight-year-old girl threatening her balance.

Mariah stepped down, one branch at a time, testing its strength before she put her full weight upon it.

And then it happened.

Miller saw the branch give before he heard the rifle-sharp snap. In nightmarish slow motion, he saw Mariah grab for the branch above her, holding them both with only one hand, one arm. He could see her muscles straining, see her feet searching for a foothold.

And then he saw her fingers slip.

"Mariah!" The cry ripped from his throat as she began to fall.

But somehow, miraculously, she didn't fall far. She jerked to a stop, still holding tightly to the little girl in her arms.

Her tool belt. Somehow the back of her belt had been hooked upon the stub of a branch—a branch sturdy enough to hold both of them. They hung from the tree, facing out, dangling like some kind of Christmas ornament.

Miller raced up the tree, the bark rough against his hands and sharp against his knees, even through his jeans.

As he drew closer, he could see that Mariah's elbow was bleeding. Her knees, too, looked scraped and the worse for wear. The belt was holding her not around the waist, but rather around the ribs. Still, she managed to smile at Miller. "That was fun," she whispered.

"Are you all right?" He saw them then—bruises on the insides of her upper arms. The tree hadn't done that to her—*he* had. That night that he'd fallen asleep on her couch. He'd grabbed her, thinking she was Domino. God, he could have killed her. The thought made him feel faint and he brought himself back to here and now. He'd have enough time to feel bad about Mariah's bruises *after* he got her down from this tree.

"I think I may have rearranged a rib," she told him. "I had the breath knocked out of me, too. Take Janey. Please? Jane Ann, this is John. He's going to take you down to your mommy and dad, okay?"

The little girl looked shell-shocked. Mariah gave her a kiss on the cheek and Miller lifted her out of Mariah's arms without a fuss. "Let me get you down from there," he said to Mariah.

"Take Janey down first," she told him, still in that odd, whispery voice. "I think you're going to need two hands for me."

Miller nodded, moving as quickly down the tree with the child as he dared. He looked back at Mariah, but she'd closed her eyes. Rearranged a rib. He knew she'd put it that way so as not to frighten Jane Ann. Her tool belt had slammed into her ribs with the full weight of her body against it. And it wouldn't take much for a broken rib to puncture a lung.

Miller felt a flash of fear as he glanced back up at Mariah. Had she simply closed her eyes or had she lost consciousness?

He practically threw Jane Ann into her father's waiting hands, then swiftly climbed back up to where Mariah was still hanging by her belt.

She opened her eyes as he approached, and he nearly fell out of the tree from relief.

"Ouch," she said. "Can I say ouch now?"

Miller nodded, looking hard into her eyes for any sign of shock. "Can you breathe? Are you having trouble breathing?"

She shook her head. "I'm still a little...squashed."

"Can we unfasten your belt?" he asked.

She shook her head. "I already thought of that, but the buckle seems to be in the back. And it's not easy to undo even in the best of circumstances."

They were going to have to do this the hard way.

Miller braced each foot on a separate branch, pressing his body up close to Mariah's. "Hold on to me," he ordered her. "I'm going to lift you up and get your belt free."

She hesitated.

"I'm a little sweaty," he apologized. "I'm sorry. There's not a lot I can do about that. Lock your legs around my waist."

"Maybe I should wait for the fire department."

"Put your legs around my waist," he said again. "Come on, Mariah. Just do it."

She did it.

Miller refused to think about anything but getting her down from there. Yes, she was soft, she was warm, and yes, she smelled delicious. Yes, she was everything he remembered from that night on her couch, but she was also in danger of falling and breaking her neck.

"Hold me tighter," he commanded as he tried to shift her up, one hand reaching behind her, searching for the stub of the branch that had hooked her tool belt and saved her and Janey's lives.

He found it. He found the wetness of blood, too—

Mariah's blood—where the sharp edge of the branch had scratched and scraped and stabbed into her back. Her ragged intake of breath told him how much it hurt.

"Try to lift yourself up," he told her. "Help me get you free."

Her legs tightened around him as he pushed her up, every muscle straining. His head was pressed against the soft pillow of her breasts, but there was nothing he could do about that.

Finally, *finally,* with a strength he didn't even know he possessed, he got the tool belt free. His muscles tensed as he held Mariah's full weight. She clung to him now, more tightly than he'd ever dreamed she'd hold him.

"I'm not feeling very secure here," she told him.

"I've got you," he said. "I won't let go."

And he wouldn't. At least not until they reached the solidness of the ground.

He helped her find her footing, helped her down to the larger, sturdier branches, but still she held on to his hand.

Her face was still mere inches from his, and her eyes were swimming with unshed tears.

"I think I have to cry," she told him.

"Can you wait just a few minutes more?" he asked. "Until we get you down onto the ground?"

She forced a wavery smile. "Yeah."

One branch at a time, they moved slowly down the tree. When they got to the bottom, Miller knew he was going to have to let her go.

Sure enough, Renee and Thomas were there, reaching out to help her, along with the entire rest of the site crew.

But she still didn't cry. She smiled at them. She made light of her scrapes and scratches. She pooh-poohed the angry-looking cut on her back. And when Jane Ann and the other little girl, Emma, leaped at her, nearly knocking her over, she hugged them back, hiding the fact that she was wincing.

Miller approached Laronda, the site coordinator. "I want to take Mariah over to the hospital," he told her quietly. "I think she might've broken a rib and she'll probably need stitches for that cut on her back. Can someone give us a lift, or do you want to give me the keys to the van?"

"I was going to have Bobby take her over, but if you're thinking about going, too..."

"I *am* going. Definitely."

Laronda nodded. "Show me your driver's license, Mr. Mills, and I'll let you take the van."

Miller took out his wallet and within moments had the keys to the van in his pocket. He briefly went inside to get his T-shirt. Pulling it over his head, he intercepted Mariah. He took her arm and led her toward the van.

She protested. "I want to wash up."

"You can wash up at the hospital."

Mariah nodded. "All right."

The fact that she didn't protest further was not a good sign. She *was* hurt worse than she was letting on.

Miller helped her up onto the hot vinyl of the bench seat in the front of the van, then went around and climbed behind the wheel. He started the engine and pulled onto the street, moving carefully over the potholes so as not to jar Mariah.

He glanced at her as he pulled up to the stop sign at the end of the street. She was sitting very still, with her eyes closed, arms wrapped around herself.

"You can cry now," Miller said softly. "No one's here but me."

She opened her eyes and looked at him and he put the van in park. It was crazy and he knew he shouldn't do it, but he held out his arms and she reached for him as she burst into tears.

"I thought that little girl was going to fall," Mariah sobbed as she clung to him. "I was sure that I'd killed her—and myself, too."

"Shhh," Miller whispered into her hair, holding her as close and as tightly as he dared. "It's all right. It's all right now."

What was he doing? This was sheer insanity. Holding her this way, giving her this kind of comfort... His body responded instantly to the sensation of her in his arms, his wanting all but overpowering his sense of right and wrong.

He couldn't kiss her. He *would not* kiss her.

"I'm sorry," she said, half laughing, half crying as she lifted her head to look up at him. "I'm getting your shirt all wet."

He wanted to kiss her. Her mouth was right there, inches away from him. Her lips would taste so soft and sweet....

Miller clenched his teeth instead. "Don't worry about my shirt."

A new flood of tears welled in her eyes. "I don't think I've ever been so afraid. But I didn't drop her. Even when all the air was knocked out of me, even when it felt like that branch went into my back like a knife, I didn't let go."

Miller smoothed her hair back from her face, knowing that he shouldn't touch her more than was necessary. Except, this felt very necessary. "You did great," he told her. "You were amazing."

"I was stupid not to wait for the fire department."

"You were brave—and lucky."

She nodded. "I *was* lucky, wasn't I? Oh, God, when I think about what might've happened..."

She held him tighter, and he felt his arms closing around her, too.

Think about what might've happened... He couldn't think about anything else—except maybe how much he wanted to kiss this woman.

It was not the right thing to do. He knew that, but he did it anyway.

She met his lips eagerly as if she, too, was as starved for his kisses as he was for hers.

God, it was heaven.

And it was hell, because he knew it hàd to end.

He forced himself to lift his head. He made himself pull back as he gazed into Mariah's whiskey-colored eyes.

"I need to get you to the hospital." His voice didn't come out more than a whisper.

She nodded, a flare of embarrassment in her eyes. "I'm sorry. I'm...doing it again, aren't I?"

"Doing what?"

She pulled away, moving back to her side of the bench seat. "Kissing you," she told him with her usual blunt honesty. "I seem to be unable to keep myself from kissing you." She wiped her face with her hands, pushing away her tears. "Come on. The hospital's not far from here. I drove José over a few weeks ago when he stepped on a nail."

Miller put the van into gear, uncertain of how to respond. He'd made another mistake by kissing her, yet she seemed to think it was *her* mistake.

He took a left out onto the main road, wishing not only that he'd been strong enough to keep from kissing her again, but that he was weak enough to be kissing her still.

John was waiting for Mariah as she came out of X ray.

He looked sweaty and hot, and with that unshaved stubble and covered with the grime of a full morning's worth of construction work, he looked dangerously sexy. He also looked as worried as hell.

"I'm okay," she told him. "Nothing's broken. Not even cracked. Just bruised."

He smiled then, one of his crooked half smiles. "Good." He looked up at the nurse who was wheeling Mariah's chair. "What's next?"

"She's got a cut on her back that's going to need a stitch or two," the nurse told him. "Unfortunately, she's going to have to wait for the doctor."

"May I sit with her?" John asked.

"Of course."

"I mean, if she wants me to," he added, glancing down at Mariah.

"Thanks," Mariah said, feeling strangely shy as she briefly met his eyes. "I'd like that."

The nurse brought them back into one of the emergency rooms. There were six beds in this one, each with a curtain on runners that could be pulled around to give them some privacy.

John helped Mariah up onto the bed. During her X ray, she'd taken off her athletic bra, and now she wore only a hospital gown over her shorts. It was tied loosely at her neck, and she could feel the coolness from the air conditioner blowing against her exposed back.

It was the front of the gown that made her self-conscious, though. The cotton was thin, and every time she moved, it seemed to cling provocatively to her breasts, outlining every detail, every curve. She pulled it up at her neck, wishing there was some way to ensure that it wouldn't fall off.

Her movement made the short sleeves of the gown ride up, and John reached for one of her arms, pushing the sleeve even further up. He turned her arm over, exposing the bruises she had there. There were five of them—little oval finger- and thumb-shaped bruises. She had a similar set on her other arm.

He looked into her eyes. "I'm so sorry about this."

"I know." She held his gaze. "What were you dreaming that night?"

He didn't look away, but he didn't speak for several long moments, as if he was deciding what to tell her. "Tony, my best friend, was…an officer of the law," he finally said. "He was executed by a drug runner's gang. Shot in the head."

"Oh, my God." Mariah couldn't believe what he was telling her. "Were the people who killed him caught?"

John nodded. "Yeah. They were caught. That doesn't keep me from dreaming about them, though. I see their faces and…" He broke off, turning away. "I shouldn't be telling you this. I must be insane."

"Did you know the men who did it?"

For a moment, she thought he wasn't going to answer.

"One of the guys working for the drug lord went to high school with Tony and me." He shifted his weight, looking away from her. "I keep wondering if his bullet killed Tony. I keep thinking I should've beaten the hell out of him—and put the fear of God in him—in high school, when I had the chance."

"That's where you got Princess," she guessed. "Tony was the friend that you inherited her from."

He nodded. "Yeah. She still misses him." He glanced back at her. "I do, too."

"So you dream about him dying. Were you there when it happened? God, you didn't see it, did you?"

He shook his head, his voice bitter. "No. I got there too late." He changed the subject. "Mariah, I'm sorry that I hurt you."

He was talking about the bruises on her arms, but for a moment, she could have sworn he was talking about the way he'd treated her at Serena's party.

"And I'm sorry about your friend." She paused. "You knew him—Tony—since high school?"

Miller pulled a chair closer to her bed and sat down. God, why had he told her about Tony? Tony hadn't been friends with high-class Jonathan Mills. At age sixteen, Tony had befriended John Miller, the new kid in school—the poor kid, the *foster* kid, the troublemaker. Tony had accidentally broken a window, and Miller willingly took the fall. It hadn't been hard to fool everyone—everyone expected that the troublemaker in foster care was the kid who'd broken the glass, anyway.

He'd been living with his current foster family long enough to know that he would be preached-at to death, but he wouldn't be hit. Tony, on the other hand, had a brute of a stepfather who didn't care enough even to keep his blows from marking the boy's face.

Miller had stepped forward, confessed to a crime he hadn't committed, and in return had won Tony's undying loyalty. Not that Miller had wanted it. Not at first. But eventually, Tony had pushed his way past Miller's hardened shell and the two boys became friends.

There was no way in hell he could tell Mariah any of this—foster families and stepfathers with iron fists didn't fit in with Jonathan Mills's world of yacht clubs and tennis lessons and stock dividends.

"How many stitches do you think I'm going to need?" Mariah asked, changing the subject after his silence had dragged on and on and on.

Miller shook his head. "I don't know."

Silence again. Miller could feel her watching him. "How are *you?*" she finally asked. "In all the excitement, I forgot that just a few days ago you were feeling ill enough to faint on the beach. And here you are, suddenly building a house and climbing up and down a tree..." She was still gazing at him, her eyes questioning now. Wondering. "Carrying Janey. Carrying me. If you're this strong now, how strong did you *used* to be?"

"I'm feeling pretty tired," he said, hoping she wouldn't notice that he hadn't answered her question. He prayed that she wouldn't think too long or too hard about the fact that he *had* moved up and down that tree with the balance and strength of a man who couldn't possibly have just completed a crippling round of chemotherapy. He knew one way to get her mind off this topic and fast. "Mariah, about before...in the van...?"

She blushed, but she met his gaze steadily. "John, I'm really sorry about that. I know—you just want to be friends. It's taking a while to sink in, but I'm finally starting to get it and—"

"I wanted to apologize to you."

"To me? But—"

"I kissed you," he told her. "You didn't kiss me until after I kissed you, and I shouldn't have, so I'm sorry."

She was gazing at him, wide-eyed. It was all he could do not to kiss her again. "It *wasn't* me."

Miller shook his head. "I couldn't resist."

"I don't get it," she said. "If you can't resist kissing

me, and *I* can't resist kissing *you,* then why aren't we doing a whole heck of a lot more kissing?''

The doctor came in, saving Miller from even attempting to answer her. He stood up, grateful for the escape. "I'll wait outside."

"John."

He stopped and looked back at her.

"Forget I ever said that, okay? We're friends. That's enough—it's okay with me."

Miller nodded and went out the door. He just wished he could close his eyes and fall asleep and wake up in a place where simply being friends with Mariah Robinson was okay with him, too.

He was seeing her, too.

He was still seeing her. They were gone all day, and she realized he must have gone to that silly house-building.

She found it amusing, but nothing to worry about.

When it was time to make a choice, he would choose correctly. There was no doubt about it.

Chapter 7

Two stitches. Two tiny little stitches, and she had to stay out of the water and away from Foundations for Families for another unknown quantity of days.

It wouldn't be so bad if she knew precisely how long it was going to be before she could get back to her routine. Two days? Two weeks? Two *months?* Nobody would give her any definite answers, and meanwhile, her entire life was on hold.

All for two little stitches.

She was working hard to control her impatience. But Foundations for Families was counting on her. She'd already missed too many of her shifts. She needed to get back and…

Mariah did one of her breathing exercises. She sounded like Marie. This was not Mariah, with her no-worries, no-stress attitude. Mariah would take these imposed days off as a gift. A chance to lie on the beach and catch up on her reading. A chance to sleep late, to take the time to cook herself delicious, healthful dinners, to watch the sunset and see the stars come out at night.

The first few days actually had been fun. Jonathan Mills had dropped by once a day, bringing her things to eat and books to read, videotapes to watch and tacky little toys from the souvenir shop to amuse her. A goofy-looking duck made from seashells glued together. A Garden Isle coloring book and a thirty-six-pack of crayons. A booklet of Mad-Libs.

Funny things. Silly things. The kind of things one friend would give another.

John's visits were nothing but friendly. In fact, he seemed to take special care that they never touched—that they never got close enough even to brush against one another by accident.

Their conversations were safe, too. They talked about books and movies and newspaper headlines. They talked about Foundations for Families and the best place on the island to get an omelet.

Mariah wasn't certain when John's latest medical test results would be coming in, but she was more than ready for him to receive a clean bill of health. From things he'd said, little hints he'd dropped, she had to believe that he'd be getting word soon. Maybe then he'd let himself give in to the attraction she still saw simmering in his eyes whenever he thought she wasn't looking.

Of course, it was entirely possible that when he wasn't looking at her, he was looking at Serena with the exact same heat in his eyes. Serena didn't come to visit, not even once, and Mariah couldn't bring herself to call her. She suspected, though, by John's noticeable absence at dinnertime, that the two of them were together. She suspected, but she hoped it was only her too-vivid imagination, fueled by jealousy, rearing its ugly little head.

She tried to stomp it back into place, but it peered at her from dark corners. She tried to bring it out into the light. So what if John was seeing Serena? He'd made it clear to Mariah that he and she were no more than friends. She could be happy with his friendship. She could be content to keep their relationship on that level.

And her Aunt Susan was the pope.

The truth was always there—a tiny voice that never failed to remind her of how she'd felt when John had kissed her. The voice reminded her of the way she'd been so ready to give herself to him in every way imaginable. The voice was always there to point out just how much she wanted this man, even despite his rejection.

She was a fool, yet every time he came to her door, she let him in. She knew damn well that in her case, being friends *wasn't* better than nothing, but she couldn't get past his illness.

What if she shut him out, what if she turned him away, refused his friendship, and he died?

He was comfortable with her. She could see him visibly relax as they sat and talked. How could she deny him that?

She was a sucker, too kind for her own good, but at least she knew it.

As of this morning, it had been nearly a day and a half since John had last stopped in.

Afraid to overstep the bounds of friendship, Mariah hadn't even called. She'd picked up the phone more than once. She'd even dialed the resort. She'd gone as far as inquiring if Mr. Jonathan Mills was still staying there. He was. But she didn't leave a message, fearful of her tendency to want too much where John was concerned.

She more than missed him. She worried about him.

Was he feeling sick? Was he relapsing? Where the heck *was* he?

A dog was barking, down on the beach.

Mariah looked up from the book she was trying her best to concentrate on, hoping it was Princess. And John.

It was Princess all right, but John was nowhere in sight. The funny-looking little dog was dancing in and out of the water, barking at the seagulls. There was no one around her for quite some distance in either direction.

Mariah laid her book aside and went down onto the beach. She whistled and the little dog looked up, ears alert. "Princess!"

Princess seemed almost to grin as she trotted toward Mariah.

"Hey," Mariah said to her, "what are you doing out here all by yourself? Where's John? Where's your master?"

The dog, of course, didn't answer.

Mariah was under doctor's orders to take it easy, but a nice, slow walk down the beach...? Now, that couldn't hurt, could it?

"Come on, Princess," Mariah said. "Let's get you something to drink and let me grab some shoes and we'll go find John."

Returning his wandering dog was clearly a friendly gesture. It was neighborly—something even just a casual acquaintance would do.

It was also the best idea she'd had all day.

Serena Westford was waiting for him in the most elegant of the resort's lounges.

Miller went slowly inside, letting his eyes adjust. Even at this time of the morning, the room was barely lit. In small bits and pieces, light filtered in through the heavy curtains that covered the windows, giving the room an odd, almost smoky feel.

Serena sat in the corner, sipping a cup of coffee, her perfect legs gracefully crossed, her dress an angelic shade of white.

Miller felt a sense of dread as he approached her. They'd met for dinner two nights ago. He'd gone directly from Mariah's house to pick her up, and he'd been late. He hadn't wanted to leave.

He'd been far too comfortable at Mariah's, far too at home, and he'd cursed himself soundly even for going there in the first place. He'd visited her for several days running—well above and beyond the call of duty. The truth was, duty had nothing to do with his visits. They were for pure pleasure—his own pleasure as well as Mariah's.

Mariah. She'd been unable to hide the flare of happiness in her eyes whenever he arrived. It was addictive, and he'd found himself visiting her more often than he should.

He'd been careful to keep his distance since their kiss in the Triple F van. But the minimum distance he *should* have maintained was at least several miles wide. The truth was, he should have stayed at the resort.

But he couldn't do it. He couldn't stay away.

And two nights ago when he'd left to pick up Serena, it had been all that he could do not to pull Mariah into his arms and tell her everything. He wanted to tell her who he really was and *what* he really was. And he wanted to kiss her until they melted into one, kiss her until time itself stood still.

Instead he'd left to meet Serena. He'd spent yesterday afternoon with Serena, too, purposely staying away from Mariah's house. They'd shared another early dinner and he'd sat in the resort restaurant, and thought about Mariah while Serena told him about her fictional past, working for the peace corps in Africa. He'd been far less attentive than he should have been. After dinner, they had a drink out on the restaurant's veranda, and he found Serena gazing at him, waiting for him to respond to some question she'd asked.

He hadn't had a clue what they had just been talking about, and that scared him. He hadn't kept his mind on his job. He'd been standing there thinking about how badly he wished he was with Mariah.

The power Mariah had over him scared him to death, and at the time he did the only thing he could think of—he took Serena into his arms and he kissed her.

He'd kissed her hard, trying to banish the ghost of Mariah that seemed to hover permanently in his subconscious. He'd tried to call up some degree of passion, but even though Serena had pressed her sinewy, lithe body against him, even though she'd responded enthusiastically, Miller had been left feeling bitterly cold—and thinking once again of the fire Mariah could start within him with just one look.

He hadn't liked kissing Serena Westford, but she hadn't seemed to notice. As he approached her now, he hoped to God he wouldn't have to kiss her again.

But Serena only lifted her cheek for him to brush with his lips, and as he sat down next to her, she poured him a cup of steaming coffee from a silver coffeepot.

"Good morning," she said. He knew the English accent was a fake, but unlike most Americans who slipped into unauthentic-sounding British accents, Serena clearly had listened quite carefully to tapes, almost as if she was learning an entirely new language. "Did you sleep well last night?"

"Like a child," he lied. In fact, he'd stared at the ceiling for hours…thinking of Mariah. And when he finally *had* fallen asleep, it was not his nightmare that had jerked him awake before dawn, but rather an all too realistic erotic dream. He and Mariah, tangled together on her couch, clothing melted away as she opened herself to him and…

He'd awakened, disoriented, reaching for her, aching with need. But, of course, she wasn't there.

Serena was gazing at him, her cat green eyes watching him closely. He managed a smile. It was time to move this game up to a new level. "I spoke to my doctor today," he told her, mentally bracing himself, knowing that upon receiving his "good news" Serena was going to kiss him again. "He had the results from my most recent blood test. So far, it looks as if I'm not going to die."

"Oh, John, that's such wonderful news," Serena said. Sure enough, she leaned forward to kiss him.

And sure enough, Miller wished he was kissing Mariah instead.

There was an ambulance waiting outside the resort. The moment Mariah saw it, her heart began to pound, and her mind flashed to the worst-case scenario. The paramedics had come because of John. He'd fallen ill again. He was dying. He was already dead.

She stopped herself cold. That was ridiculous. It was extremely unlikely. Thinking that way wasn't going to do her one bit of good. Still, she went quickly toward the front desk, holding tightly on to Princess's collar. Through the window, she could see the ambulance pulling away. "Excuse me, can you please tell me which room Jonathan Mills is in?"

The desk clerk was cheerfully apologetic. "I'm sorry,

we can't give out room numbers. But we can ring a guest's room for you, if you like.''

"Yes, please. Jonathan Mills.''

The clerk handed her the telephone. It rang. And rang. And rang. No answer.

The fear was returning, lodging in her throat, when Princess pulled free.

"Hey!'' Mariah tossed the phone back to the clerk with a quick thanks and ran after the dog. Just because John wasn't in his room, she told herself, didn't mean that he was inside that ambulance.

Princess slipped out the doors that led to the deck by the pool, and Mariah followed. She hurried down the steps and ran nearly smack into Jonathan Mills.

He caught her elbows to hold her steady. "Mariah?''

"John!'' She threw her arms around his neck. "Thank God!'' He felt so warm and solid and he smelled so good—like sunblock and coffee. He always smelled like coffee. Maybe if he stopped drinking so much coffee, she thought inanely, maybe then he'd be able to sleep.

He pulled her even closer, held her even tighter for just a fraction of a second. It was so brief, she wondered if she'd imagined it, but she knew she hadn't. He'd held her like that before—almost desperately—all those mornings ago, on her couch. But instead of kissing her, the way he'd done that morning, he quickly moved back, away from her.

And that was when she saw Serena.

Looking cool and impossibly young and pure in a white sundress and hat, Serena moved to rest her hand possessively on John's arm. "Mariah,'' she said. "What a surprise.''

Daniel, John's assistant—the slender young Asian man Mariah had met the day John had fainted on the beach—was also standing nearby. At a nod from John, he took Princess by the collar and led the dog away.

"We were...uh, we were just going to have lunch out here by the pool," John told Mariah. "Would you, um, care to join us?"

"Mariah's on some kind of macrobiotic diet," Serena told him. "There's nothing on the menu here that she could possibly want."

John and Serena. They were standing there, looking very much like a couple. Although the truth was that she was too short for him—they didn't look quite right together. Still, there they were. About to have lunch. Together.

Mariah could easily imagine them having spent the morning together. The morning—and maybe even longer. Maybe even the night before. When *had* she seen John last?

Mariah cleared her throat, gazing up into his eyes, knowing that he could clearly see her hurt, knowing she had no right to feel hurt, but unable to hide it. "I found Princess on the beach. Alone. I haven't seen you in a few days, so I was worried. I thought maybe you were sick or hurt or...and I can see right now that you're definitely not, so I guess I'll just...go."

She backed away.

"Did you hear the good news?" Serena asked as if she was totally unaware of the tension that seemed to leap and crackle between Mariah and John. "Jonathan got the first of his test results this morning. His doctor is almost certain the cancer's gone." She smiled up at John. "He's going to live to a ripe old age, aren't you, darling?"

This morning. He'd known this morning and he hadn't even bothered to call. "That's such good news," Mariah managed to say. She even managed a smile, despite the tears in her eyes. "John, I'm so glad for you."

True, she'd imagined him getting the news and coming to *her,* not Serena. Still, that didn't make the news any less wonderful. But now he was going to have lunch with Serena, and Serena had made it clear that their table was only for two.

"I better go," she said. She gazed into John's eyes for just a moment longer. "I'm *so* glad."

Miller couldn't believe it. Despite his careful talk of friendship, Mariah clearly had had expectations that were now dashed upon seeing him here like this with Serena. Yet her words were sincere and heartfelt. He'd hurt her, probably badly, yet she was honestly happy for him.

She looked out of place at the resort grill, dressed the way she was in cutoffs and a T-shirt. Her hair was wind-blown—her soft curls tumbling down to her shoulders. Her eyes were filled with tears—still she was smiling.

"So glad," she whispered again.

As Miller watched, she turned and walked away.

He wanted to follow her. He was dying to follow her. But he couldn't. He couldn't even take a moment and feel like crap for hurting her this way because Serena was watching him. He had to smile and pretend that the expression he'd seen on Mariah's face wasn't making his heart ache.

His heart *was* aching.

A surprising turn of events for a man who wasn't sure he even had a heart just a few short weeks ago.

"Shall we have lunch?" Serena murmured.

Miller nodded and gave her another smile. Tonight he was planning to ask her to marry him, and sometime in the next few weeks, she would try to stick a knife into his heart.

Even if she succeeded, he suspected it would not be a new sensation.

"Hi, it's me. Is this a good time to talk?" Mariah asked.

There was a brief silence on the other end of the line, then Serena's cool voice answered, "If you're wondering if I'm alone, yes, I am. But I'm a little busy right now. I'll call you back."

The line went dead, and Mariah stared for a moment at the phone in her hand. Instead of hanging up, she pressed redial. But this time, Serena didn't answer. This time, her answering machine didn't even come on.

That was odd. Serena was nearly obsessive about getting her phone messages. Why she should leave the house without turning her machine on was a mystery.

But the phone rang before Mariah even started clearing her lunch dishes off the table. She picked it up. "Hello?"

It was Serena. "Sorry—I had to get *out* of there. I'm calling from the pay phone in front of the Northbeach pizza parlor. My place is *crawling* with bugs. I've had an infestation of some kind of disgusting cockroaches. *Awful.* I'm going off island for the rest of the afternoon and evening. To Atlanta—I have some business to take care of. Can I get you anything from the real world?"

She didn't let Mariah answer. "God, I can still see those nasty little bugs when I close my eyes. There were so *many* of them. The exterminator came and said they had to spray some awful poison, and even then, they'd need to come back every few days or so to spray again. I told the rental office that I *wouldn't* be coming back. Not to *that* cottage."

"Will you be coming back?" Mariah asked, hardly daring to hope.

"Of course. I'll probably stay at the resort for a few days until I can find something less populated by the native insect life."

The resort. That would put Serena closer to John. How convenient.

Mariah took a deep breath. "Serena, I wanted to talk to you about John."

"Jonathan Mills?"

"Yes."

"He was *so* excited when he received those favorable test results," Serena told her. "Just like a little boy. Of course, one set of favorable tests doesn't necessarily mean he's in remission or whatever. He still could die."

"If you think that, then what are you doing with him?" Mariah asked. "You want a husband who's alive, don't you?"

Serena laughed. "A husband? Who said anything about a husband?" Her voice changed. "Has Jonathan mentioned anything to you about wanting to get married?"

"No."

"Well, see? We're just friends. You're his friend. Can't *I* be friends with Jonathan, too? Really, Mariah, it's nothing serious. The man hasn't done more than *kiss* me," Serena pointed out. "He's had plenty of opportunities to come home with me or take me back to his place, but he hasn't." She paused. "Yet."

John had kissed Serena. Mariah closed her eyes as she fought the wave of jealousy and hurt that threatened to consume her. "It might be nothing serious for you, but..." She knew John pretty well by now. "John's *always* serious. And he's fragile in a lot of ways. His cancer has made him vulnerable. And he has those awful nightmares."

"Are you trying to scare me away—or give me instructions on how to hold his hand and warm his milk for him at night when he has a bad dream?"

"These aren't bad dreams. These are violent nightmares. Hasn't he told you?"

"Maybe he's afraid he'll scare me away if he tells me all of his dark secrets," Serena said.

Or maybe when he was with Serena, he didn't spend any time talking.

"He should realize that I don't scare easily," Serena added. "What are the nightmares about? Being sick?"

"No," Mariah told her. "A friend of his was a police detective and he was killed in the line of duty. It haunts him."

"Isn't that interesting," Serena mused. "A police detective, you said?"

"Actually, John said his friend—Tony—was a cop. Tony was killed on the orders of an organized crime boss."

"Well, that certainly adds a new dimension to the game."

"Serena, if this is just a game to you—"

"Life is a game," Serena said. "You play it, and then you die. No matter what rules you play by, dying is the one given. Everyone dies sooner or later. Some, sooner. If the cancer doesn't kill Jonathan—who knows—maybe he'll be hit by a bus."

"That's a terrible thing to think!"

"Oh, please, Mariah," Serena said. "The Pollyanna act gets old after a while."

"Maybe when you leave today, you shouldn't come back."

Serena laughed. "Maybe I won't." She paused. "Was

that really the most awful thing you could think of to say to me?''

Mariah gazed out over the ocean, curbing her impulse to say the words that were really on her lips. "No," she admitted. "But we're friends. I don't want to say anything that—"

"Did you get that negative back from the photo lab?" Serena interrupted.

"No. I haven't been off—"

"Now I've *got* to come back." Serena sounded annoyed. "Have it ready for me tomorrow, please. I'll come by to pick it up."

"Tomorrow? I'm sorry, I can't—"

The line was dead. Serena had hung up without even saying goodbye.

Chapter 8

A light was on in Mariah's cottage.

Miller stood on the beach, gazing up at the house, wishing he'd been able to sleep. He wished he hadn't given up and climbed out of bed. He wished he hadn't roused Princess and brought her out onto the beach. He wished he'd walked in the other direction.

Most of all, he wished he could erase the memory he had of Mariah's face as she turned away at lunch. But the hurt and disappointment in her eyes had been burned into his brain. There was no escaping it.

He shouldn't have come out here.

But something had pulled him in this direction. Something strong. Something he couldn't resist.

Nothing had gone right tonight. He'd planned to take Serena to dinner and ask her to marry him. But she'd called and left a message, canceling their date. She hadn't told him where she was going or when she'd be back—

just that she had to go to the mainland to take care of business and that she'd be back soon.

His first thought was that she was on to him. Somehow, she'd made him. She knew he was FBI.

She was dangerously smart, and he had screwed up all over the place with this case, starting with his obsession with Mariah and continuing with his failure to stick to his cover story and play the part of the invalid at the Foundations for Families building site. He knew what chemotherapy did to a person, and it was highly unlikely that, had he had the treatments he was pretending to have had, he would've been able to rescue that eight-year-old from the tree, let alone Mariah.

Yeah, and then there was his telling Mariah about Tony. That was a real stroke of genius. He'd actually told Mariah that Tony was a *cop*. What had he been thinking?

He *wasn't* thinking. He was reacting. He was feeling. He was wanting. He was leading with a part of his anatomy that didn't have a very high IQ.

And that was how agents got themselves and their partners killed. And God help him, he may not give a damn about his own life, but he would not—*would not*—bury another partner.

He gazed out at the horizon, squinting to make out where the sky ended and the ocean began. A light haze obscured all but the brightest of the stars, and a steady breeze blew off the water, carrying with it a salty mist. It was almost cold.

He was exhausted, bone weary, yet he still couldn't sleep. He couldn't sleep because he was afraid to sleep. He was afraid to fall into his nightmare. Afraid to gaze down into Tony's sightless eyes. Afraid to hear Tony's voice, tight with fear. Afraid to face his own guilt.

Princess was halfway up the path that led to Mariah's, looking back at him with a quizzical expression on her fuzzy face. *Aren't you coming?*

"No," Miller said, softly but firmly. "Come back here, Princess. *Now.*"

But the dog either couldn't hear him over the wind and the surf, or maybe she simply chose not to hear. She trotted steadily toward the shelter of Mariah's deck.

Miller went after her, breaking into a run, but she was too far ahead. As she started up the wooden steps of the deck, she barked sharply. Once. Twice.

Damn. That was all he needed—for Mariah to know he was here, skulking around outside her house, hoping for what? To get a glimpse of her? To talk to her? To kiss her? To fall back with her onto her bed? To lock her bedroom door and never come out?

All those things. *Dammit,* he wanted *all* those things.

"Princess, get your butt down here," he hissed, starting up the stairs after her.

The door slid open. "Hey, what are *you* doing here?" Mariah greeted his dog. Her voice was not so friendly when she turned and spotted him, frozen on his way up the stairs. "John?"

He climbed up the last few steps, silently cursing Princess, silently cursing himself. "Hi. Yeah, it's me. I'm sorry—I didn't mean to bother you, but the dog has a mind of her own."

Mariah looked incredible. She was wearing those same cutoffs she'd had on at lunchtime, the same clingy T-shirt. Her legs were long and tanned and looked as if they'd be deliciously smooth to touch. She'd pulled her hair up and off her neck, holding it in a messy bundle on top of her head with one of those giant bear-trap-type clips.

But she also looked tired—her normally sparkling eyes were shadowed. She looked wary and leery and not at all happy to see him.

As he watched, she took a breath, and the slight movement made her breasts strain against the cotton of her shirt. God, what he wouldn't have given to pull her into his arms.

She glanced back inside the house, twisting slightly to look at the clock on the wall. "It's after one. Couldn't you sleep?"

Miller shook his head. "No. I never can. Sleep, I mean. Except for that one time here..."

She was silent for several long moments, just gazing at him. He couldn't read her eyes, couldn't read her body language. He had absolutely no idea what she was thinking.

"It's cold tonight," she finally said. "Why don't you come inside?"

She turned and went in, not waiting for him to answer.

Miller knew he should take Princess and go. But he'd left everything he knew he should do behind a long time ago. And Princess was already curled up in the dry, protected corner of the deck. So instead, he followed Mariah into the house and closed the door tightly behind him.

It was outrageously bright in there after the darkness of the beach. Mariah had brought most of the lamps from other rooms over to the dining table near the sliding doors, and that part of the house seemed to glow. He stepped past the lights and into the dimness of the living room.

"How's your back?" he asked awkwardly, wishing that she would ask him to leave. It would make everything so much easier if she just kicked him out.

"It's fine." She was standing in the middle of the room, arms folded across her chest, watching him.

"What are you doing...you know, up so late?"

"I couldn't sleep, either," she admitted. "I thought I'd put some of my pictures in albums. I've been trying to organize them." She gestured back toward the dining-room table. Photos of all shapes and colors were spread across its surface, along with albums of all sizes.

Music was playing softly in the background. It wasn't soft music; it was just turned down low, as if she'd adjusted the volume when she heard Princess out on the deck. A slide guitar wailed over a heavy country backbeat. Vocalists in tight harmony came in—singing about a girl with a tattoo in the shape of Texas. Miller had to smile.

"You know, I always pictured you as being so serene, with your stress reduction exercises and your crystals," he told her. "I guess I always imagined that when you were alone you'd listen to New Age music—not kick-ass country."

She smiled very slightly. "Oh, please. I thought you knew me better than that. New Age music puts me to sleep."

"Maybe we should both try listening to it, then."

Mariah turned away from him and sat on the end of the couch, her legs underneath her, tailor-style. It was dim in the living room, with all the lights moved into the dining area. She looked mysterious sitting there, shadows falling across her face. "Tell me about the test results."

Miller stepped away from the table and farther into the darkness of the living room. He sat down in the rocking chair opposite her and cleared his throat before he told her a lie. Another lie. There had been so many, yet at the same time, he'd told her more about himself than he'd ever told anyone. All those memories of his mother...

"There's not much to tell. My blood tests show vast improvements. If it keeps going like this, I'm going to be considered in remission. If the cancer doesn't recur in five years, I'm going to be considered cured."

He sounded bitter. He *was* bitter. He knew so much about Hodgkin's disease and about the so-called survival rate because his mother had been one of the ones who hadn't survived. She'd been in remission. She'd even been pronounced cured. And still, she'd relapsed and the second time around, the cancer had won. She'd died.

"Five *years...?*" Mariah leaned forward. "John, you've got to stop worrying about it. You can't not sleep for five years." She sighed. "Have you considered going into therapy?"

He wanted to sit next to her on the couch. God, he wanted her so badly he could barely speak.

Why was he here? What was he doing here? There was nothing—absolutely nothing—good that could possibly come of this. Nothing but a few brief moments of comfort, a temporary respite from the hell his life had become. Mariah could give him that. But what about her? What about all that he'd be taking away from her in return?

"I know you don't think so, but I'm okay about the Hodgkin's. It's not even real to me." Miller stood up swiftly, aware that he was saying the wrong thing again. What was he telling her now? Damn right the cancer wasn't real to him, because it *wasn't* real. But it *was* real to Jonathan Mills.

Except he *wasn't* Jonathan Mills. He was John Miller. John Miller was the one who couldn't sleep, the one with the terrible nightmares. He was the one with all the guilt, all the suffocating blame. He was the one who had come here tonight, seeking her out.

Mariah stood, too, looking at him, her eyes wide. "John, are you all right?"

He shook his head. "No. I have to..." What? What did he have to do? Run away. God, he never thought he'd ever run away from anything. But here he was, forced to run from the one person who maybe could save him, given the chance.

But he couldn't give her—or himself—any kind of a chance.

She was moving toward him slowly, the way someone would approach a frightened animal. "John, when was the last time you slept?"

He shook his head. "I don't know." But that was another lie and he was tired of lying to her. He knew damn well when he'd last slept. "It was here," he said. "That time I was here."

Her eyes widened. "That was over a week ago!"

"I've had some naps since then, but..." He shook head.

"But you wake up with that nightmare, and then you can't—or won't—go back to sleep, right? My God, you're shaking!"

He was. He jammed his shaking hands into the front pockets of his jeans and turned toward the door. "I have to go."

Mariah blocked his path. "Let me call Daniel to come and get you."

"No, I'm fine."

"You are so *not* fine. Look, just sit down. On the couch."

Miller didn't move.

"Please? John?"

He sat.

She sat down next to him. All he could think about was how badly he'd wanted to sit next to her. Well, now here he was.

"Talk to me," she said quietly. "Tell me about Tony. Why do you blame yourself for his death? What really happened, John?"

Miller turned to look at her, and with a flash of clarity that nearly pushed him down onto the floor, he knew why he wanted to be here, why he wanted to be with Mariah so desperately.

Why do you blame yourself for his death?

He did. He blamed himself. And yet he knew that Mariah would forgive him. He knew that without a doubt. Mariah would tell him that even if it *was* his fault that Tony had died, even if he *had* been to blame, even if there was something he could have done to save his partner and best friend, she would *still* forgive him.

He should have gotten out of the van sooner. He should have known there would be a snafu with the backup. He should have anticipated the fact that the choppers wouldn't arrive. His list of recriminations went on and on, but regardless of its length and content, the bottom line was the same.

He'd failed.

But Mariah, with her gentle smile and warm eyes, would forgive him for failing. She would forgive him his mistakes, forgive him for being human.

God help him, he wanted that forgiveness. He wanted to hear her say it. And he knew with that same flash of clarity, brighter than all the lights gathered around the dining-room table, that he had to get out of here, and soon, or he'd break down in tears, crying like a baby. Crying for Tony, and crying for himself—for everything that he'd lost that awful night two years ago. Crying because the one time it had really mattered, the one time his reputation of never failing, of not accepting the word "impossible," of being "The Robot" with his superhuman ability to get the job done—the one time that would have really made a difference, reality had stepped in and Tony had died.

He knew he had to get out of there, but Mariah reached out and took his hand, and he couldn't move.

"I couldn't save him," he told her, his voice hoarse.

She touched his face. "But you tried, didn't you? You *were* there."

Miller had to close his eyes to keep his tears from escaping. "I didn't see it. But I heard them kill him. God, I heard him die!" He turned away as more than two years of pain and grief and rage erupted in an emotional cataclysm. His tears burned his face and his lungs ached for air and his body shook as he broke down and wept. "I was too late. I got there too late."

Miller felt Mariah's arms around him and he tried to pull away, tried to stop his tears, tried to shut himself off and push everything he felt back down inside him. He might've succeeded had she not held on to him so tightly.

"What if you'd gotten there earlier?" she asked, her voice as soothing as the gentleness of her hands in his hair. "How could you have stopped them from killing him? What would you have done?"

He knew the answer—and he knew that she knew it, too.

"You probably would've been killed, as well, wouldn't you?" she asked quietly.

"Yes." Not probably. Definitely. He would've died. It was only because he'd arrived after most of Domino's men had emptied their bullets into Tony's head that he'd managed to take them all out without being killed himself. If he'd shown up any sooner, he would've been lying on that concrete floor, just as dead as Tony.

"John, you've got to forgive yourself for not dying with your friend."

That was why he'd come here, wasn't it? For absolution. For the relief of his soul. But he wanted relief for his body, too. He wanted it so badly he was afraid he'd give in to the temptation. God, it wouldn't take much to push him over the edge.

He tried to pull free from her hands, well aware that her touch was giving him far more than comfort. Her touch was lighting him on fire, reminding him of the sweet oblivion that awaited him if only he gave in. He had to get out of here.

But she wouldn't let him go. "It's all right," she murmured, her hands in his hair, on his face, soothing his shoulders and back. "Let it out, John. Let it go. It's okay to feel angry and hurt. It's okay to grieve. If you don't, it'll poison you. Just let it all go."

Miller couldn't stop himself. Mariah held him even more tightly as he clung to her desperately. Please, God, don't let her kiss him. If she did, he'd be lost.

He closed his eyes as she began talking to him soothingly, softly, walking him through that same relaxation exercise she'd helped him with last week. And once again, like last week, his exhaustion crashed down upon him.

He was barely conscious as she pulled him back onto the couch with her, her arms tightly around him, his back pressed against her front.

"Forgive yourself," she murmured. "I'm sure Tony does."

* * *

Mariah couldn't sleep.

The couch wasn't meant to hold two people lying down—especially not two people her and John's size. But she wasn't uncomfortable. In fact, she liked the sensation of John's body pressed against hers, their legs intimately intertwined.

She liked it too much.

She listened to the steady, quiet rhythm of his breathing and cursed herself for being a fool.

At least she hadn't had sex with him. Although, that was really only because he hadn't asked. If he'd wanted to, she probably wouldn't have been able to turn him down.

God, what had happened to her since that first morning she'd set eyes on this man? Where on earth had Jonathan Mills gotten the power to transform her so totally into some kind of doormat?

He stirred slightly, and she took the opportunity to pull her arm out from underneath him.

It was the cancer thing. The idea that this man had faced—and was still facing—the very real possibility of his imminent death did her in. His plight reduced her to a quivering mass of emotions and reactions.

It had to be that. Because she'd fallen in love before without losing her sense of self, her strength and...

Fallen in love.

She looked down at John's face. He looked impossibly young, improbably innocent, his lips slightly parted in sleep.

She was in love with him.

Mariah knew in that instant that her doormat days were done. She was in love, and yet she was more unhappy than she'd ever been in her entire life. She hadn't felt this bad even while she was going through her divorce from Trevor.

She couldn't do this to herself anymore.

She wasn't crazy. And yet here she was, holding John while he slept when she knew for a fact that he'd been sharing more than meals with Serena. From now on, he was going to have to go to Serena for the comfort he needed to get him through the blackest hours of the night.

Mariah peeled herself away from him, climbing off the couch. He stirred again, but he didn't wake up as she stood there, looking down at him.

She should have felt better. Pushing him away from her like that should have been empowering.

But without his body next to hers, warming her, all Mariah felt was cold.

She came back to the hotel quite late. She'd closed the bar down, drinking and dancing.

Her dress smelled of smoke and sweat, and she peeled it off, letting it fall in a heap on the soft, expensive carpeting. She wouldn't take it with her when she left in the morning.

She was going to have to go back. She needed that negative. Except the stupid cow hadn't sounded as if she was going to go out of her way to get it back from...

Where was it she kept her negatives? B&W Photo Lab. Just over on the mainland from Garden Isle. It would be easy enough to find, easy enough to walk in there and get hold of her entire collection of negatives.

She caught sight of herself in the mirror and stopped for a moment to admire her body, her face.

She'd had plastic surgery to remove all but one of her scars. One she kept—a little one, just along the line of her left eyebrow.

The first one had done that to her. The first one had given her all her scars—at least all the scars that her father before him hadn't given her.

She closed her eyes, remembering the thrill she had felt when the policeman had come to her door, waking her in the middle of the night to tell her that the first one was dead. A car accident. He'd drunk himself into a stupor, and instead of coming home and beating her to a pulp, he'd driven his car into a tree.

The undertaker's wife, mistaking her round-the-clock vigilance at his coffin for grief, cut her a lock of his hair to remember him by.

But it hadn't been grief keeping her there—it had been fear. Fear that unless she watched him, unless she made damn sure he stayed right there in that wooden box until they nailed it shut, he might somehow escape. He might jump up and run away and come back to haunt her.

She'd nearly thrown the hair into the toilet, but on second thought, she'd kept it, wrapped in cellophane, at the bottom of her jewelry box.

The insurance money, along with a stash she'd found in a suitcase in the garage, had been enough to get her to St. Thomas. She'd picked herself a new name, afraid that whoever owned the money that had been in that suitcase would come looking for her.

That was when she'd met the second one.

He was rich and old and nearly as mean as the first one. Except the abuse *he* dished out wasn't physical. And when a piece of chicken caught in his throat during dinner, she had stood by and watched him choke.

She didn't call for help. She just watched—watched the look in his eyes as he knew she would do nothing to save him, watched as he realized he was, indeed, going to die. She'd liked it—liked the power, liked the feeling of control.

The third one she'd married with the intention of killing.

It had been laughably easy. She was so much smarter than all of them.

Smarter than Jonathan Mills, who wasn't really named Jonathan Mills.

She knew that sooner or later the police would try to trap her. She'd been watching for them. She'd been ready. And when she'd found their clumsily hidden microphones all over her house, she knew that Jonathan Mills had been sent to stop her.

Instead, she'd escaped.

She climbed between the crisp hotel sheets, feeling a flare of regret.

She would have liked pushing her knife blade into Jonathan Mills's heart.

Chapter 9

Miller opened his eyes to the sound of the telephone ringing.

It was daylight. Bright, gleaming morning. The sun had been up for at least an hour and he simply lay for a moment on the couch, staring up at the light playing across the ceiling, hazily wondering why that should seem such an amazing thing.

"Yes." He heard a soft voice from the other room. "Yes, he's here. I'll see if he's awake."

Then he heard the sound of footsteps coming into the living room, and he sat up, automatically raking his hair back with one hand, pushing it from his forehead. Except the hair his fingers connected with was shockingly short, and he remembered instantly both where he was and who he was supposed to be.

Dear God, he'd slept all night again. This time, without even a trace of his nightmare.

"Phone's for you," Mariah said quietly, handing him a cordless telephone.

She didn't meet his gaze. She hardly looked at him at all.

Miller quickly played back the previous evening in his mind. God knows he had plenty to be embarrassed about, what with breaking down and crying the way he'd done. But he couldn't recall a single thing Mariah had done that should make her so uncomfortable.

She hadn't even kissed him.

God help him—he'd somehow managed to spend all that time here last night without ever kissing Mariah. Although he had a very definite memory of falling asleep cradled in the softness of her arms.

He brought the telephone to his ear, still watching Mariah as she opened the sliders to let in the fresh morning air. Last night's coolness remained, but it wouldn't for long, not in the heat from the sun. She stayed for a moment, just looking out at the ocean, her fatigue evident in the way she stood, in the set of her shoulders.

He might have slept well last night, but she clearly hadn't.

"Yeah?" Miller said into the phone.

"John, it's Daniel. I'm sorry to have to call you there, but Serena appears to have gone for good."

Miller didn't move a muscle. He just sat and watched Mariah watch the ocean. "Based on…?"

"Based on the fact that yesterday she notified her rental agent that she was terminating her lease agreement. Her place is empty, John. All her things are cleared out. I went over there early this morning. All the surveillance microphones are still in place—it doesn't look as if she touched any of them, but that doesn't mean anything. I've got to believe she found 'em, got spooked and ran."

Miller swore sharply. Mariah glanced back at him, but quickly looked away. "Call Pat Blake," he told Daniel. "Advise him of the situation and then get back to me."

He should've proposed marriage to Serena yesterday at lunch, when he'd had the chance. But he'd hesitated, and now she was gone. And in his experience, when a suspect fled, that suspect was gone for good.

The case was over—at least this stage of it was—with the suspect still at large. But other than that first sharp flash of annoyance, all Miller felt was relief. Because, for the first time in his life, he had found something that he wanted even more than he wanted to solve this case.

He'd found Mariah.

He pushed the button to disconnect the phone, then set it on the end table. He stood up stiffly, stretching out his legs and back. "Mind if I use your bathroom?"

Mariah turned to face him. "No, of course I don't," she said stiffly, politely. "But afterward, I think you should leave."

He froze mid-stretch. Leave?

He'd found Mariah—who wanted him to leave.

She turned swiftly, disappearing into the kitchen.

It was too damned ironic. For the first time since he'd met her, Miller finally felt free. True, the case wasn't officially over. He couldn't tell her who he was or what he'd been up to—not yet anyway. But he could pull her into his arms and kiss her without knowing for damn sure that she was going to end up hurt.

Miller didn't believe in happily ever after. He had no misconceptions regarding his ability to make Mariah happy in the long run. He knew damn well that kind of future wasn't in his cards. But he was sure that he could make her smile in the short term. He was *very* sure of that.

He went into the bathroom, relieved himself, then washed up. As he splashed cold water on his face, he caught sight of himself in the mirror. Despite the sleep he'd gotten, he still looked tired. For the first time in years, he found himself longing to crawl back into bed. For the first time in years, sleep beckoned invitingly instead of looming over him dangerously, like some snarling, vicious beast.

With Serena out of the picture, he had nothing to do, nowhere to go—at least not until Daniel contacted Pat Blake. Knowing Blake, he'd call a meeting, maybe even come down here himself to inspect the scene of the disaster firsthand. But that wouldn't be for hours, maybe even days.

Mariah wanted him to leave, but Miller wanted to stay. And for the first time, he *could* stay.

He took a deep breath before he opened the bathroom door. Mariah was in the kitchen. He could hear the sound of water running.

"I gave Princess some water," she told him without even looking up as he paused in the doorway.

"Thanks," he said. He hesitated, suddenly oddly embarrassed, a picture of the way he'd wept last night flashing into his head. "And thanks...for last night, too. I feel..." He smiled crookedly. "I feel *okay.*"

Mariah turned to face him then. "You slept for a long time."

He nodded. "First time in over two years I've slept through the sunrise."

"You never let yourself grieve for him before, did you?" she asked quietly, talking about Tony.

Miller squinted slightly as he looked out the window at the brightness of the day. "No."

"It wasn't your fault that he died."

He shook his head very slightly. "No. No, it wasn't." He laughed very softly. "I know it wasn't. Logically. Rationally. I guess I just don't quite *believe* it wasn't." He paused, gazing at her, feeling that familiar ache of longing. He wanted to pull her into his arms, but she was sending out all kinds of signals warning him to keep his distance. "Maybe you could help me work on that."

"Gee, I'm sorry, but I can't." She took a deep breath. "I don't want to be your therapist anymore, John," she said bluntly. "What you're dealing with isn't going to be solved by breaking plates or silly little relaxation exercises. You need to find someone professional who can really help you. And I..." Her voice broke. "I need you to stay away from me. I can't pretend to be your friend anymore. Maybe that's petty of me, because I know you really need me as a friend, but I can't do this anymore. I respect myself too much to play this crazy game with you. Do you want me or don't you? Every time I think that you do, you back away. And just when I'm convinced that you don't, you look at me like...like...*that*. Don't look at me like that, dammit, because I'm not going to play anymore. I want you to leave."

He stepped toward her. "Mariah—"

Mariah lifted her chin, folding her arms across her chest, holding her ground despite the tears that filled her eyes. "The door's in the other direction."

John stopped moving toward her, but he didn't retreat, either. He just gazed at her. In spite of his long, quiet sleep, he still looked weary, his chiseled features in high relief. His chin was covered with dark stubble, making him look doubly dangerous. But it was the bright blue of his eyes that caught her and held her in place. Beneath the heat of desire that nearly always simmered there, his eyes were filled with apology and darkened with a haunting vulnerability.

"Whatever you do, don't think that I don't want you," he whispered. "Because I do. I've wanted you right from the start—and every minute from then till now."

She couldn't believe what she was hearing. She laughed, but it came out sounding more like a sob. "Then why have you been kissing Serena?"

He didn't seem surprised that she knew—and he didn't try to deny it. "I can't... I can't explain that."

"Try."

John just shook his head.

He was blocking the only way out of the room, but Mariah couldn't stand to be there a moment longer. She tried to push past him, but he caught her arm, his fingers locking around her wrist. "Mariah, wait—"

"Let *go* of me!"

Miller let go. No way was he going to risk hurting her again. Seeing those bruises on her arms had made him sick to his stomach. "I kissed her because I hoped it would make me stop wanting *you*." That was only part of the truth, but he hoped it would be enough.

She turned to look back at him, her eyes filled with anger, her lips tight with disgust. "You are so full of—"

Miller kissed her. He knew it wasn't playing fair, but he didn't give a damn. He knew kissing her would melt her anger and ignite her passion, leaving the arguments and harsh words far behind. He knew he was good at word games, but Mariah had told him point-blank that she didn't want to play games anymore.

This kiss would eliminate everything but the most basic of truths—that he wanted her and she wanted him.

And yes, she still wanted him.

He tasted it in the fire of her kiss, in the heat of her

melting embrace. He kissed her harder, sweeping his tongue deeply into her mouth, and she met him with a fierceness that took his breath away. She pulled him closer, her hands gliding up his back, her fingers on his neck, in his hair, even as his own hands explored the softness of her body, cupping the fullness of her breasts.

"Make love to me, Mariah," he whispered, kissing her again. Her response was clear from the strength of her answering kiss.

She pulled back slightly, and he could see molten desire in her eyes. "If I do, I'm going to regret this, aren't I?" she said huskily.

"No," he said. "This is going to be too good to regret."

Her smile was tinged with sadness. "I just made up my mind to stay away from you, and now you go and totally mess me up. I mean, God! Give me one good reason why I shouldn't kick you out right here and now."

He couldn't. There was no reason, other than he wanted to stay, and she wanted him to stay, too. He leaned forward to kiss her again, but she stopped him with a finger against his lips.

"I don't know, maybe I haven't made this totally clear, but I'm emotionally involved here. Taking you into my bedroom and getting naked with you is going to be more than just great sex to me. It's going to be making love. Love, John—do you understand what I'm trying to say to you?" Mariah took a deep breath and let it all out in a rush. "In plain English, I'm in love with you. So if you're going to get all freaked out and scared about that, maybe you should just run away now—*before* you tear my heart out."

Miller couldn't move. He couldn't speak. He couldn't breathe. Mariah was in love with...*him?*

He gazed down into her eyes, unable to look away, feeling an odd tightness in his chest. "That sounds like a good reason for me to stay," he whispered.

He wanted to be loved. God, how he wanted that. He was shaken by how badly he wanted that, wanted more than just lust, more than physical gratification. He wanted to be cared for, to be cherished. In the past, he'd run away from such emotions, but as he looked into Mariah's eyes, he only wanted to move closer. He wanted her to love him. He wanted *her*. And somehow she knew. He could see in her eyes that she knew.

Still, it wasn't quite enough.

"I need you to promise me something," she told him.

"Mariah, I can't promise much—"

"I'm not looking for any major commitment or anything like that," she countered. "Just..." She had to start again. "Don't sleep with Serena, okay?"

That was easy. "I won't," he said. "I promise."

That was all she needed. Taking his hand, she led him to her bedroom.

The morning sun shone through green curtains, giving the room a greenish tint. The ocean breeze made the curtains move, and the light seemed to shift and dance across the ceiling. It was like being underwater. Or maybe up in heaven.

Mariah's bed was in the center of the small room, the headboard pushed against the wall. It was rumpled, unmade, the white sheets exposed beneath a green spread. Miller knew that Mariah had spent much of the night in here, unable to rest while he'd been fast asleep on the couch.

Mariah kissed him, and he knew his second assessment was right. This was definitely heaven.

She kissed him slowly, deeply, shifting her body

against his in a way that made him groan. He knew from the burst of heat in her eyes that she liked the involuntary sound of his desire.

Her hands slid up underneath his T-shirt, traveling slowly up his back, and Miller closed his eyes.

This was too good, too intense, and too damn slow. But if she wanted it like this, dammit, he was going to curb his raging impulses and make love to her slowly.

He knew without a shadow of a doubt that he'd go to superhuman degrees to give her anything she wanted, anything at all.

She tugged at his T-shirt and he helped her pull it up and over his head. But when he reached for her shirt, she stopped him.

"Have you noticed that when it comes to sex, guys don't like to get naked first?" she said, kissing his shoulders, his neck, his chest. Her fingers moved down to the waistband of his jeans, lightly brushing against his stomach as she unfastened the top button. "It's a dominance thing," she added, smiling up at him as she slowly unzipped his pants, "a power thing. It makes sense, doesn't it? The person still dressed has a certain amount of power over the person who's naked."

"Are you, um, into that?" Miller asked.

She pushed him back onto the bed, pulling his jeans down his thighs. "And then there's the female thing," she continued as if she hadn't heard his question. "Women tend to be afraid to take the lead for fear of coming on too strong. Socially, we're taught to lie back—let the man take off our clothes. Let him set the pace. Let him choose the time and place and position. Let him do the work. Hence the passive phrase 'to be made love *to*.' I much prefer 'making love *with*.'" She tossed his jeans onto the floor. "*That's* what I'm into."

He reached for her, pressing her back on the bed with the force of his kiss. But then he moved away, suddenly remembering. "Your back—is it all right?"

"It's fine." She pulled him toward her for another kiss, molding herself against him.

The sensation of the smoothness of her legs intertwined with his nearly overwhelmed him. He pulled her T-shirt up, over her head, and this time she didn't protest.

He gazed down at her and she smiled back at him, just letting him look. She was impossibly sexy, lying there like that. Her bra was white, covering her full breasts with some kind of stretchy lace material that allowed him tantalizing glimpses of dark pink nipples. He covered her breasts first with his hands, then with his mouth, suckling her through the lace of the bra, tugging on the desire-hardened tips with his lips, with his tongue.

She moaned, opening herself to him, cradling his swollen sex against the heat between her legs.

Miller reached for the button on her shorts, and she let him unfasten them and pull them down her legs. They soon joined his jeans on the floor.

Mariah closed her eyes. For all her liberated talk, she was lying there, letting him undress her. And cringing because she was nearly naked—and afraid he wouldn't like her because she didn't have the body of a Barbie doll.

She felt John's hands skimming her body. She knew he was looking at her.

"God, you're incredible," he breathed.

About to protest, she opened her eyes, but then she saw the fire in his gaze, the sheer admiration on his face. He was serious. He honestly liked what he saw.

He wasn't one of those men who went for boyishly figured women like Serena. He wasn't like Trevor, who had been forever trying to get her to go on a diet, to lose weight, to shrink herself down to his height.

No, John clearly liked *women*. Real women. And maybe especially women who were six feet tall, and generously—and appropriately—proportioned for their height.

As Mariah watched John's face, her shoulders were no longer too broad. Her thighs weren't too big, her legs too thickly muscled. Her hips weren't too wide, or her breasts too full.

Mariah sat up and unfastened the front clasp of her bra—for the first time in her life voluntarily exposing herself to the eyes of a man without hiding in the cover of the darkness of night.

The look in John's eyes was well worth the risk. He smiled, a short, hot smile that nearly scalded her, as he pulled her up toward him.

The sensation of the hard muscles of his chest pressed against her bare breasts and his rock-solid arousal against the softness of her stomach was dizzying as she knelt with him, there on her bed. His kiss made her sway, and she clung to him as he slipped one hand beneath the lace of her panties, his exploring fingers touching her lightly, intimately.

She reached between them, too, finding him hard and sleek and hot.

He groaned. "Mariah..."

She opened her eyes to find herself gazing directly into his. The connection was just as physical as his touch.

"You said you had protection," he said.

At just the same moment, she asked, "Will you put on a condom?"

They both laughed.

"I'll get one," Mariah said, pulling free from his grasp.

She rummaged through her bedside-table drawer, searching for the packet of condoms that her aunt had given her, complete with a note telling her to have a *very* good vacation. Mariah had rolled her eyes and tossed the box into her suitcase, hardly expecting to find call to use it. As she found the box, way down at the bottom of the drawer, John came to stand behind her, pressing himself intimately against her, covering her breasts with his hands and kissing her neck. It felt delicious—a hard promise of things to come.

And Mariah knew that she didn't want to wait a moment longer. He'd taken off his briefs and now he slipped her panties down her legs, as well, as she turned to face him.

They were both naked, but she was more so—because she'd told him that she loved him.

This should have been strange—standing here like this, just looking at this beautiful, naked man, letting him look at her. But it wasn't strange at all, despite the fact that it had been years since she'd been with a man this way. She'd been attracted to John from the first moment she'd laid eyes on him. She'd liked him from the first time they'd talked. And somewhere between then and now, she'd fallen deeply in love with him, too. And it was that love she felt that kept this from being strange, that instead made this moment perfect.

She knew he didn't love her—she didn't try to kid herself about that. But he liked her. She knew he really liked her. And on many levels, she preferred that steady, milder emotion to the short, hot, quick-burning flash of infatuation that many people mistook for love.

She pressed one of the condom packets into his hand.

"Put this on," she told him. "Then lie down and close your eyes."

John laughed softly. "What are we doing? Pressure Cooker Release? Seabirds in Flight?"

Mariah gently pushed him onto the bed, unable to hide her smile. "You'll see." She was going to make this an experience he'd never forget. "I'll be right back."

She pulled on her robe and went quickly into the living room. She unplugged her boom box from the wall, found the CD she wanted, then carried both back into the bedroom.

John was on the bed, as she'd asked. He was gorgeous—all dark hair and sleek, hard muscles beneath his tanned skin. Lying there against the white sheets, he looked impossibly healthy. How could this physically perfect man have been in a hospital fighting for his life just a few weeks ago?

He was up on one elbow, watching her as she set the CD player on her dresser and plugged it in.

Miller's blood was burning with anticipation. He'd barely been able to get the condom on, he was so aroused. And now Mariah was putting a CD into her portable player, her brightly colored silk robe hanging open, revealing tantalizing glimpses of her incredible body.

When he'd first seen her picture, he'd thought of her as a goddess. He'd had no idea how completely right he had been.

With a swirl of turquoise silk, she turned to face him. "One more thing," she said, giving him a smile that put dimples of mischief and amusement in her cheeks. A small square that looked something like a speaker sat on the bedside table. She touched it, adjusted it, and the sound of flowing water filled the room. "A waterfall," she said. She smiled at him again as she let her robe flutter to the ground. "Close your eyes."

Miller didn't want to. He wanted to look at her—he'd never tire of looking at her.

She moved back to the CD player and turned it on, too, adjusting the volume.

It wasn't music that came on. Miller listened closely, trying to identify the sounds that were playing over the high-quality speakers.

Birds.

They were birdcalls. Sweetly melodic chirping and tweeting.

Mariah sat next to him on the bed, leaning forward to kiss him. "Close your eyes," she said again.

Miller closed them.

He felt her straddle him, felt her kiss him again, her stomach pressed against his erection, the tight beads of her nipples brushing erotically against his chest. He was on fire, but he wanted to please her, so he did what she asked. He stayed on his back and kept his eyes closed. But he couldn't keep from touching her, his hands sweeping down the softness of her skin. He filled his palms with her breasts, loving the sound of her breath catching in her throat.

And then she moved her hips, covering him with her soft heat, and he couldn't help himself. He pressed himself up, wanting more, needing to feel himself inside her. Now. *Now.*

She kissed him again and he groaned. "Mariah, please…"

She shifted her hips again, granting him access, and with one velvet-smooth thrust, he was ensheathed by her.

He held on to her hips, pressing himself more tightly inside her, praying that she wouldn't move even the slightest bit, sure that if she did, he would lose control. Too soon. It was too soon.

But she didn't move. She kissed him instead, her lips gentle against his mouth, his cheek, his chin and jaw, his ear.

"You are now in a very special place," Mariah said softly, laughter in her voice, her breath warm against his ear, "with birds singing and a waterfall trickling...."

Miller opened his eyes to find her smiling down at him, amusement dancing in her whiskey-colored eyes.

"The next time someone tells you to close your eyes and picture yourself in your special place," she continued, "you'll have no problem imagining yourself *right* here. And I mean right here." She moved her hips for emphasis.

Miller had to laugh. And then he had to kiss her. As he claimed her mouth, she began to move slowly on top of him. Each stroke was sheer heaven as she took her sweet time.

She was driving him mad, and she knew it, too. He could tell from the little smile she gave him as she sat up above him.

He reached for her, pulling her down against him, drawing her breasts toward his hungry mouth, pulling hard on her desire-swollen nipples.

She moved faster then, harder, and he moved with her, filling her again and again as she cried out her pleasure. Time seemed to stop as his entire world shrank completely down to this one woman who was touching him, loving him. Nothing else existed, nothing else mattered. He filled himself with her, all his senses working overtime as he watched his own ecstasy mirrored on her face, as he heard her cries and murmurs of pleasure, as her softness and warmth surrounded him completely.

He felt the shuddering thrill of her climax and he buried his face in the softness of her breasts as he, too, went up and over the edge. The rush of his release engulfed him, rocketing him to a dizzying height.

Mariah collapsed upon him as slowly, very slowly, the roar subsided, leaving him warm and relaxed and peacefully calm.

He became aware of Mariah's soft hair against his face. He became aware of the way her breath caught slightly as she sighed contentedly. He became aware of birds singing and the sound of water splashing enticingly down a steep hill.

A special place. Yes. This was a *very* special place.

Mariah turned her head and brushed her lips against his neck. She didn't say the words, but she didn't have to. He knew that she loved him.

This was what it was like to make love with someone who really cared. It was incredible—being loved so completely, on so many levels. It made the rather ordinary act of sex seem a miracle. It heightened all his senses and made his heart seem ten times as big. It took his breath away and filled his lungs with sheer joy and laughter. It made him want to smile—all the time.

Miller wondered if Mariah felt the wonder of this miracle. He wondered if she knew, if she felt it, too.

He didn't say the words, either. He didn't know how. But he knew without a doubt that he loved her.

She left the photo lab carrying the box of negatives.

The nice man had seen no problem in letting her take them to her friend.

Once inside her car, she lifted the lid and looked inside. One by one, she held the strips of film up to the windshield, using the sunlight to illuminate them. She went through about twenty of the plastic-encased strips before she gave up.

She was going to have to burn the entire box.

She looked down into the box and saw there was a paper folder—the kind that drugstores use to enclose color prints. She pulled it out, almost on a whim. There were no photos inside, but there were several smaller strips of negatives.

She held one to the light and…

Quickly, she pulled out another and another.

These were other photographs of *her*. Somehow that bitch had taken more pictures of *her!*

Her rage was laced with fear. If there were negatives, then somewhere there were photographs.

She was going to have to go back.

She took a deep breath, calming herself. It didn't matter. She was smarter than they were. She could get the photos. She *would* get the photos. She would destroy the evidence and punish the bitch who had brought her this trouble.

Her calm soon turned to anticipation. She *was* smarter than they were. She could do all that, and more.

She put the lid back on the box and threw her car into gear. She had lots to do. *Lots* to do.

Chapter 10

Mariah focused the lens of her camera on John. "Smile," she said.

He laughed as he glanced over at her. "You're taking a picture of me doing the dishes?"

She snapped several photos in rapid succession before looking up from the camera to smile at him. "No, I'm just taking pictures of you. The doing-the-dishes part isn't important. You know, I really wish I'd developed those pictures of you I took that day we first met."

He lifted an eyebrow as he drained the soapy water from the sink and dried his hands on a dish towel. "What? You mean you took pictures of me when I was lying with my face in the sand?"

She had to laugh. "No. I took pictures when I first saw you—when you were out on the beach with Princess. I wonder what I did with that roll of film. It's probably around here somewhere. But I wish I had those pictures to show you for comparison. It's amazing—you look so different now. You look so relaxed and...happy."

"That's because I got lucky this morning." John pulled her close and kissed her below the ear. "And I happen to know that the esteemed Dr. Gerrard Hollis recommends that particular activity we took part in as his number one means of relieving stress. So, yeah, I'm extremely relaxed."

"I'm not sure Dr. Hollis put it in quite those words," Mariah said, laughing in dismay. "Getting lucky."

He kissed her again, on the mouth this time, so sweetly she felt herself start to melt. "I got lucky all right," he said, searching her eyes. "I don't think I've ever felt this lucky in my entire life. I really hit the jackpot when I met you, Mariah."

Mariah's throat felt tight as she gazed back at him. What was he telling her? There was a softness, a gentleness in his eyes that, were she feeling foolhardy enough, she might interpret as love. But she didn't want to interpret it. She didn't want to hope or wish or even *think* about it.

The telephone rang, and she pulled away from him, grateful for the interruption.

It was the doctor's office, finally returning yesterday's call. The doctor seemed to think she could resume normal activities—provided she didn't push herself too hard.

Miller poured himself another cup of coffee as he watched Mariah talk on the phone. He wished he could take *her* picture. Dressed the way she was in only her silk robe, her hair still rumpled from the time they'd spent in bed, she looked incredible—as warm and welcoming and as satisfying as the breakfast they'd made together and shared out on the deck in the soft morning sunlight.

Normally, he resented anyone's intrusion into his

morning routine. The morning was his private time. But as he gazed at Mariah, he knew he would enjoy having all of this on a regular basis—breakfast, watching her across the table, even doing the dishes. It was relaxed and easygoing. It felt right. Even the silences were comfortable.

He could easily imagine seeing Mariah's beautiful face first thing every morning, feeling her luscious body next to his every night. He could imagine coming home each evening and losing himself, *submerging* himself in her sweet warmth and love.

That was a dangerous way to be thinking. Mariah had done and said nothing to let him believe she was interested in anything more than a vacation romance. And before they could progress to anything beyond a casual love affair, they both had to come clean and confess as to why they were using false names.

Miller smiled wryly. It was only a matter of time before this investigation was declared defunct. But what was the best way to tell a lover that she didn't know his real name? When was the best time? Right after making love? Or maybe over a quiet dinner? *By the way, darling, you don't really know who I am....*

And he wasn't the only one working under an a.k.a. Mariah, too, had something of her own to share during show-and-tell. Marie Carver. Former CEO of Carver Software out in Phoenix, Arizona.

He'd checked the files. The company was doing fine. There'd been no reports of embezzlement—and no reasons for it either. Marie—Mariah—had inherited her father's share of the company when he had died and under her hand it had thrived. Even though she was no longer CEO, she still owned a large percentage of the business—which, if it was sold right here and now would easily put fifteen million dollars into her personal bank account. No, Mariah had no reason to turn to embezzlement. And according to the IRS, both her personal and business taxes had all been paid both accurately and on time.

So what was she doing, living under an alias, all these thousands of miles away from her home?

Miller had tried to find out during breakfast. Asking leading questions, giving her a clear opening to tell him the truth. But she'd sidestepped all his questions about her business, and somehow they'd ended up talking about Princess instead.

As she hung up the phone, he tried again.

"Mariah is such a pretty name," he told her, leaning back against the counter as he sipped his coffee. "What made your parents name you that?"

"Actually…"

Here it came. She was going to tell him the truth.

"Actually, my parents didn't name me Mariah," she said. "My grandmother did." She took his mug from his hands and set it down on the counter, then slid her arms around his waist.

Miller closed his eyes as she held him tightly, as his body leapt in response to her sweet softness.

"Mariah was *her* grandmother's name," she told him between dizzyingly delicious kisses. "My great-great-grandmother. She was born not far from here, in Georgia, before the Civil War. According to my grandmother, by the time Mariah was twelve, she was an active member of the Underground Railroad. That's partly why I came to Garden Isle. To see where she lived. I've always been fascinated by the stories Grandma told about her."

Miller was wearing only his jeans, and her silk-covered breasts felt incredibly smooth against his bare chest—but not as sinfully good as her skin would feel. Her belt was already loose and it opened easily as he parted the front of her robe and slipped his hands against the softness of her skin, pulling her against him.

She pulled his mouth down to hers and Miller lost himself in her kiss.

He felt her fingers on the button of his jeans and experienced a wave of euphoria. Was this great, or was this great? She wanted him again. Her own attraction to him was clearly as insatiable and intense as his was for her. Mutual overpowering lust.

True, undying love.

That thought came from out of nowhere, and Miller shook it away, unwilling to think about the way he'd felt as he'd held Mariah in his arms after making love.

But it was the way he still felt. It hadn't faded. It hadn't disappeared.

He kissed her harder, wanting only to feel the intense physical pleasure she gave him. It was overpowering, unlike anything he'd ever felt—desire of a caliber he'd never really thought existed. He'd heard people talk about the sensation of being hit by a truck, of being blinded to everything but need, but he'd always thought they were weak. They were weak, and he was strong, except here he was, unable to see anything but Mariah, unable even to catch his breath from the weight of the desire that bore down upon him like a runaway train.

He thought his need for this woman would be abated by making love to her, but that had only served to make him want her more. He'd had a taste of her heaven, and he was shamelessly addicted now.

He lifted her right onto the counter, and she willingly opened her legs to him as he kept on kissing her, his mouth trailing down her neck toward her luscious breasts, one hand working to free himself from his pants and...

Mariah pulled back. "John! We need to get a condom."

What the hell was he doing? He had been mere seconds away from thrusting deeply inside of her with absolutely no protection—without one single *thought* of protection. God help him, this woman drove all sane thoughts clear out of his head.

Mariah looked at the expression on John's face and started to laugh despite the adrenaline that passion had kicked into her system. He looked thoroughly, adorably stunned. "I don't want you to stop," she told him. "I just want you to get a condom." She slid down off the counter, pressing herself against him, loving the sensation of his arousal hard against her stomach. She kissed him quickly. "I'll get one. You wait here."

Mariah's heart was still pounding as she ran down the hall to her bedroom. Her bedside-table drawer was still open, the box of condoms on the top. She grabbed one and the phone rang.

Damn! The cordless phone was there in her bedroom, so she quickly picked it up, praying it wouldn't be one of the ladies from the Garden Isle Historical Society, wanting to talk on and on for fifteen or twenty minutes about the latest event at the library. "Hello?"

"I'm sorry to bother you again, Ms. Robinson, but is John still there?"

It was Daniel with the Asian-sounding last name—the dark haired young man who was John's personal assistant.

"Um, yes, he is, actually." Mariah carried the phone into the kitchen. "Just a moment, please." She covered the mouthpiece with her hand as she held out the phone to John. "It's for you. It's Daniel."

He fastened his pants before he took the phone—as if Daniel would somehow be able to tell that he was standing there nearly naked and mere moments from sexual fulfillment.

"Yeah," John said into the phone. "What's up?" He met Mariah's eyes briefly and smiled. Even with his jeans zipped, it was still very obvious—at least to the two of them—exactly what was up.

Mariah hadn't bothered fastening her robe, and John's smile faded and his eyes turned even a deeper shade of blue as he looked at her. Another woman might've found the intensity of his expression frightening. But Mariah loved it. She loved the way he seemed to burn for her. She stepped toward him, and he reached inside the thin silk to touch her.

"When?" he said into the phone. He glanced at the clock on the stove and swore softly. "That soon?" Another pause. "Yeah, all right. I'll be there."

He ended the connection with a push of a button, and Mariah took the phone from him, pressing the condom packet into his hand.

He swore again. "Mariah, I'm sorry, I have to go."

"Daniel can wait five minutes, can't he?" She unbuttoned his pants.

"Mariah—"

She pulled down his zipper. "*Three* minutes…?"

He groaned as she touched him, then crushed his mouth to hers. Before she could even blink, she found herself back up on the counter. She heard the tear of the wrapper, felt him pull back for just a second, and then she felt him fill her with a hard, fast thrust that took her breath away.

He groaned, too, still kissing her as he drove himself into her again and again, setting a wild, delirious, feverish pace. It was raw, almost savage sex, and Mariah dug her fingernails into his back, urging him on, wanting more, even more.

It was breathtakingly exhilarating. She had never been made love to like this before. She'd never had a man go so totally out of control over her before. It was more exciting than she'd ever dreamed. He was touching her everywhere, kissing her, caressing her in ways that filled her with fire, and she exploded almost instantly with pleasure, crying out his name.

He followed her lead, and she felt the power of his release as it rocketed through him, shaking him, pushing her even higher to a place of even more pleasure.

He held her tightly, his face buried in her neck as they both struggled to catch their breaths.

''I know you have to go now,'' Mariah said, when she finally could speak. ''But is there any chance I can bribe you with the promise of dinner so that you'll come back later and do that again?''

He lifted his head and laughed. ''The hell with dinner. I think we've discovered an entirely new use for the kitchen.'' His smile softened. ''You know, I can go for days without a meal, but I don't think I can go for more than a few hours without making love to you.''

John gently touched the side of her face, tracing her lips lightly with his thumb, as if he could see from her eyes how much she melted inside when he said things like that. And why shouldn't he see? She wasn't trying to hide anything from him. She'd told him she loved him. It wasn't a secret.

And for one heart-stopping moment, Mariah seemed

almost sure that he was going to tell her that her feelings were mutual, that he loved her, too.

But he only said, "I'll be back by seven at the latest."

Still gazing into her eyes, John leaned forward and kissed her gently on the lips, then pulled her forward and helped her down from the counter. He kissed her again before disappearing for a moment into the bathroom as she straightened her robe and tied her belt. When he came back down the hall, he was pulling on his T-shirt.

"I've got to hurry now," John said, stopping to kiss her on the mouth—a quick brushing of the lips that turned into a much longer, lingering kiss. He groaned softly, forcing himself to pull away from her. "I'll see you later, okay?"

"Seven o'clock," Mariah said.

As he moved toward the sliding doors, past the dining-room table, he suddenly stopped short. "My God!"

"What?"

John picked up one of the pictures that were spread out on the table. It was a color photo she'd taken of Serena with that cheap, disposable camera. "Where did you get this?"

"I took it—I think it was a few weeks ago. Why?"

There was an intensity in his gaze that she'd never seen before. It made the blue of his eyes seem hard and flinty. He swore sharply, almost excitedly, adding, "This is good. This is *very* good. Do you have any other pictures of her?"

Mariah gazed at him, her heart sinking like lead into the pit of her stomach. Why should John care if she had photographs of Serena? Unless he was still... No, she refused to think that way.

"Yes," she said, moving toward the table and turning on several of the lights that were still positioned around that part of the room. "I managed to take four or five of them without her noticing. She's amazingly photogenic. Still, she doesn't like to have her picture taken. It's kind of strange."

"Yeah, I know," he said. He looked down at the seemingly haphazard piles of pictures as if he wanted to search through them but was afraid to mess up her organizational system. "Where are the others? Do you still have them?"

Unless he was still infatuated with Serena... This time she couldn't prevent the thought from coming through.

"They're here somewhere," Mariah said, quickly flipping through one of the piles, again cutting off that errant thought. He didn't want Serena. He wanted *her*. He'd told her that—she knew it was true. How could he have made love to her the way he just had if it wasn't true? "Probably close to where you found the first one." She unearthed three more pictures of Serena.

One photo caught the blond Englishwoman in nearly perfect profile. The three others were either three-quarter or full face.

"May I have these?" John asked.

Mariah laughed. "You're kidding."

He suddenly seemed to realize the inappropriateness of his request. Just a short time ago—mere *minutes* ago—he'd been making love to Mariah, yet now he wanted her to give him pictures of the woman he'd last dated. Dated—and at the very least, kissed. Mariah didn't want to think about the possibility that John had made love to Serena, but it was far too easy to imagine the two of them together.

John shook his head. "It's not what you think."

"It's not? Then please, tell me. What exactly *is* it? I'd like to know. Why do you want these pictures?" She was willing to give him the benefit of the doubt. Maybe he *did* have some genuine reason for wanting those pictures.

But John shook his head. "Look, I'm sorry. Never mind, all right?" He put the pictures back on top of the pile she'd found them in. "It's just...I was going to send one to a friend of mine up in New York. I think the two of them would really hit it off—she's just his type and..."

He was lying through his teeth. He was standing there and telling her some lame *lie* as if he actually thought she would accept it. But she didn't buy it, and he knew it.

He swore softly. "I can't tell you why I really need them, Mariah, but I promise you, my wanting those pictures doesn't have anything to do with you and me."

"I really don't want you to take them," Mariah said. "I'm sorry. Serena didn't know I took them, and...I don't want you to have them."

"That's all right." He nodded. "That's okay. I understand. Just...trust me, please?"

Mariah folded her arms. "You're going to be late," she said. "You better go."

But he hesitated. "I'm going to tell you everything really soon, all right?"

She tried to smile. "I'm not certain just what happened here, but sure. Whatever you want to tell me, whenever you want to tell it to me, would be nice."

"I will." John gazed at her steadily, real consternation in his eyes. "I'll tell you soon." But then he squinted out the door, up at the hazy blueness of the sky. "Damn, I don't have any sunblock with me," he said, and when he turned to look back at her, she could see a hint of that same dishonesty in his eyes. "I'm going to fry without it. Do you have anything number fifteen or higher that I could use?''

Mariah knew that if she left the room, he was going to pocket those pictures of Serena. He was going to *steal* them, even though she'd told him point-blank that she didn't want him to have them. Trust me, he'd said. Trust me.

She cleared her throat. ''Yeah, it's in the bedroom—in my beach bag. I'll get it.'' She turned away. What could she do? Short of accusing him of theft or denying him the use of her sunblock? *Please let me be wrong.*

Miller watched Mariah walk down the hall and into her bedroom.

Quickly, he took two pictures of Serena—the profile and the best of the full-face shots—and slipped them into the back pocket of his jeans. He hated the fact he had to do it this way—to take them without Mariah's permission—but these photos would be invaluable in tracking down Serena Westford. With a photo of this quality on an APB sent to all law enforcement agencies, the FBI would actually have a chance of finding her again before she altered her appearance. It was a slim chance, but a chance just the same.

And it wasn't going to be long until this part of the case was deemed over and done with, and he'd be able to tell Mariah everything. Surely if she knew the truth, she wouldn't deny him access to the photos.

She returned with the sunblock, and he quickly spread it across his nose and cheekbones.

He kissed her again, one last time, trying to tell her with his kiss the way she made him feel. Despite the wariness in her eyes, she kissed him warmly, sweetly.

''I'll see you later,'' he said. He slipped out the door and onto the porch where Princess was napping in the shade. "Come on," he said to the dog. "We've gotta run. We're already late."

He set off down the beach at an easy jog, Princess loping beside him. His legs felt weak, his body still buzzing from the pleasure he'd allowed himself to partake of only moments before.

On impulse, he turned to look back at the cottage. Mariah was standing on the deck, watching him. He waved, lifting an arm, and she waved back.

Picking up his speed, he smiled. Yes indeed, he was going to be late to this meeting with Pat Blake. When Daniel had called the second time, Blake's plane had already landed at the little airport on the mainland. His car would be pulling into the resort driveway in a matter of moments, and Miller would arrive a good five minutes after him—unshowered, unshaved and smelling distinctly like Mariah. Sweet, sexy Mariah. What a reason to be late....

Blake would nearly swallow his teeth at the sight of him—Miller couldn't remember ever attending a meeting such as this one in anything other than a dark suit and tie. But all would be forgiven the moment he produced these photographs.

Miller hoped Mariah would be as quick to forgive when he told her the truth. God, he wanted to tell her the truth soon. And maybe then she'd tell him why she was here on Garden Isle using a fake name.

So Mariah was just a nickname. What did your parents call you? That's what he should have asked. He should've pushed the conversation in that direction, but he'd been waylaid by her kisses. He'd been overcome by the promise of ecstasy. All rational thought had simply ceased to exist.

Damn, she drove him out of his mind.

He turned to look back once more at Mariah's house, but this time she was gone.

Mariah watched in the dim darkroom light as the photos she took just that morning slowly developed. She was feeling that familiar gnawing of worry and upset that she'd worked so hard to eradicate over the past few months.

Stress was making her shoulders tight and she rolled them, silently chanting her mantra: No worries. No problem.

But she was lying to herself. She *was* worried. There *was* a problem.

She was in love with a man who'd not only lied, but had stolen from her.

As she rinsed the chemicals from the paper, Jonathan Mills smiled directly up at her from the photo, his eyes warm and flashing with amusement. Mariah looked more closely at his eyes, trying to see if maybe his dishonesty had been captured through the camera's lens. She wanted to know if he'd been lying right from the start. But all she could see was warmth and life.

The pictures she'd taken in her kitchen were sharply in contrast to the shots she'd taken on the beach the day they'd met. Mariah had found that roll of film and developed it first. Those pictures now hung, drying. John's gaunt silhouette against the backdrop of a lightening sky. His profile—a face etched with pain. He looked cold and distant. But he didn't look deceptive.

She wasn't exactly sure what she was looking for— perhaps a shiftiness in the eyes. Or a glint of malice. In reality, it was probably the case that the most deceptive people gave away nothing at all. Her stomach started to hurt and she rolled her shoulders again. *No worries.*

Mariah carefully hung the more recent pictures of John next to the ones from the first roll of film. Someone glancing at them all would find it hard to believe this smiling man was the same person as in the others.

Mariah looked again into John's laughing eyes. This was the man who'd come to her for comfort as he'd finally allowed himself to grieve for his friend's death. This was the man who had made love to her so passionately. This was the man who had told her he wanted *her*, not Serena. She found it hard to believe that this was the same man who lied to her, who had actually *stolen* from her.

Mariah hadn't allowed herself to look through her piles of photos after he'd first left. And she'd hated herself for mistrusting him when she'd finally given in to the temptation. But she'd been right to mistrust him. Two pictures were missing. John had taken two of the photos of Serena even after Mariah had specifically said she didn't want him to have them.

The phone rang, and Mariah picked up the cordless extension she'd brought downstairs with her, half hoping it was John and half hoping it was not. "Hello?"

"Hey, girl, how's your back?" It was Laronda, the site coordinator from Foundations for Families.

"It doesn't hurt at all anymore," Mariah told her. "And I just got the all clear from the doctor this morning. I'm allowed to go back to work."

"God is truly watching over me," Laronda exclaimed melodramatically. "I'm in desperate need of roofers. Tropical storm Otto is heading on almost a direct path to the Washburtons' house. It wasn't supposed to rain—at least not hard—until the end of the week, and we gambled and took advantage of a local electrician who had some time off. We had the electrical work done before the roof was finished. But now the weather bureau is saying oops they made a big mistake. We're gonna get high winds *and* flooding rain. We need to get that baby sealed up tight before old Otto makes some bad voodoo by mixing water with those wires. Can you help? We're doing a blitz—round the clock from now until we're done. I'll take you for as long a shift as you can give me."

As usual, Mariah wasn't wearing a watch. "What time is it?"

"Nearly noon. Just say yes and I can have the van pick you up in fifteen minutes. Door-to-door service today."

"I'll be ready. But, Laronda—"

"Bless you, girl!"

"I have to be home by seven."

"We'll get you there."

Mariah took one last look at her pictures of John before she turned off the light and went up the basement stairs. She'd be back by seven, all right. And then she was going to get some answers.

Chapter 11

Mariah's sliding glass door was open, the screen unlocked.

"Mariah?" Miller called.

No one answered. Nothing moved.

Miller stepped into the house and closed the screen door behind him.

Without Mariah to brighten the place up with her laughter and life, the room seemed almost shabby. Miller moved quietly to the dining-room table, intending to slip the two photographs he'd borrowed and had copied back into the pile. She'd never even know they were gone.

In theory, it worked, but in theory, Mariah hadn't checked up on him. In reality, she had. The other pictures of Serena had been separated out from the stack. She knew he'd taken two of them. He set the two in question down on the table with the others.

It didn't really matter. He'd had every intention of telling her the truth—and he could now. During his short meeting with Pat Blake, this portion of the case had been officially closed. Hanging around here and waiting for Serena to return had been deemed a waste of time and finances. Even at this moment, Daniel was back at the resort, packing up the equipment.

Miller had been helping him, determined to get the work done and his report filed in time to meet Mariah for dinner at seven. But something Daniel had said during the meeting had started him thinking. Daniel had pointed out that in the past, Serena had always been so careful about having her picture taken. Was it possible that she knew about these pictures?

Miller knew it damn well was possible that she was on to him. She could have found the bugs in her house and correctly identified Miller as FBI. And if that was the case, she might've purposely left these pictures behind as part of some kind of weird game she was playing.

But what exactly was that game?

Had she left intending to alter her appearance so thoroughly that leaving photos behind didn't even matter? Was this possibly some kind of arrogant challenge?

Or had she truly slipped up? Had she found the microphones in her house and run scared? And after she calmed down enough, would she realize that because Mariah was a photographer it was more than likely she had pictures of Serena, taken either intentionally or unintentionally? And if that was the case, would Serena come back? And if she did come back, would Mariah then be in danger?

That thought had made Miller break out in a cold sweat, and he'd called Mariah, but she didn't pick up the phone. Thinking she might be on the beach enjoying the early-afternoon sunshine, Miller had left Daniel to deal with the equipment as he took the car and drove out to Mariah's cottage as quickly as he could.

"Mariah?" he said again, moving into the kitchen.

A jar of peanut butter was out and open on the kitchen counter. She'd told him the first time they'd met that leaving food out in the kitchen was an invitation to disaster. Ants or enormous American cockroaches would come in almost immediately and they were nearly impossible to get rid of.

A plate with bread crumbs sat nearby—as if she'd made herself a sandwich there, then taken it with her as she'd left.

Left to go where? Her bike was leaning up against the side of the house. He'd seen it when he'd arrived. There was no sign of her in the yard or out on the beach.

Wherever she'd gone, she'd left in a hurry.

Miller made a complete circuit of the house. There were signs in the bathroom that Mariah had taken a quick shower—a wet towel had been tossed onto the floor along with the robe she'd been wearing this morning. A tube of toothpaste was open and left out on the sink. In her bedroom, the bed was unmade, the sheets still rumpled from their lovemaking.

Miller sat down on the edge of the bed, letting himself lie back among the sheets. He closed his eyes, breathing in the sweet scent of Mariah's perfume. Where had she gone in such a blessed hurry?

Even with his eyes closed, he could picture the house and all its telltale signs of a hasty exit. He was known for his ability to take the clues he'd been given and hypothesize the most likely scenario. Only this time, he didn't much care for the scenario he'd almost instantly come up with.

He had one Mariah Robinson living under an assumed

name, telling him specifically that he could not have those pictures of Serena. He had Mariah go through the photos after he'd left, pulling out the shots of Serena and discovering that he had, in fact, taken two of those pictures with him. He had Mariah quickly take a shower, quickly make a sandwich and then leave the house in such a hurry that she didn't even lock the back door.

Going where? To meet Serena? To warn her that Miller had those pictures?

Miller could place Mariah—or Marie Carver, her real name—in Phoenix, Arizona, three years ago, during the time Serena had been there, too, preparing to off husband number five. The possibility that the two women had met at that time opened the door to all kinds of nasty questions, such as: Had Mariah/Marie come here to Garden Isle to act as some kind of accomplice or assistant? Was Mariah/Marie some kind of Black Widow killer-in-training?

Miller sat up. Dammit! He'd obviously been working for the FBI for too long. How could he possibly think such things about Mariah? Sweet, gentle Mariah...

He hadn't checked the basement because it was dark, but now he went down there anyway, hoping to find something that would tell him where Mariah had gone.

He'd never been inside her darkroom, and he turned on the light as he pushed open the door. It was a small room, with built-in counters lining the walls. It had a sink and shelves for chemicals and other supplies—even a small refrigerator for storing film. Different kinds of equipment were set up on the counters, including something big that looked like an enlarger.

Miller knew with just one glance that this room—combined with the beachfront property and the incredible view of the ocean—was the reason Mariah had rented this particular cottage. Dozens of places were more lavishly furnished or nicely decorated, but Mariah cared more about having a place with a darkroom.

There were photos hanging from some kind of clothesline assembly, curling slightly around the edges as they dried. Miller looked closer. The pictures were of him.

They were black-and-white photographs, but they still managed to capture the beauty of the sunrise. He and Princess were just silhouettes in many of them, but in several, Mariah had used her zoom lens, and he could clearly see his face, etched with relentless fatigue. The pictures echoed his pain.

But there, right in the middle of these pictures of his bleakly grim face, was a close-up. It was one of the pictures Mariah had taken just that morning. He was smiling at her, smiling into the camera.

Miller stared at the picture. It was him. He knew it was him. He remembered her taking the picture. He remembered smiling. But he'd never seen himself looking quite like that before. His eyes were reflecting the morning light coming in through the window and they seemed to sparkle with warmth and life. His smile was wide and sincere.

He looked nothing like a man who had been dubbed "The Robot."

And he wasn't, Miller realized. When he was with Mariah, he *wasn't* a robot. He was a real, live, flesh-and-blood man, capable of feeling—and releasing—deep emotions.

He closed his eyes, remembering the way she had held him as he'd given in and cried for Tony for the first time in two years. He remembered the strength of the emotion he'd felt as he'd held her in his arms after making love.

That man, that flesh-and-blood man would never have

entertained such doubts about Mariah. It was only "The Robot" who could think that way—mistrusting everyone.

God, he wanted Mariah to come back. He wanted her to transform him once again into that real man. He despised himself for being this way, for having all these doubts about her.

With one last look back at Mariah's photographs, Miller turned off the darkroom light and went upstairs. As he locked the back door, he heard the crunch of tires in the gravel driveway and turned to look out the front window, hoping it was Mariah.

It wasn't.

It was *Serena's* car pulling into the driveway. It was Serena. My God, she'd come back. Miller's heart nearly stopped. Then it kicked back in, beating double time with a vengeance.

As he watched, she parked next to his car and got out. She didn't seem perturbed by the fact that his car was there—she knew he and Mariah were friends. And Miller knew from the time he'd spent with her that Serena had complete confidence in her sexual allure. Miller had no doubt that Serena didn't view Maria as any kind of a rival.

He moved to the front door, intending to step outside when Serena rang the bell. But she didn't ring, she just opened the screen and came in.

"Mariah's not here," he told her. "I stopped by to see how she was doing. The back door was unlocked, and—"

Serena kissed him. It was a kiss meant to curl his hair, to thoroughly numb him, to drop him—dizzy with passion and desire—to his knees.

Instead, Miller had to fight to hide his revulsion. She'd caught him off guard, that much was true. He kept close track of her hands, suddenly keenly aware that this woman might very well have killed at least seven times by forcing a knife blade into her husbands' hearts. It was true that he was not her husband, but it was possible she knew he was FBI. Although if she *did* know that, this was one hell of a dangerous game she was playing by returning to Garden Isle.

"Did you miss me?" she murmured.

"Absolutely," he lied.

As quickly as she'd started kissing him, she broke away, making a quick circuit around the room, stopping to look at the photos on the dining-room table. She picked up one of the pictures of herself.

"Oh, good," she said. "Mariah must've set these aside to give to me. I'd asked her about them last week. She's a remarkable photographer, isn't she? I mean, for an amateur."

"Yeah," he said. "She's pretty good."

"For an amateur," Serena repeated.

As Miller watched, she slipped all four of the pictures into her purse.

"So where did our little Mariah—or should I say *big* Mariah—go off to?" Serena mused. "Her tool belt's not by the door. I'll wager she's off trying to save the world, one family at a time."

Miller couldn't believe it. For all his highly touted skills as one of the FBI's top agents, he hadn't thought to check and see if Mariah's tool belt was missing. Sure enough. Her belt and her backpack were both gone.

"I've never been down this hall past the loo," Serena said, disappearing down the hallway that led to Mariah's bedroom. "What's down here? Her bedroom probably."

Miller followed her. "Serena, don't go back there."

"Why not?"

"Because you're invading Mariah's privacy."

"She left the door unlocked, didn't she?" Serena said almost gaily, sitting down on Mariah's unmade bed, surveying the small bedroom. "I don't know why she lives in a little dumpy place like this. She has plenty of money, you know."

Miller stood in the doorway. "We should leave."

He would've had to be a fool not to catch the meaning of the glint in her eyes. She was coming on to him. She was attempting to seduce him right there in Mariah's room, on Mariah's bed.

"I suppose we could go to your place." Serena leaned back on both elbows as she gazed up at him. "But I confess I like it here. Think of the excitement from knowing that Mariah could come home any moment and find us here together."

God, the thought made him sick, but he couldn't deny that this was what he'd wanted for so long. He'd wanted an opportunity to be in a position where it would seem natural for him to propose marriage to this woman.

But he hadn't wanted to do it like this.

Not here in this room where he'd discovered such pleasures with Mariah.

But he couldn't take Serena back to his room at the resort where Daniel was packing up crates of electronic equipment. They'd brought the gear into the resort in inconspicuous suitcases, but there had been no need to leave with it that way, so most of it was clearly labeled with its destination, Quantico—FBI headquarters—in big black, official-looking letters.

"Why don't we take a walk on the beach?" Miller suggested.

"In these shoes?" Serena reached for his hand, tug-

ging him down so that he was sitting next to her on the
bed.

Mariah's bed.

It took everything Miller had in him not to stand up,
not to pull away. Apprehending Serena was his job.
Catching a killer was never fun. He didn't have to like
it, he just had to do it.

He tried to convince himself that he wasn't betraying
Mariah as he let Serena push him back onto the bed. He
tried not to think about what Mariah would assume if she
came home to find him here with Serena, entangled in
an embrace in the very bed in which he'd made love to
Mariah just mere hours earlier.

This wasn't real. He felt distant, removed both physically and emotionally from this woman who was kissing
him so passionately. That distance worried him—surely
she'd be able to tell that she left him feeling cold. Surely
she'd realize that he wanted to kiss her about as much
as he wanted to kiss Daniel. Less.

He'd made one hell of a mistake in assuming that Serena had gone for good. He'd messed things up royally.
He'd made love to Mariah this morning, and this afternoon he was going to propose marriage to Serena.

Serena ground herself against him, and, suddenly
giddy, Miller knew the truth. He didn't want to do this.
But what was he supposed to do? Was he supposed to
tell both Daniel Tonaka and Patrick Blake that he was
taking himself off the case? How could he do that after
coming this far? The setup had worked after all—he had
the suspect exactly where he wanted her.

Or maybe she had *him* right where she wanted him.

Daniel was sure to understand and forgive him. But
Blake wouldn't. Not after getting to this point. Blake
would send him in for that psych evaluation, assuming

that Miller had finally snapped. The unit shrink was sure to find him crazy—crazy in love with Mariah.

Miller was just about to push Serena off him when she spoke.

"Please," she said, kissing his face and his neck as she sat straddling him, her head bent over him, her golden hair finding its way into his mouth. "Please, John. I know that you want me, darling, but please, can't we wait to do this until after we're married?"

Miller was astonished. He nearly laughed aloud. *She* was on top of him. She was the seductress, yet her words sounded as if she were an innocent being seduced. She was overpowering, yet she was presenting him with the illusion of being the powerful one. The approach must've worked well for her in the past. He'd never once—in any of their conversations—mentioned marriage, yet she spoke of it as if they'd been discussing it for weeks.

He spit her hair out of his mouth.

"Please, darling," Serena whispered. "We can fly to Las Vegas—be married by tonight."

It was too easy. He couldn't turn her down. He'd been after her for too long.

Still, he hesitated. Mariah would be devastated.

Yet to turn Serena down meant that when the photos of her next victim—and there was sure to be a next victim—crossed Miller's desk, he would know he could have prevented that death. And the next one, and the next one. He would know that he could have stopped her. And he wouldn't be able to bear that. He wouldn't be able to handle having failed. He *could* stop her, right now, right here.

"I'll charter a flight," Miller said to Serena.

He didn't want to do it, but he didn't have a choice.

Chapter 12

Mariah could hear the phone ringing and she took the stairs up to the deck two at a time.

Maybe it was John. Maybe he was finally calling to tell her why he'd left a message canceling last night's dinner plans.

His insomnia was contagious. She'd spent most of last night tossing and turning—sometimes feeling hurt, sometimes concerned, sometimes terrified that she'd been played for a fool.

She scooped up the phone, praying she'd reached it before the answering machine kicked on. "Hello?" she said breathlessly.

"Oh, good. You *are* there." It was Serena. "Can you come over and see my new place?"

Mariah cursed silently. "Now's not a really good time because I've—"

"I've rented that house right up the hill from you," Serena told her.

"The big one?"

"I suppose compared to *your* place, it might be considered big—"

"Serena, that house is a palace. You've wanted to live there since you first came to the island. How on earth did you manage to arrange to move in there?"

Serena lowered her voice. "Oh, I've only got it for a short time. There was a week-and-a-half block in between renters. It's expensive, but considering that this is my honeymoon—"

"Your *what?*"

"I flew out to Vegas last night and got married," Serena said with a silvery laugh. "It was rather unexpected."

Married. Serena was married. Who did she know well enough to marry? Not Jonathan Mills? Dear God, had she gone and married John? Mariah felt a flash of disbelieving heat followed quickly by a blast of cold fear. "Who's the lucky man?" she managed to ask, somehow sounding casually nonchalant.

Serena just laughed again. "That's my surprise. I want you to come over and meet him."

Serena's new husband couldn't possibly be John. He wouldn't do that to her. Mariah refused to believe that he was capable of such a thing. He'd told her he wanted *her*, not Serena. He'd promised her he wouldn't sleep with Serena. Of course, she hadn't made him promise that he wouldn't *marry* Serena....

"Serena, just tell me who he is."

"If you ride your bike, it'll take you even less than three minutes to get up here," Serena said, laughter bubbling in her voice. "See you in a few."

Mariah stared at the telephone receiver, listening to the

buzz of the disconnected line. With a curse, she hung up the phone.

She was going to have to go up there.

Not to please Serena, who clearly wanted to show off the house, but to put her own mind at ease.

She'd go up there, see for herself that the man Serena had married wasn't John. She'd see for herself that he was probably some older man with the ability to write million-dollar checks without blinking.

This was good, Mariah told herself as she tied the laces of her sneakers and went out to where her bike was leaning against the side of her house. With Serena safely married, Mariah wouldn't have to worry about the blonde actively competing for John's time and attention.

Provided, of course, he came back from wherever he'd gone. And provided he came equipped with a good explanation as to why he'd stolen those photographs.

"What are you looking at?"

Miller turned to see Serena standing in the door to the elegantly high-ceilinged formal dining room. "Just... checking out the view from the windows."

She pointed through the treetops. "Look. There's the roof of Mariah's little cottage."

Miller nodded. He knew. That's what he'd been looking at.

He hadn't planned on living quite so close to Mariah. But Serena had rented this monstrously huge example of modern architecture on the morning before they were married and had insisted they return here for their "honeymoon."

He'd intended for them to stay in Nevada. He'd planned to call Mariah from a pay phone in one of the casinos to tell her that he was sorry, but he'd been pulled out of town on business—he wouldn't be back for a few weeks. He'd hoped Mariah would never have to find out about his charade of a marriage to Serena.

But...Serena hated Vegas.

And when he'd offered to take her on a honeymoon anywhere, *any*where in the world, she chose Garden Isle. She was adamant about returning there, and although Miller had put up a good fight, he'd eventually had to give in for fear she'd become suspicious.

That, of course, was assuming she wasn't suspicious of him in the first place.

"I love this room," Serena said, circling the banquet-sized table. "We ought to throw a dinner party."

"Sounds good to me."

She stepped closer to him and slipped her arms around his waist, embracing him from behind. "Or maybe we should just have our own *private* dinner party."

He tried to sound sincere. "That sounds even better." Miller gently pulled free from her arms. "Look, Serena, I called my doctor this morning," he told her. "He said it could be a few months before I'm...back to normal." He cleared his throat tactfully. "You know..."

He'd told her last night—their wedding night—that he was still suffering from the side effects of the chemotherapy he'd recently undergone. He'd informed her that one of those side effects was impotence. He'd told her it was a temporary condition, and he'd apologized for not telling her sooner.

She'd offered to see what she could do to arouse him, but he'd quickly made up some story about how he'd been advised not even to try since trying and failing could cycle into a more permanent psychological problem.

She hadn't been too upset.

They'd spent the night watching old movies on one of

those classic-movie cable channels. Miller had stayed awake even when Serena had dozed off. He didn't much like the idea of waking up with a cold blade of steel in his chest. Or not waking up at all.

He'd slept some on the plane back east, knowing that Daniel was awake and watching out for him.

"I've decided what I want for a wedding gift," Serena told him.

"You have?" This time, he encircled her in his arms, brushing his lips against her forehead. Her perfume was too strong, too floral, too cloying. He forced himself to smile down at her.

"Yes," she said. "This house. It's on the market, you know."

This was good. This was very good. According to her pattern, she would ask him for a check or a transfer of funds into her private account. She would tell him that part of the gift would be the thrill of making the purchase herself from the money he had given her.

"I'll call the broker first thing tomorrow," Miller said.

She pulled back slightly. "You know what I would really love?"

"Something more than this house?"

She laughed. "No. But I'd like to negotiate this deal myself. I'd love to be able to write a check for a substantial deposit from my own account."

Miller kissed her again, as condescendingly as possible. "If that would make you happy, I'll simply transfer enough money into your checking account."

She kissed him again.

"Oh, my God!"

There was a clatter in the doorway, and Miller looked up from Serena's lips and found himself gazing directly into Mariah's horrified eyes.

Her bike helmet spun on the hardwood floor where she'd dropped it.

"Oh, hello," Serena said. "Funny, I didn't hear the bell."

"There was note on the door saying to come in," Mariah said, her eyes never leaving Miller's. Somehow she managed to sound completely calm.

"Isn't this the most exciting surprise ever?" Serena enthused, taking Miller's hand and pulling him toward Mariah. "Introducing Mr. and Mrs. Jonathan Mills. Can you believe it?"

"No." Mariah shook her head. "No, I can't, actually." She laughed, and as Miller watched, the sheer hurt in her eyes turned to scorn. "Or, God—maybe I can. Maybe the sad thing is that I *can* believe it. Excuse me, I have to go."

She scooped her helmet up off the floor and headed for the stairs.

Serena followed her. "Mariah, don't you want to see the house?"

"No," Mariah said, her voice echoing in the three-story entryway. "No, Serena, I don't want to see your house. I'm very happy for you. Just be aware of the fact that your husband doesn't think twice about breaking his promises, and you'll be fine."

"What is *that* supposed to mean?" Serena asked plaintively.

Miller opened the sliders that led to the small deck outside the dining room. There were stairs that led down and connected to the master bedroom's deck, and more stairs that went to the ground. He quickly went down them, intercepting Mariah just as she reached her bicycle.

"I don't have anything to say to you," she said tightly.

He held the handlebars of her bicycle to keep her from moving. "Yeah, well, I have something to say to you."

She threw her helmet onto the ground in anger. "Oh, yeah? Like what? What could you possibly have to say to me?"

"Mariah, I can't tell you what this is all about, but please, just trust me, okay? You *have* to trust me—"

She tried to jerk her bike away from him. "I don't have to do *any*thing—and the last thing I'm ever going to do again is *trust* you. You son of a bitch!"

Miller held tightly to her bike, talking fast and low. "Mariah, listen to me. Go away. Leave the island. Go to New York, or I don't know, back to Phoenix—it doesn't matter where you go. Just stay away from here for a week or two—"

She interrupted him with a terse phrase that instructed him to do the anatomically impossible as she wrenched her bike away from him. But she paused, looking back at him, heartbreaking hurt in her eyes. "To think I actually wasted my love on you," she whispered.

Miller watched her ride away, clenching his teeth to keep from calling out after her.

He turned back to the house, catching a flutter of movement out of the corner of his eye. Gazing up at the dining-room deck, he had to wonder. Had Serena been up there, watching them? And if so, what exactly had she seen?

This was going to be fun. More fun than she'd imagined.

There was something between them. Something strong. From the level of her upset, it seemed pretty obvious that he'd done It to her. Silly cow. Didn't she know men were pigs?

She deserved to die—to melt along with all of those stupid pictures she shot, day after day.

And he... She was going to make him watch before she separated his ugly soul from his even uglier body.

Yes, this *was* going to be fun.

Mariah stood in the basement, smashing dishes against the wall.

Maybe this would help. Each plate she threw was an outlet for her anger and hurt. Each plate she threw was accompanied by a bloodcurdling scream of rage.

Her voice was hoarse and her throwing arm was sore, but she kept at it, hoping, *praying* that eventually this raw wound where her heart used to be would begin to scab over.

She'd fallen off her bike on her way down the hill and scraped one elbow and both knees. But she hadn't cried. She *refused* to cry.

She cleaned up her scrapes in the bathroom, then took her suitcases down from the bedroom closet. She packed most of her clothes before she found herself here, breaking plates.

John had broken his promise.

Clearly, when he'd made it, that promise had meant nothing to him. *She* had meant nothing to him. He'd no doubt made love to her—no, not made love, had sex. It had been nothing more than sex, with the intention of never seeing her again. He'd probably already made his wedding plans with Serena.

Another piece of china hit the wall, shattering into a thousand pieces, just the way her heart had been broken.

And Mariah couldn't hold back her tears any longer. She crumpled onto the basement floor and cried.

* * *

"Can you hear me?" Miller said into the flower vase, making an adjustment to the miniature receiver he wore in his right ear.

"Roger," Daniel said from his position about a quarter mile to the south of the house. "Let's check those babies in the dining room once more before we move on into the bedroom."

Miller went into the elegant dining room where he'd planted a number of nearly invisible microphones underneath the huge table, along the sideboard, on several of the chairs and on the edges of one or two picture frames.

He stood in the center of the room. "Do you have me?"

"Loud and clear," came Daniel's reply. "Hang on a sec. Just let me fine tune this puppy... Got it."

The surveillance device in Daniel's car had been designed to look like nothing more than an intricate and expensive car stereo system. It was incredibly complicated to program—Miller was glad Daniel was the one doing it. He preferred the straightforward equipment that came inside the tinted glass of a surveillance van.

He wouldn't be able to wear his in-ear receiver tonight. Not as long as there was a possibility that Serena might find it.

"You know, I'm going to be fine here tonight. You could do this surveillance in comfort from the resort. She's not going to try anything until my bank transfers that money into her account," Miller told his partner.

"Yeah, I know," Daniel said. "I'd just feel better being close—at least for now. There's something in the air that's making my hair stand on end."

"Storm's coming," Miller said, moving to look out the window at the ocean.

A bank of dark clouds was gathering on the horizon.

The late-afternoon sun was still shining, but the air was heavy with humidity and hard to breathe.

"Yeah, maybe that's it," Daniel said. "Whatever the case, I'll be out here, mainlining coffee and listening to every word you say. So don't say or do anything you don't want me to hear."

That wasn't going to be a problem. Miller found himself gazing down at the roof of Mariah's house. Was she in there right now, tearing all her pictures of him into tiny shreds? Was she in her bedroom, packing up her clothes and her CDs and her funny little speaker that made such realistic-sounding water noises? *Imagine yourself in a special place...*

"Any sign of Mrs. Mills?" Daniel asked.

Miller snapped himself back to the present, listening hard for any signs of movement in the house. When Serena had announced that she was taking a walk on the beach, he'd begged off. He claimed fatigue, but in fact wanted to use the opportunity to plant and test the surveillance system. He'd managed to get quite a number of the nearly invisible mikes placed while she was there in the house, but it was much easier doing it this way. He looked at his watch. Serena had left fifteen minutes ago. It was entirely possible that she was on her way back.

"I, um, haven't exactly been keeping track," he admitted.

There was a long silence from Daniel's end of the line. "John, I need you here one hundred percent," he finally said. "If you can't do that—"

Miller cleared his throat. "Look, Daniel, *I* need you to run over to Mariah's and encourage her to leave the island. Can you do that for me?"

"I'm a step ahead of you," Daniel told him. "I tapped into the phone lines and I've been monitoring her outgoing calls. It occurred to me that she might be in a position to jeopardize your cover if she decided to share with Serena the fact that you and she spent the night together on the eve of your wedding." He paused. "I may be assuming too much here, but I know that you like this lady an awful lot. That and your lateness to the meeting with Blake clued me in to the fact that you and she—"

"What's your point?"

"The fact is, she *is* leaving. I heard her call for a taxi for this evening. For seven o'clock. She asked for a cab with plenty of trunk room. She told the dispatcher she had quite a bit of luggage."

"Thank God." Miller closed his eyes in relief. Mariah was leaving the island. He could stop worrying about her safety. He knew it was highly unlikely that Serena would hurt anyone other than her targeted victim. Still, he would breathe easier with Mariah off the island.

He would stop worrying about her, but he wouldn't stop thinking about her—and wondering if the truth would be enough to make up for the heartbreak.

Chapter 13

Lightning forked across the sky, thunder boomed and the power flickered and went out.

Mariah swore like a sailor, bumping her shins on her suitcases as she felt her way into the kitchen where she knew there was a candle over near the toaster.

The matches were a little bit harder to locate, and with the candle held tightly in one hand, she felt along the counter with the other. She found the book of matches on the windowsill and lit the candle.

It had been burned down pretty far. Mariah estimated she had only about an hour or two of wax left at most. After that, it was going to be very, very dark in here.

But the kitchen clock was stopped at 5:37. With luck, her cab would arrive before the candle burned completely down.

She took the softly glowing light back downstairs into her darkroom. That was the last of the rooms she had left to pack. Her clothes were all ready to go, and she was going to leave what was left of her food behind for the cleaning lady.

She gazed around the darkroom at all of her photographic supplies—at the pictures of John, long since dried.

Tears filled her eyes, and she shook her head in disgust. She'd thought she'd already cried herself dry. She had, she tried to convince herself. These tears were just leftovers—kind of like an earthquake's aftershocks.

She'd cried, she'd gotten it out of her system and she was okay now. So she'd made a bad call. She'd guessed wrong, misjudged someone. Life was going to go on.

She could hear the rain pelting against the roof. Mariah thought about the Washburtons' house. She thought about the way she'd worked on that roof all yesterday afternoon, along with nearly two dozen other volunteers. They'd all worked in perfect cooperation, their common goal to get the job done and done well.

If she left Garden Isle, she wouldn't be able to see the completion of that house. She wouldn't go to the housewarming, wouldn't watch Frank and Loretta Washburton's eyes fill with joy and pride as they welcomed friends and Triple F workers into their home.

If she left, she would be leaving behind the friends she made, the work team she'd come to know so well. Laronda. There couldn't possibly be another site coordinator as cool as Laronda.

If she left Garden Isle, if she let herself be pushed out, chased away from her great-great-grandmother's childhood home, she'd never forgive herself.

Why should *she* be the one who was forced to leave? If Jonathan Mills was uncomfortable living two doors away from her, let *him* be the one to move.

Hell, she had the rent on this cottage paid through to the end of the month.

Thunder boomed, and she knew she was only kidding herself. What was she going to do? March up to John and Serena's house, interrupt their honeymoon and demand that they leave?

No, she couldn't do that, but she could just stay here, quietly keeping to herself—and feeling like crap every time John or Serena's car drove past, praying that she wouldn't run into them in the supermarket, dreading seeing them together on the beach, knowing that she still wanted him.

She still wanted him.

Jonathan Mills was a son of a bitch. The fact that he was confused, that he was tormented by painful nightmares, that he was stressed out from the strain of dealing with a potentially terminal illness—none of that gave him the right to make love to her one night and then marry Serena the next.

Yet she still ached for his touch.

She was a fool.

With a sigh, Mariah began packing up her darkroom equipment by candlelight, deciding what she had to take and what could be left behind.

Yes, she could refuse to leave the island. But as much as she hated the thought of slinking away, beaten down and defeated, she wasn't into self-torture.

She tossed the photos of Jonathan Mills into the trash can. Those could definitely be left behind.

"Wow, this is fancy." Miller stepped into the candlelit dining room.

Serena had cooked a gourmet meal and set one end of the heavy wooden table with elegant china place settings, a myriad of wineglasses and what looked to be the entire silverware drawer. There were salad forks, shrimp cocktail forks, dinner forks, dessert forks.

Miller had to wonder—was she actually planning to serve dessert tonight, or did she have something a little more macabre up her sleeve?

Actually, she wasn't wearing any sleeves. The dress she wore was black and sleeveless, timelessly chic, complete with an innocent-looking string of pearls around her neck.

"Fortunately, we have a gas stove," she told him as she opened a decanter of wine and poured them each a glass. "Or we'd be sending out to McDonald's for double cheeseburgers." She smiled at him. "And *that* wouldn't have done at all. I wanted this meal to be…special."

Special. The Black Widow's M.O.—*her* M.O.—was to serve her husband an elegant gourmet meal, drug him so that he couldn't fight back, then stab him in the heart shortly after the main course.

His nerves were strung much too tightly. Miller was as certain as he could possibly be that, just as he'd reassured Daniel that afternoon, Serena wasn't going to try to kill him tonight. It was too soon. She would wait until she had his money in hand—to do otherwise would be outside of her pattern, outside of her rules. And serial killers of this type rarely strayed from their set of rules.

"You should have told me we were going to have a formal meal," Miller said for Daniel's benefit. "I would have dressed for dinner."

Serena handed him one of the two wineglasses. "Let's have a toast, shall we?"

Right then and there, Miller knew he'd been dead wrong. She'd poured him a glass of red wine, but it smelled much too sweet and the liquid in the glass was much too thick. Opium. She was trying to drug him by putting opium in the wine. Right now. Tonight. Without having received a penny from him, she was preparing to kill him.

"I don't feel very much like red wine tonight," he said, setting the glass down on the dinner table.

Serena smiled at him. "Let's not be cute," she said. When she put her own glass down, he realized she was holding a gun. The rules were all changing, and changing fast.

"Is that a gun?" he said.

She laughed. "Yes, it's a gun," she told him. She raised her voice slightly. "Did you hear that, Daniel? Or, oh my. Maybe you're not listening. Maybe you're not *able* to listen. Maybe someone smarter than you *and* your partner waited until the call of nature pulled you out of that car you've been sitting in. Maybe someone much smarter sweetened that coffee you've been drinking to stay alert all night long—sweetened it with more than sugar. Maybe you're leaning against the steering wheel right now, drooling, about to slide into a narcotic coma. Eventually you'll just stop breathing, poor thing. What a shame to die so young...."

Miller took a step toward her and she lifted the gun, aiming directly for his head. "Sit down at the table," she ordered. "And keep your hands where I can see them."

He slowly sat down. Sitting down was good. It put his hands that much closer to the gun he had hidden in his boot.

"Hands on the table," she warned.

If she would only get close enough, if she would stop aiming directly at his head, he might have a chance to go for his gun. But she was carefully keeping her distance. Her aim seemed sure, her hands steady. Outside the windows, lightning flashed and thunder roared, but she seem oblivious, almost inhuman in her concentration.

But she may have finally met her match because there was no way in hell he was going to let Daniel die. No *way*.

"Drink the wine," she ordered him.

"No."

"Funny, I don't believe I phrased that as a yes or no question."

"I'm not drinking it."

She closed one eye as she aimed her gun and fired.

The slap of the bullet going into his arm nearly knocked Miller out of the chair. She *shot* him. He didn't let his disbelief get in his way as he went with the force of the bullet, pushing back his chair and landing on the floor, hoping to get a chance to grab that gun from his boot. But the chance never came as Serena moved around the table, aiming her gun at his head. He swore sharply as pain from his wounded arm rocketed through him.

"Get up." From somewhere, she'd procured a pair of regulation handcuffs. "Sit down. Put your hands behind you."

Miller sat back in another chair, aware of blood streaming down his left arm, aware of the teeth-clenching pain, aware of Serena's gun aimed, once again, directly at his head. He no longer had any doubts that she would use it. And once one of those bullets smashed into his brain, he'd be of absolutely no help to Daniel or anyone else.

Mariah. He closed his eyes briefly, praying that she was safe. She was due to be picked up at seven by a taxi that would take her off the island. He wasn't certain what time it was, but he knew it was close to seven. Please, God, let her be long gone....

He felt Serena cuff one of his wrists, felt her weave the metal through the heavy wooden back of the chair and then cuff his other wrist.

And then he felt her tug slightly at the hair growing at the nape of his neck. She was cutting a lock—probably as some kind of sick keepsake. A souvenir. She probably had an entire collection of hair, and once he found it, it was going to be the evidence he needed to tie her to *all* of the murders.

"I'm not going to let you keep that," he told her.

She just laughed. "Are you sure you don't want that wine?" she asked. "It works as a painkiller, you know." She sat on the table, her gun in her lap, but too far away for him even to consider going for her.

"I can't drink it by myself," he told her, willing her to get closer, to try to force-feed him that wine.

But she laughed again. "You don't really think I'm going to let you spit it in my face, do you?" she scolded him. "This is a designer dress. No, I think we'll do this another way."

She set the gun down on the table as she lifted one of the domed plate warmers. Instead of a roasted chicken, there was only a syringe lying there beside the parsley garnish.

"Morphine," she told him. "It'll make your arm feel all better in, oh, about five minutes." She moved behind him, and he felt the cold steel barrel of her gun pressed tightly against the base of his head. "If you as much as move," she warned, "I'll shoot you."

He felt her tug at his shirt, felt the sharp stab of the needle into his back. Dammit, he hadn't had a very good look at that syringe. He had no idea how much she'd given him. He suspected it would be enough to paralyze, but not enough to kill. She would want the pleasure of skewering him with her sharp little knife.

"You'll have to forgive me for not disinfecting the area of injection," she told him. "But I think that stray germs are the least of your problems."

Miller watched her walk around to the other side of the table. Backlit by the stormy sky, she looked entirely in her element.

Five minutes, she said. In five minutes, he'd be stupid and drooling, just like all her other husbands had been. Or maybe he wouldn't be. Maybe he could hold on, fight the dizzying effects of the drug. Maybe he could make her believe he was weak and vulnerable. Maybe then she'd get close enough. Maybe she would let down her guard and he could overpower her....

"Oh, by the way, I have a little surprise for you," she said. "I want to tell you about it before the morphine starts working. It won't be as much fun to tell you if you don't really understand what's happening." She paused. "Are you listening?"

"I'm listening."

Serena smiled. "I put a bomb in Mariah's basement. All those pesky photographs that she had—I got her negatives out of storage and realized she'd been lying to me. She'd taken quite a number of pictures of me without my knowing it. I put the negatives next to some extremely flammable chemicals in her darkroom. This way, they all go up in flames—photos, negatives...and photographer, too."

Miller felt the cold fingers of death clutching at his heart. Mariah... "No."

"Don't worry, darling, the morphine I've given you will ease the sting." Serena looked at her watch. "The timer's set for six-thirty. That's in another six minutes.

From where you're sitting, you'll have an excellent view of the fire. Of course, by then you probably won't care.''

"Serena! God!" Miller's voice sounded harsh to his own ears. "Mariah doesn't know anything, I swear to you. Don't bring her into this."

"Too late."

"No, it's not. Call her. Call her and tell her to get out of the house. All you really want is to destroy those photos. You don't need to kill her!"

"My, my, my. You *do* care, don't you? You should have thought of that *before* you came after me. *Before* you listened in on me and stalked me like some kind of wild animal."

Her fingers tightened on the trigger of the gun and Miller nearly stopped breathing. Please, God, don't let her kill him now. Not yet. Not while there was still a chance that he could talk her into saving Mariah.

Her face was taut with anger. "Did you really think you could outsmart me? Did you really think I wouldn't notice that my house was *infested* with hidden microphones—just like the ones you hid here!"

"Mariah had nothing to do with that. Call her. Tell her to get out of there. Serena, she was your *friend.*"

Something shifted in Serena's face. "Four minutes," she said. "And I can't call her. The phone lines went down when the power went off." She smiled. "Come on, John. I want to hear you scream."

Miller could feel a vein throbbing in his neck. It was an odd sensation, countered by a feeling of floating, of drowsiness, of numbness. God help him, the drug was kicking in.

God, this was his worst nightmare happening all over again. Except this time, it wasn't Tony in a warehouse he wasn't going to be able to save. This time, it was

Mariah, in a cottage where a killer had planted a bomb. This time he wouldn't hear her die. Instead, he'd see the flames that were devouring her. He'd see them over the tops of the trees.

Rage blinded him, and he used it to fight the unbalancing effect of the drug as he strained at his handcuffs, praying Serena would step just a little bit closer....

That was funny. Mariah couldn't remember putting that box down here, next to her supply of chemicals. The box had B&W Photo Lab's familiar logo on the side, and she pulled it off the shelf and opened it, holding the candle up to illuminate what was inside.

Negatives. The box was filled with dozens of plastic sleeves that held her negatives. That was weird. She'd been storing these over at the photo lab on the mainland. How on earth had they found their way back here? Who could have put the box on this lower shelf, where in the darkness she probably wouldn't have noticed it even with the power working and the overhead light turned on and...

She held the candle up again and looked deeper into the darkness of the bottom shelf. What the heck...?

She looked closer, then started backing away.

Whatever was in there, it looked a *hell* of a lot like a bomb. Not that she'd ever seen a bomb before—not up close and personal like this. But it looked like the bombs she'd seen in movies—some kind of sticks of explosive tied together, hooked into an alarm clock that was ticking quietly....

Mariah grabbed her candle and ran. She ran up the basement stairs, through the living room and out into the pouring rain. The candle went out the moment she burst through her front door, and she threw it down onto the lawn. She grabbed her bike from the side of the house and jumped on it, pedaling furiously down the driveway, taking a left to head toward town, toward the police station, toward somebody, *any*body who might have some sort of idea why there was a *bomb* in her basement.

The rain soaked her almost instantly, and the wind ripped at her hair and tore at her clothes. She had to squint hard, to squeeze her eyes nearly shut to see through the driving rain, but still she pedaled standing up, muscles straining.

Somebody wanted to kill her. Somebody wanted to *kill* her.

She hadn't gone more than a tenth of a mile before she saw car headlights up ahead. They weren't coming toward her, but rather, they were motionless, the light pointing crazily into the heavy underbrush that grew along the side of the road. As she drew closer, Mariah could see that the car had skidded off the road and slammed into a tree.

There was no way she was going to stop. Someone had planted a *bomb* in her basement. Someone wanted her dead, and she wasn't going to stop until she reached the safety of the police station downtown.

She would have gone past with a silent apology and a promise to herself to tell the police about the accident right away when she recognized the car. It was *Daniel's* car. And God, that was Daniel, still in the front seat, slumped over the steering wheel.

Cursing, she braked to a stop and dropped her bike along the side of the road. She cursed louder still at the sting of the branches that whipped against her legs in the wind. She moved as quickly as she could through the sodden underbrush, and bracing herself for the worst, she jerked open the driver's-side door of the car.

It looked as if the air bag had been inflated, and Daniel had somehow deflated it again. But he was resting his head against the steering wheel as if he had some kind of injury. Or as if he were drunk.

The radio was on—some kind of a talk show or a dramatized broadcast—a man and a woman were talking. And what looked to be close to half a dozen large thermoses of coffee littered the floor, along with an empty doughnut shop bag.

Mariah felt Daniel's neck for a pulse. It seemed uncommonly slow. But there was no sign of blood, no sign of any kind of injury. She touched the side of his face. "Daniel?" God, he *was* drunk. She smacked him lightly, then a little bit harder. "Daniel, wake up!"

He roused slightly. "Mariah!" he said. "Gotta warn you! A bomb!"

Mariah pulled back, aghast. "What did you say?"

"FBI," he mumbled. "Me an' John. Tracking a killer. Gonna blow up Mariah."

"Who's FBI?" Mariah was shocked. "*You're* FBI? You and…" John?

"Gotta save John, too." Daniel was fighting to stay awake, but it was clearly a losing battle.

"What's wrong with you?" Mariah shook him, feeling a flare of disbelief, of unreality. This couldn't be real, it couldn't be happening. "Are you drunk? What are you saying to me?"

"Somethin' in the coffee," Daniel breathed. "Gotta get help, gotta save John."

"Where is John?" Mariah asked, suddenly terribly, horribly afraid. Daniel's eyes were closed and she shook him again. "*Dammit, where's John?*"

But he didn't answer.

Something in the coffee. Someone had put something in his coffee—and a bomb in her basement.

Soaked to the skin and sobbing with frustration, Mariah used all her strength to push Daniel over into the passenger seat. She climbed in behind the steering wheel and tried to start the car. *Get help.* Unable to drive from the effects of whatever the hell had been put in his coffee, Daniel had crashed his car as he'd tried to go get help. Or maybe not to get help. Maybe to warn her. Maybe he was coming to warn her about the bomb.

Although how would he have known?

She turned the key in the ignition and the engine almost turned over. Almost. She tried again, but this time it only wheezed and died.

She tried again, but there was only silence. Silence, and those infernal radio talk show hosts talking and talking and talking and...

"Less than a minute now," the woman's voice was saying. "Thirty seconds and Mariah and her stupid photographs will be nothing more than a smudge of smoke in the sky."

"I'm going to kill you," the man's voice said. His speech was slightly slurred, slightly slow, slightly shaking with rage, but the voice was unmistakable. It was John. "I'm going to break free from this chair, and I'm going to kill you."

And the woman's voice was Serena's.

Mariah couldn't breathe.

"Twenty seconds," Serena said. "Shall we count down together?"

"No!" John said. "No!" It was a howl of rage and pain nearly identical to the cry Mariah had heard the night he'd had a nightmare when he'd slept on her couch.

"Ten," Serena said. "Nine, eight, seven, six, five, four, three, two, one—"

The explosion rocked the car as flaming bits of shingles and wood rained down around them, extinguished almost instantly by the deluge. Mariah looked back up the road. Where her cottage had been was roaring flames—the fire too big and too hot to be put out by the rain.

"Oh, my God," she breathed.

Over the radio, she could hear John, his voice little more than a keening cry. "No," he said over and over again. "No!"

"Oh, please," Serena scoffed. "I know the morphine tends to make one overly emotional, but show a little backbone, won't you? I would've expected more from someone sent to catch *me*."

Mariah's heart was in her throat. John thought she was dead.

"I'm not dead," she said aloud, but, of course, he couldn't hear her.

"Mariah…" he whispered. "Oh, God, Mariah…"

"You really expect me to believe you cared that much about that great, huge *cow* of a woman?"

"You *bitch*," Mariah exclaimed. "I am *not* a cow!"

"You can stop the act," Serena continued. "I know what you're trying to do. You're trying to make me think that you're thoroughly anesthetized—totally helpless. You want me to come close enough so that you can try for me. What are you planning to do with your arms bound behind your back, John? Snap my neck with your legs?"

"Mariah…" he breathed. "No…"

John's arms were somehow tied. Serena had somehow managed to overpower him and tie him up. She'd given him morphine, too. That's what was making John's speech sound so slurred. Maybe Serena had put something similar in Daniel's coffee.

"I think I'll wait another few minutes or so before I get too close," Serena said. "I don't care to have my neck snapped today."

John took a deep, shuddering breath, then spoke softly, quietly. "Just do it, Serena," he said. "Just get out your stiletto and get it over with. Because I'm already dead. You killed me when you killed Mariah."

"No!" It was Mariah who cried out this time. "Oh, God, no!"

Whatever she was going to do, she had to do it fast. She tried to start the car again to no avail. She tried to rouse Daniel, but he was as unresponsive as the car's engine.

FBI, he'd said. He and John were FBI.

And FBI agents carried guns....

Mariah searched through Daniel's pockets and through his clothes. It wasn't until she pushed him over and patted around his waist that she found what she was looking for. A gun, in some kind of holster at the small of his back.

"I'm really sorry, but I think I need this," Mariah said to the unconscious man, as with shaking hands, she pulled his shirt free from his pants and drew out the gun. It was small and deadly looking, and warm to the touch from Daniel's body heat.

She pushed open the car door and stepped out into the driving rain, pushing the gun into the back pocket of her shorts, praying that it had some kind of safety attachment that would keep her from shooting herself in the butt by mistake.

She picked up her bike and pointed it back up the

hill—away from town and the police. Her muscles strained as she started up the slight incline. She started to gather some real speed as she went past the still flaming ruins of her cottage.

The neighboring house that lay between hers and Serena's was silent and empty, and the last of her hopes for getting help sank. There was no one home there. There was no way anyone could be home and not be out on the porch, or at least at the windows, watching the inferno next door.

Still, Mariah kept pedaling up the hill. She didn't understand *half* of what was going on, but she knew one thing for damn sure. Serena wasn't going to kill John. Not if *she* had anything to say about it.

Chapter 14

"*I* never quit," Tony said sternly. "I confess I did a stupid thing, I got myself into a situation that there was no getting out of, but I spit at Domino as his boys were squeezing the triggers of their guns to blow me away."

Miller's mouth was dry, his stomach queasy and his head felt as if it were floating a good twelve inches above his body. "Mariah's dead," he said. "She killed Mariah."

"No talking," Serena said sharply. "No more talking!"

Tony moved closer, lowering his voice. "You know, she's having some kind of ritualistic meal, getting into some kind of sicko trance while she's getting ready to skewer you, pal. And look at you. You've got your head on the table in a puddle of drool."

"I don't care," Miller told him.

It was amazing, actually. He had a bullet in his left arm, but it didn't hurt. He couldn't feel it. He couldn't feel anything. Nothing hurt. Nothing mattered. He honestly didn't care.

"I can't believe it," Tony said. "This bitch killed Mariah, and you're going to let her get away with it? You're going to just quit? I don't know what happened in the past two years, baby, but you're not the John Miller *I* used to know."

"I loved her," Miller said.

"Yeah, right, maybe." Tony didn't sound convinced.

"I told you to shut up!" Serena snapped.

"I did," Miller insisted. "I loved her more than anything."

"Not more than you love yourself," Tony pointed out. "If you did, you wouldn't quit. But you're scared because you know it's going to hurt you more than you can bear to wake up tomorrow morning and still be alive while Mariah's not. You *want* this bitch to shish-kebab you because Mariah's dead, because you couldn't save her, and because you can't deal with that."

"Damn right I can't deal with that! God, every day for the rest of my life?"

Serena clapped her hands together and the noise seemed to thunder around him. "I'm warning you!"

Miller lifted his head, working hard to focus his eyes. "Go to hell," he snarled.

"Attaboy," Tony murmured. "Get mad. Fight back."

Mariah was dead. Mariah was dead. Christ, Mariah was *dead.*

The pain of reality came stabbing through all of the layers of drug-induced numbness and apathy. Sweet, beautiful Mariah was gone forever, and Miller knew that Tony was right. As easy as it would be to quit, he couldn't do it. He couldn't just put his head down on the table and die.

Not without making Serena pay.

So instead, he put his head down on the table and waited for Serena to come closer.

With his eyes opened and focused, Tony was gone. He was on his own here, without even his dreams and hallucinations to back him up. He tried to formulate a plan, tried to make his brain turn back into a brain again, rather than the soggy basket of wet laundry it had become.

She would come close, and he would use every bit of strength he had left in his jellolike muscles, and he would...do something.

No, no! He had to come up with something specific. He had to figure out the details. He was always so good with details, good with alternate plans. He was good at making plans for every variable, every difference in every detail.

But for now, he'd have to skip the little details. For now, he'd focus on an overall plan. His mind was too foggy for anything but the big picture. It was hard enough to concentrate on how exactly to get from where he was sitting right now to being the one in control of the gun.

Gun.

There was something about a gun that he should remember....

He had a gun. He could...shoot her with the gun that was still inside his boot! Yeah. That was a great idea.

Except his hands were cuffed behind his back and he couldn't reach his gun.

Miller fought a wave of dizzying fatigue by calling to mind Mariah's beautiful face, her gorgeous smile. He focused on the dimples that appeared in her cheeks, the flash of laughter that danced in her eyes. That was gone, all gone, forever gone. Serena had stolen Mariah from him. Serena had taken all his hopes and his dreams when she'd so casually snuffed out Mariah's life.

He used the pain to bring himself back from the edge, to push back the fog that threatened to overpower him.

Think. He had to *think*.

He had to figure out what he had to work with, his strengths as they were—not an easy task since he was finding it harder and harder to remember his name.

His legs.

His legs were free. They weren't tied.

He could kick the dining table over on top of her. Crush her. Or, like she herself had suggested, he could put her in a leghold and snap her neck.

He had the chair. He could throw himself forward, chair and all, and use the chair he was cuffed to as a weapon.

And the morphine. He could take that which weakened him the most and use it to his advantage. He could break his legs from the force of the blow he intended to deliver, and he wouldn't feel any pain.

Miller forced his eyes open. He could see Serena sitting way down at the other end of the table, eating her elegant dinner. She was halfway through the main course, and he knew that when the main course was through, she would take out her razor sharp little knife.

And then she would come closer.

If he was lucky, he *would* break her neck. He'd take her out for good.

And if he was really lucky, she'd take him out with her and he wouldn't have to wake up tomorrow and know that Mariah was dead.

The house was dark and quiet.

Mariah stood in the pouring rain, straining to listen for something, *any*thing at all.

All she heard was the rain.

She'd rushed over here as fast as she could ride on her bike, but now that she was here, she wasn't quite sure what to do.

Ring the bell? Knock on the door as she pushed it open, calling, "Yoo-hoo, Serena, did you just try to blow me into a million little bits by planting a bomb in the basement of my house, and are you about to murder your husband and my lover—who, in fact, seems to be some kind of federal agent?"

Stealthily, she tested the doorknob. The door was unlocked. She turned the knob slowly and just as slowly pushed the door open.

It was as dark inside as it was out.

Darker.

Mariah silently closed the door behind her and stood for a moment, letting her ears adjust to the now muted sound of the rain on the roof, hoping her eyes would adjust to the eerie, smothering darkness, as well.

She became aware of a new sound—the sound of water dripping from her clothes and onto the Mexican-tiled floor. And as she took a step farther into the entryway, her sneakers squished. Moving as quietly as she could, she stepped out of them.

Her eyes *were* starting to adjust to the dark. She could see a dim light coming from somewhere upstairs. She looked around for a place to hide her sneakers, but gave up as she realized she might be able to hide them, but there was no way she could hide the puddle of water she'd brought inside with her. She might as well leave them by the door and pray she found Serena before Serena realized she had uninvited company.

Mariah heard a voice speaking sharply, echoing from an upstairs room. It was Serena. She couldn't make out what the woman was saying, but she sure as heck didn't sound happy.

Mariah went up the stairs as quickly and quietly as she could, reaching into her back pocket and wriggling free Daniel's deadly little gun.

Dear God, she had no idea *what* she was going to do. She pictured herself leaping through the doorway, gun raised and held in both hands, like one of the cops on *NYPD Blue,* shouting for Serena to freeze.

And then what? What was she going to do if Serena had her own gun? Was she going to shoot Serena?

Now *there* was an unlikely scenario. Mariah had never fired a gun before, let alone fired one at a living, breathing human being.

As she drew closer to the top of the stairs, she saw that there was candlelight coming from the dining room—the room where all her dreams had come crashing down around her just this morning. It was the same room where she had found Serena and her new husband—Jonathan Mills.

She crept toward the door, careful to stay out of the light, pressing herself against the wall, gun raised. She held her breath and closed her eyes briefly, waiting for the trembling in her knees to stop, hoping that she would hear John's voice, praying that he was still alive.

The next move was hers. It was totally up to her. She could stand here for another two minutes, or she could get ready and—

"My gun is aimed at Jonathan's head." Serena's voice was crisp and clear, echoing in the silence. "I know you're out there, and if you don't step into the light with your hands held high, I'm going to kill him right now."

The next move wasn't Mariah's after all. Dear God, Serena must have heard her coming up the stairs.

"Do it now!" the older woman said sharply, "or I swear, I'll kill him."

Mariah stuffed the gun back into her back pocket and stepped into the light, hands held up over her head.

"You?" Serena laughed. Sure enough, she held a gun trained with steady confidence directly at John's head. "Well, well, look who's come to rescue you, John. It's Mariah, back from the dead."

"Run!" John shouted. "Mariah, run!"

Mariah couldn't move. It was as if she'd stepped into some scene from a horrific nightmare, and she couldn't move an inch.

John was sitting behind the long dining table, his hands behind his back. His left arm was soaked with blood. It looked as if it was all he could do to hold his head up. And Serena was standing across the room, perfectly dressed as usual in an elegant black sheath dress, with pearls and a gun as accessories.

It was unreal. Mariah didn't understand. What the hell was going on? Why was the FBI after Serena? What had she done? Why would she want to kill John and drug Daniel? Why would she put a bomb in Mariah's basement? It didn't make any sense.

But Serena held the gun calmly, confidently, as if she was accustomed to it. Clearly, she wouldn't hesitate to shoot—obviously she'd shot John once tonight already. She swung the gun toward Mariah.

"No!" Miller was drowning. The shock of seeing Mariah whole and alive had transformed rapidly from near euphoric joy to screaming fear. She was alive—but she wouldn't be for long if she didn't get the hell out of here.

"Well, isn't *this* different," Serena said. "You *are* a

fool, aren't you? He married *me,* and yet here you are, rushing to his rescue, empty-handed. You know, he was only using you to get closer to me. Did you know that Jonathan Mills isn't even his real name? God, Mariah, I'm sure absolutely nothing he's told you is true."

Mariah took one step and then another and another toward Miller. "John, are you all right?" She was soaking wet, shivering slightly as she knelt next to him, as she touched his blood-soaked sleeve. He could smell her perfume, and reality shifted. For one incredible moment, he was back in her bed, making love to her and... He shook his head, trying to bring his focus back to here and now.

"Gun in my boot," he whispered, praying that she would understand, knowing that he had to act, and act fast. As much as Serena was loath to kill him with a gun, she'd have no problem using a bullet to kill Mariah.

"Of course, Mariah was playing her own game," Serena continued. "Mariah Robinson isn't her real name either. I wonder, John. Did you consider her a suspect because of that?"

Miller looked directly into Mariah's eyes. "Gun," he started to whisper again.

She cut him off. "I know. I'm really mad at you," she added, reaching behind him to touch his hand. Except wait—those weren't her fingers that touched him. It was something cold and...

It was amazing, but somehow she'd managed to get the gun out of his boot without his noticing. Without Serena noticing. Miller's hands were numb, but he took the safety off, preparing the gun to fire.

Still, this gun wasn't going to do him a whole hell of a lot of good as long as he was holding it behind his back. He was a good shot—at least he was when he wasn't pumped full of narcotics—but trick shooting had never been his forte.

"Take it back," he told Mariah.

She shook her head. "I can't."

Serena's gun was still pointed loosely at Mariah, yet now she brought her hand up higher, taking better aim. "What are telling her?" she asked him sharply, then said to Mariah, "Move away from him."

"Take it," Miller said. *"Now!"*

Mariah didn't want that gun. She knew damn well there was no way she could aim it at Serena and pull the trigger.

But John dropped it into her hand as he used both of his legs and kicked the enormous table onto its side. A shot rang out as he tipped his chair over in front of her, and Mariah realized Serena was shooting at them. She lifted the gun, closed her eyes and squeezed the trigger.

The recoil knocked the gun out of her hands and she screamed.

Miller tried to shield Mariah as the shot she fired went wild. He could feel the dry wood of the old chair he was cuffed to splintering, and he pulled himself free of it.

His wounded arm should have hurt like hell as he contorted to slip his cuffed hands past his legs and around to the front of him, but he didn't feel even a twinge, thanks to the morphine Serena had given him. Weakness as strength. He was superhuman now. Nothing could hurt him, nothing could stop him—not even Serena's bullets.

He felt the force of one plow into his leg as he covered Mariah with his body, as he reached for the gun she had fired and dropped. He felt another bullet strike him as he took aim, and he saw Serena's eyes as she realized that only a direct hit to his head would take him down.

He fired.

And Serena fell instead, her gun falling from her hand.

In the sudden silence, he could hear the sound of sirens.

It was the sound of fire trucks, rushing to extinguish the blaze that once had been Mariah's cottage.

But they didn't stop down the street. They came all the way up the hill, all the way into the driveway. He heard the door burst open, heard the pounding sound of heavy footsteps on the stairs.

He leaned back, resting against the toppled-over table as Mariah tried to stop his bleeding.

Backup had arrived. Somehow Daniel had managed to call for backup, and they had arrived.

"I'm going to close my eyes now," he told Mariah.

"Don't," she said, tears in her own eyes. "Please, John, don't quit on me. Stay with me—"

He touched her cheek. It was wet with tears. "Don't cry. I never meant to make you cry. I'm so sorry," he murmured. "So sorry..." I love you, he wanted to say, but his lips didn't seem to be able to move.

"We need that stretcher up here stat!" he heard someone shout as the world went black.

Chapter 15

It was thirty-six hours, seventeen minutes and nine seconds before John opened his eyes.

Mariah knew, because she'd been counting every second. The nurses had brought in a cot for her, and she'd slept fitfully, not convinced that she would be roused if John woke up.

But he hadn't.

He had an IV dripping steadily into his right arm. He was hooked up to machines that monitored his heart rate and his breathing. Doctors came and went, seemingly satisfied with his progress despite the fact that he slept on and on and on.

Daniel came to before John did, and he sat quietly for a while, next to Mariah. He told her about Serena, about all her other husbands, about the years John had spent tracking her down. He told her how, after Mariah had left him in the car, he'd roused himself and crawled out into the rain. He'd forced himself to keep awake, keep moving, and eventually, he'd flagged down a passing car. The driver had taken him to the Garden Isle police station, where a team of local cops had donned their bulletproof vests and driven like bats out of hell to John and Mariah's rescue.

Except by the time they'd arrived at Serena's place, John and Mariah had pretty much managed to rescue themselves.

He told her that Serena was in custody, expected to recover from her gunshot wound. He added that her real name was Janice Reed and that they'd found her keepsake collection of hair, which tied her to nearly a dozen murders.

Daniel managed to answer only some of Mariah's questions. He said she'd have to wait for John to answer the others. Before John woke up, Daniel had been discharged from the hospital and he'd returned to the resort to finish packing their equipment.

And still Mariah sat next to John's bed.

Then, finally, he stirred and opened his eyes.

He just looked at her, and she just looked at him, fighting back the tears that immediately sprang to her eyes.

"You're not dead," he said when he finally spoke, and she realized that there were tears in his eyes, too. "I'm not really sure what I dreamed and what was real, but I'm glad as hell that you're not dead."

His mouth was dry, and she helped him by lifting the cup of water the nurses had left for him. She aimed the bendable straw so he could pull it into his mouth and take a long sip.

"My real name is Marie Carver," she told him without hesitation, "although my nickname has always been Mariah. I've spent the past few months on Garden Isle using the name Mariah Robinson because I read in a book that going on vacation and leaving your name behind was a good way to reduce stress.''

He smiled very slightly as she put the cup back on the table next to the bed. ''It's also a good way to make the local law enforcement officials very suspicious.''

''I never even thought of that.'' She paused. ''You didn't really think I was…a killer?''

''We pretty much knew it was Serena right from the start.''

''I can't believe you married someone you suspected of being a serial killer! Is that part of your job description as an FBI agent?''

He laughed, then winced, holding tightly to his side where one of Serena's bullets had cracked a rib. ''No. No, that was above and beyond the call of duty.''

Mariah was quiet for a moment. She almost didn't ask, but she had to know. ''How could you…sleep with her, knowing that she'd killed all her other husbands?''

He took her hand, interlacing their fingers. ''I didn't sleep with her—I didn't want to sleep with her. Besides, I promised you that I wouldn't, remember? I told her I was impotent—that my condition was a side effect of my chemotherapy.''

Mariah gazed into his eyes. Chemotherapy. Cancer. ''You never really had cancer,'' she realized aloud. ''That was all just part of your cover.''

He nodded. ''That's right. I'm sorry—''

''Sorry?'' She laughed, leaning forward to kiss him hard on the mouth. ''Are you kidding? That's *such* good news! It makes all this hell we've just been through worth it. You're not going to die!''

Her reaction was pure Mariah. She was focusing on the good, not the bad. Miller felt his heart flip-flop in his chest. God, he loved her.

He caught her chin, pulling her mouth down to his for another kiss. This kiss was more lingering, and when she pulled away, her eyes looked so serious, so solemn.

"I don't even know your real name," she told him.

"It's John Miller."

"I don't know anything about you—who you are, where you're from—"

"Yes, you do," he told her. "You know more about me than anyone in the world. I told you more than I've ever told Daniel. More than Tony ever knew."

"Tony was real?" she asked.

"Yeah."

She looked down at their hands, their fingers still intertwined. "Serena said you were only using me to get close to her."

"If you really believe that, what are you doing here, sitting next to my bed?"

She looked up at him then. "I don't know," she confessed. "I honestly don't know. I just...I had to know you were all right before I...left."

Before she left. God, he didn't want her to leave. But if she *was* going to leave, he wanted her to know the truth.

Miller took a deep breath. "I did meet you to get close to Serena," he told her. "Yes, that's true. But I kept coming back—I couldn't stay away—because I fell in love with you."

Her eyes were so wide, so beautiful.

"I love you, Mariah," he told her quietly. "I have almost from the very first day we met. I made a lot of mistakes in this case—even though I tried my damnedest to keep away from you, I couldn't. And when Serena left the island, I was so sure she had gone for good. And then after we made love, and she came back..." He exhaled noisily. "I made some very wrong choices. I knew that marrying her would hurt you, but I couldn't stand the thought of letting her get away, and I nearly got you killed because of that."

He took a deep breath, afraid that what he was about to say was going to drive her away for good. "You see, that's who I am," he continued. "I'm a man who can't stand to fail. I have a record of arrests that's unrivaled in the bureau. I have a reputation for always catching the bad guys, for never letting them get away. I'm supposed to be some kind of superhero—the toughest and meanest in the field. I have a nickname—the other agents call me 'The Robot,' because nothing matters to me outside of my job. They think I have no heart and no soul, and maybe they're right, because the truth is I have no life outside of the work I do. I have no family and no friends—"

"Daniel is your friend."

Miller nodded. "Yeah. I don't get it, but yeah. He's my friend."

"I'm your friend, too."

Miller had to swallow. He had to take another deep breath before he could say, "That's all I can really ask. That you be my friend."

She was very quiet, just watching him.

"I had this crazy dream," he told her, "that morning we made love. I was thinking, this could be my life. I thought, maybe I could feel this good every single day. This woman could love me, and I could become this peaceful, relaxed, happy man. I could be so much more than I've ever been before—than I'd ever thought I'd be. And I could picture us, forty years from now, still making love, still holding hands, still laughing together. I really liked that picture."

Mariah's heart was in her throat as he looked away from her, as he was silent for several long moments. As she watched, he swallowed hard, and when he looked back up at her, his eyes were luminous with unshed tears.

"But I'm not that man. I'm 'The Robot.' And I don't blame you if you can't love me—if you don't want to love me. I'm hard, and I'm driven, and my job matters too damn much to me. I wouldn't wish myself on anyone—maybe especially not on you." He took another deep breath and forced a smile as he squeezed her hand. "So, go on. Get out of here. You've seen for yourself that I'm okay. You can leave."

Mariah couldn't move, couldn't speak.

"It's okay," he said. "I'm okay. I'm just…I'm glad I had the chance to love you. To, you know, know that I could actually feel this way and…"

One of his tears escaped, rolling down his cheek and splashing onto Mariah's hand. He swore, turning away and tightly closing his eyes. But that only served to make more of his tears fall.

"John," Mariah said quietly, gently touching his face. "Robots don't cry." She leaned forward and kissed him and when she pulled back, she whispered, "What would Jonathan Mills think if I told him that I made a mistake, too? What would he say if I told him that really, all this time, I've been in love with a man named John Miller?"

He could feel all his emotions cross his face. Disbelief. Amazement. Confusion. Jubilation. She loved him. She *loved* him!

He made a sound that was something like a laugh as he fought to keep his eyes from filling with tears again. And then he didn't fight anymore. Hell, with Mariah, he didn't need to fight it. He wanted her to know, wanted her to see the way she made him feel.

"He would wish you the best of luck," he told her, "and he would warn you that with me, you're probably going to need it."

Mariah touched his cheek, touched the tear he knew was shimmering there. "And what do *you* think about that?"

"I think that if you still have the urge to change your name, you should consider changing it to Miller."

He'd caught her off guard. "Are you asking me to *marry* you?"

"Yes," he said. "Yes, I am."

This time, the tears that fell were Mariah's. "Yes," she whispered, "I'd love to change my name." She leaned forward and kissed him.

It was the sweetest kiss Miller had ever known.

* * * * *

Take 4 bestselling love stories FREE

Plus get a FREE surprise gift!

Special Limited-time Offer

Mail to Silhouette Reader Service™

3010 Walden Avenue
P.O. Box 1867
Buffalo, N.Y. 14240-1867

YES! Please send me 4 free Silhouette Intimate Moments® novels and my free surprise gift. Then send me 6 brand-new novels every month, which I will receive months before they appear in bookstores. Bill me at the low price of $3.34 each plus 25¢ delivery and applicable sales tax, if any.* That's the complete price and a savings of over 10% off the cover prices—quite a bargain! I understand that accepting the books and gift places me under no obligation ever to buy any books. I can always return a shipment and cancel at any time. Even if I never buy another book from Silhouette, the 4 free books and the surprise gift are mine to keep forever.

245 BPA A3UW

Name	(PLEASE PRINT)	
Address		Apt. No.
City	State	Zip

This offer is limited to one order per household and not valid to present Silhouette Intimate Moments® subscribers. *Terms and prices are subject to change without notice. Sales tax applicable in N.Y.

UMOM-696   ©1990 Harlequin Enterprises Limited

As seen on TV!
Free Gift Offer

With a Free Gift proof-of-purchase from any Silhouette® book,
you can receive a beautiful cubic zirconia pendant.

This gorgeous marquise-shaped stone is a genuine cubic
zirconia—accented by an 18" gold tone necklace.

(Approximate retail value $19.95)

Send for yours today...
compliments of Silhouette®

To receive your free gift, a cubic zirconia pendant, send us one original proof-of-purchase, photocopies not accepted, from the back of any Silhouette Romance™, Silhouette Desire®, Silhouette Special Edition®, Silhouette Intimate Moments® or Silhouette Yours Truly™ title available at your favorite retail outlet, together with the Free Gift Certificate, plus a check or money order for $1.65 U.S./$2.15 CAN. (do not send cash) to cover postage and handling, payable to Silhouette Free Gift Offer. We will send you the specified gift. Allow 6 to 8 weeks for delivery. Offer good until March 31, 1998, or while quantities last. Offer valid in the U.S. and Canada only.

Free Gift Certificate

Name: _____

Address: _____

City: _____ State/Province: _____ Zip/Postal Code: _____

Mail this certificate, one proof-of-purchase and a check or money order for postage and handling to: SILHOUETTE FREE GIFT OFFER 1998. In the U.S.: 3010 Walden Avenue, P.O. Box 9077, Buffalo, NY 14269-9077. In Canada: P.O. Box 613, Fort Erie, Ontario L2Z 5X3.

FREE GIFT OFFER   084-KFD
ONE PROOF-OF-PURCHASE
To collect your fabulous FREE GIFT, a cubic zirconia pendant, you must include this
original proof-of-purchase for each gift with the properly completed Free Gift Certificate.

084-KFDR2

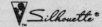